Against a wonderfully evoked
Canadian background, Elizabeth Holland tells the story of
a young girl growing up first on
a farm and later at college in
Winnipeg. Peggy is intelligent,
sensitive, wilful and attractive
and sharply aware of the people
in her life. Her encounters with
her male cousins, a terrifyingly
awful evangelist in a kilt, and
her brilliantly-portrayed old
grandmother, add delight to a
first novel which is funny, per-
cipient and wise.

A SEPARATE PERSON

BY

ELIZABETH HOLLAND

One's-self I sing, a simple separate person.
WALT WHITMAN: '*Leaves of Grass*'

LONDON
MACMILLAN & CO LTD
1962

MACMILLAN AND COMPANY LIMITED
London Bombay Calcutta Madras Melbourne

THE MACMILLAN COMPANY OF CANADA LIMITED
Toronto

PRINTED IN GREAT BRITAIN

To

THE EDINBURGH BOOKSHOP

BROWN'S & GRANT'S, GEORGE STREET,
EDINBURGH

Chapter One

I WAS born in Canada, not thirty years ago, on a farm forty miles from Winnipeg. It was snowing heavily, I am told, and the drifts piled up around the house; the soft fall of snow obliterated the sky and the countryside, the sharp bitter winter held its grip on the land. Inside our house, however, it would all be safe and warm, for in the winter there was always a bright fire burning in the great iron range in the kitchen. It was a comfortable house, built of wood, two stories high, and provided with storm windows to put up in winter; and for the summer we had frames of mosquito netting to put over the windows, and there was a little bluff of trees to shelter us from the merciless summer heat.

Outside there stood one of the finest barns in the district, painted red, with a great hooped roof, and beside it stood a little windmill to generate our own electricity, a fan on a small steel pylon, which began to revolve with a sudden whir whenever the wind started up across the plain. The cows and horses used the bottom of the barn, the harvest was stored in the top. This was our only farm building except for some sheds where the milk cans, the vehicles and the machinery were kept, and a few hen-houses. We had no piggeries. There was another little building up a path through the scrub behind the farmhouse, which was our plumbing.

Here you sat on a plank with two holes — a choice of

sizes for you — and read a page torn from a catalogue hanging on a nail. It was always difficult, here, to decide whether to open the door and risk the arrival of Cousin Joe, Cousin Ernest, or, worst of all, Cousin Peter: or to shut it and put up the hook and be safe, but unable to read, except by means of the one shaft of sunlight that fell through a crack in the planks of the hut, passing by the cobwebs and their dead flies to shine on the print and pictures of the catalogue. Experience of Cousin Peter convinced me at last that it was better to hook the door.

The farm belonged to my uncle. My father, who was English, had died already in England, and my mother, who had only just come to Canada, did not live long after I was born. I lived on the farm with my aunt and uncle and Joe, Ernest and Peter: and the cows, horses, hens, cats and dogs, and Benjamin, the hired man: and the mice and the rats and crickets and beetles.

Life began, then, about ten years before the war. But it began to my own consciousness when I was a year and a half old and had been put in my cot on the verandah to sleep, and suddenly I awoke and looked up and saw the long faces of two of Uncle's Percheron horses peering at me through the mosquito netting covering the open window. I began to cry, and my aunt came and shooed the horses back into the field from which they had escaped. I remember the picture quite clearly, the horses as large as elephants and the gigantic whispering trees around the house; and I remember that not only did I know that *I* was there that afternoon, in a vague way I felt also that I had never been there before, had never awoken before into any morning or afternoon. This was my first own day in this sad world.

And later on, still as certain as ever that I was myself, I would toddle around the farm or make my way into the growing wheat that waved high above my head, or would chase the hens that seemed as large as dogs to me. Later still I would lie at the edge of the fields and watch my uncle coming into sight across a mile and a half of land, the great wings of the binder turning slowly and the noise of the tractor droning on under the bright sun. And often when I was a child I lay awake and heard that tractor rumbling on as my uncle worked half the night at the ploughing, half-sleeping the length of the field, waking up in time to turn the tractor, a slave to the powers of his land.

But in these days his work meant nothing to me, and I earnestly carried out my own small projects, and would catch the crickets and other little insects at the field's edge, and pop them into boxes, and through a hole in the box I would peer down into the dark prison, with one round brown eye, eagerly regarding them. I carried my loot carefully away behind the little hut up the path, and sat in my favourite spot just behind it, where a growth of rank grass made a cushion, and the branches of the small silver birches formed an obliging little bower. Here I would take the lid off my boxes, and would chat to my little captives and tell them stories, to which they listened with melancholy attention, and I would take the dry lacy wings down out of the spiders' webs at the eaves of the hut, and feed them to the prisoners. But soon I would forget, and put the box down; and the inmates would hasten away, while I found some other task to pass the days while my two elder cousins went to school.

At six years old I joined them and we went to school together, and in another year Ernest came with us. Our childhood was not too troubled, except that to live at all is a trouble. We trudged to and fro to school across the squeaking snow in winter, and along the dusty track in summer, crossing four times a day over the unfenced railway line that ran across my uncle's land to Winnipeg.

It ran straight and level across the flat countryside, and

to me Winnipeg seemed to be only a mythical destination; the trains ran, I felt dimly, like man's life, out of nothing into nothingness, appearing suddenly on the horizon, gathering like a cloud, approaching with a shrill cry as they scorched through the township station, rushing past us, a small observant group of children, with mighty bustle and importance, and then suddenly fading away into limbo in the east or west — leaving behind them utterly uninterrupted the great flat plain, the sun, the vast sky, and the intense busyness of four small children and a dog.

Only once did they assert a substance and will of their own. My uncle had this group of Percheron horses, oh, terrible horses they were, mighty bay animals that hung around the trough near the pump and snuffed at me over the wire with long breaths through their soft nostrils, and followed me on immense platelike feet when I tried to reach the barn. They were a source of terror to me from the beginning. One day they had made out through a loose place in the wire, and were feeding on the far side of the railway track, when the usual sensation and bustle began. They started homewards then by way of a cautionary measure. They reached the track and broke too late into a canter. The train caught them fair and square, sock, it caught three of them in the flank, and tore away to nonentity in the pale apple-green border of the evening sky, leaving obliterated three bay Percheron horses. On the inerasable tablets of my mind there is a mark evoking the dispersed bloody limbs of three strong horses, and my cousin Peter's brown hand tugging at the collar of a desperately panting, sniffing dog.

And as I moved about like an ant between the flat earth and the great sky, or played in the shadows of my room under the sloping roof, I carried a pack of images with me, small prototypes of life. We had a Reader at school describing animals of various kinds, with a picture of each one to head

4

each page and a little character sketch of the animal below. These creatures became very real to me. The crocodile, for instance, which can snap off an arm or leg with one clap of its mighty jaws. This crocodile lived under my bed. Under the bed also was the chamber-pot, for, as I have said, there was no indoor plumbing. This raised the problem: how to reach the chamber without losing an arm or leg to the intrepid crocodile? I kept a piece of string coiled up under my pillow with a bit of bread tied to the end, and I would lower this cautiously over the side of my bed and dangle it about invitingly to make sure that the crocodile was asleep. Then I would grab the chamber in a fearful rush and heave it up and plant it on the quilt. The quilt was a beautiful patchwork device made by my great-grandmother from scraps of old dresses interspersed with pieces of turquoise satin from her wedding gown; I felt a kind of guilt at having to give it such a burden, but I was driven by a stern choice: I must sacrifice the quilt, or lose my arm or leg.

The lion, on the other hand, lived behind the bushes near the far end of the barn. My cousins never seemed to understand this. 'Hide behind the barn, Peggy,' they would shout. 'Race you round the barn!' they cried. 'Go find the little white cat,' they said to me, 'she's sneaked off around the end of the barn.' 'Come on, Peggy,' they called to me, 'there's a skunk in the bushes past the barn.' How could I explain to them the danger that lay there, not for them, but for me? That lion had been waiting there all my life; it was a hungry, hungry, hungry lion. I stayed away from those bushes. I went through them for the first time when I was thirteen, looking for one of my uncle's new turkey chicks. Happy to say, the lion was not there.

Of all our pictures, I cared most for the Devil, in another of our books, complete with horns and tail. We had Pan, too, playing away at his pipes, a musical goatlike

5

person who was obviously only somebody else's portrait of the Devil. The Devil was a great comfort to me when I was young: 'I will respect you,' I said to him, 'and you look after me.' The Devil took me past the muscular carthorses. He bore me through the little river when we waded through it up to our waists, and stood me up to my aunt when she scolded us for our wet muddy clothing. He did innumerable pages of homework for me and he recited my pieces to the class; he helped me to sing when we each had to perform a solo, and he even made my uncle give me a bicycle for my tenth birthday. I don't know what I should have done without him.

My uncle and aunt had been born at a time when religion was coming to a low ebb, and other religion than my good friend the Devil did not have much place in our house. My uncle was Irish, of a family which had turned Protestant and left Ireland, and he did not spare much thought either to the new faith or the old, while my aunt cared chiefly for housekeeping. And yet quite a few of the older Canadians were still staunchly religious, especially my grandmother. Most certainly my grandmother was a religious woman! She lived in Merrilee town itself, in a house as Victorian inside as you can imagine, polished to the remotest corners, the front windows hung with net curtains from behind which she might better observe her neighbours. She had the highest moral principles, and questioned us closely about all our doings whenever she saw us, and told us just what she thought of our accounts of ourselves. She was a stout, resolute old lady, terribly deaf. 'Gee whiz!' muttered Joe one day, exhausted by bellowing. 'Is she ever deaf!' 'No, I am not,' Grandma replied tartly, 'I can hear if you speak properly.' Her opinions were as definite as her deafness. She hated Roman Catholics and Episcopalians. She hated drink. 'If your father,' she used to say to me, 'had spent more time on his knees and less at the bottle, he would never have been called below when he was.' My cousins used to play a game featuring Grandma and Uncle. The cousin playing Grandma sat on the woodpile, and in came the cousin playing Uncle. 'Mother,' he said, 'I've took a beer.' 'Arthur!' cried Grandma. 'You wicked wicked boy!', and she burst into floods of tears. Each cousin was allowed this major role in turn.

My cousins were not much troubled by the pangs of imagination nor of conscience. They were hard, muscular boys, resolute as their grandmother. Ernest, a year younger than myself, was small, fair and insignificant-looking, with sunbleached yellow hair seeming rather odd above his brown eyes, very much like Auntie, but Joe's dark hair and Peter's pitch black curls came straight from Grandma's family. Peter, tall and muscular, with bright blue eyes looking straight at everything and a firm considering mouth, was the eldest, three years older than myself. Joe came next. Although no doubt he was just as strong, he was altogether rounder and softer than Peter in appearance and in behaviour; his face was fuller, his complexion brighter, his eyes were dark soft brown and his hair was smooth. He never said very much but thought a great deal, rather slowly. Peter had to be always engaged in planning or organising something, but when nothing special was going on Joe would simply sit down on the nearest bucket or tree-stump or box and would think carefully about something or other, a piece of wood he was whittling, maybe, or an old piece of string that he was carrying in his pocket until he had time to get the knots out of it.

They were quite useful boys, helping Uncle every day on the farm: and when there was no work to do they pursued endless practical courses of action. We dammed the little river, made a swimming pool, and built a hut on the bank

7

where we roasted potatoes and eggs. We built innumerable other huts in the bush, bigger and better each year; and we ambushed other children and trotted them away on the back of our pony and tormented them in the latest hut. Sometimes it even came to a pitched battle and we flung stones freely, myself keeping well to the rear. We carried out our plans in harmony, because the organisation was directed and order was enforced by Peter. If Joe or Ernest disobeyed him he would not wait to argue; seizing the advantage of size and quickness he leapt on them and rolled them in the dust, sitting astride their body with his hands at their throat. Better guidance soon dawned on a boy in this position. As for myself, I would not disobey him. I was overawed into a way of life quite foreign to my tastes: but at least I learnt to build an excellent hut.

We found an occasional diversion in making booby-traps for Benjamin. Benjamin was soft. He had been dropped on his head, people used to say. He had a loose, shapeless look about his face and mouth; his head drooped from side to side, and sometimes he would sit and stare at one and then giggle helplessly, short nervous giggles which made his body jerk up and down. I had a perfect horror of Benjamin. If he found me alone he used to whisper to me. 'Gee, I wish I had you alone in the barn,' he whispered. 'That would be fun, eh? That would be great!' And then he leered at me and rolled his eyes at the barn in idiotic perseverance. I did not agree with the pleasantness of his ideas, whatever they were. I fled when I heard his heavy tramp coming. But the boys hung round him like mosquitoes and tormented him; and Peter made subtle booby-traps for him, which provoked Benjamin to stand and giggle mirthlessly, while Peter watched with a calculating eye.

Peter's little contrivances were endless. I was glad whenever it was possible to escape from him. I waved goodbye to him joyfully when Benjamin and the boys set off to do some work on the farm. They would go to work at the harvest, for instance, and this was a splendid way to get rid of them, as it kept them busy all day.

I stayed behind with Auntie — after Peter had explained to me, one day, that I ranked after the boys, only being a cousin, I gave up calling her Ma; and I felt rather proud and affected to call her Auntie — and helped in the house, ironing the sheets or shelling peas or doing whatever else was necessary. Fetching in the sheets from the line erected over the patch of grass behind the house, I could stand under the trees and look out into the bright acres of sunshine, and feel glad not to be with the boys. This was because of the nature of the boys, and because the weather was so hot, not because I thought it such a difficult job to drive a tractor round and round a field of wheat.

Peter had showed me how to do it: there were two or three levers to pull and push, and the steering-wheel to hold on to, and that was all. The artful part, he explained, was turning at the corners, because to bring the reaper around you had to swing the tractor out a little, and then come round, and then swing in a little, and straighten out; and if you swung out too far you would swing in too far, and cut a deep half-moon in the ranks of standing grain, and as you righted yourself you would come out too far again, and then the tale of your wanderings was written into the wavy edge for everyone to see — not that anybody cared what the field might look like, but it wasted time to roam about like that.

Although it was not a very complicated task, I did not take the time to learn to master it, and of course Peter was delighted at my lack of success, and explained that as I was only a cousin and a girl I could not expect to imitate the sons of the house; and then he demonstrated the beautiful precision with which he could drive round and round, never traversing an inch of ground too much. He had already been doing it for several years, but he did not allow for this when he leapt down in triumph from the tractor, his black hair taking up all the brilliance of the sun, and shouted out, 'There! There! There's skill for you! There's art!' So I left his art to him: it required too much sitting in the heat.

However, even I had to face the harvest sun in the fields at least once a day, for everyone working outside had to have tea and scones in mid-afternoon. I carried a billy-can of tea in one hand and in the other a bucket with buttered scones in a white cloth, and went out towards the noise of the tractor, the full heat striking me the moment I left the shadow of the trees. It was a long, hard, crunchy walk, and the stubble poked up through my sandals and cut my sockless feet, especially in the instep, and I was distracted by the sight of the insects jumping away on every side and wanted to stop and catch them, but did not dare to put down the tea or the scones. As soon as they saw me approaching afar off, everyone would stop work and would cease driving the tractor or pitching the sheaves of grain or whatever they were doing, and drop down by the stooks in a few square inches of shadow, like the hens that would squat in the shade behind the hen-houses or under a small tattered tree all afternoon. After the tea was finished, I carried the empty pails back, quite pleased to leave them all to their men's employment.

Altogether, small attempts at imitating the boys at work always proved to be enough for me. There was for instance the second episode of the horses — though this was my own secret. Everyone had been busy, and Uncle had remembered that it was time to bring the horses back to the watering trough. He picked on me. 'Peggy,' he declared, 'you'll call the horses in to water.'

'Gee whiz, Uncle,' I said, 'you know I hate them horses.'

'You'll call them in for water, all the same,' he said. 'They haven't been back all day, and I want to look them over before supper.' He was quite short and firm about it. Perhaps he took after Grandma too. I set off. For a while I felt brighter about it. After all, I could do as well as the boys by myself any day. I did not need to be always ordered about by them! I strolled along whistling some of Peter's favourite tunes: but it was another miles-long walk; and in place of the sharp stubble the adamantine ridges of baked mud in the cart-track made the going very hard.

I passed one after another little knot of trees and bushes and still could not catch sight of the horses, and now I would gladly have abandoned all imitation of the boys. I picked a few wild flowers and watched a hawk hovering monotonously in the sky, and wondered what to say to Uncle if I could not find his horses at all. I found a bush of blackberries and ate some, and wondered if it would be wise to live out in the scrub for ever and never see Peter or Uncle or Auntie again. But then a wandering coyote might find me and eat me up. I pressed on.

At last as I came between two clumps of silver birch trees, like stout Cortez, silent in relieved amazement, I saw them over half a mile away across the flat open ground, standing in the shelter of another small clump of trees beside the line of wire fencing that marked the farthest extent of Uncle's land. I approached them, and after a while they raised their heads and watched me coming.

As I came nearer I could see them very clearly. They were big heavy animals, all compounded of muscle, and one or two of them were still chewing, like cartoon horses in the cinema, with a big hairy underlip moving grotesquely to and fro, keeping regular time except when a sudden gulp and shuffle on the pulp they were eating let out the odd trail of green slime, and reminded one of the long, useful yellow teeth inside.

They recognised me and they knew very well that I had come to fetch them, but they were too indolent to move and they knew I was afraid of them. I circled around them at a good distance and wished they would start for home. I whistled a bit and cried 'Harroo!' and 'Harrup!' but they listened in bored amazement. I came nearer and waved my arms and they swished their tails at the flies. Then I picked up a few clods of sunburnt earth, ammunition that would have done for cannon balls, and threw a couple at them. Their eyebrows shot up. I came nearer and threw another and it broke in two at the feet of the largest horse. He flung his head up and gazed at me deeply and then he took a few steps towards me. He was a very large horse indeed. I immediately reconsidered the whole position. Uncle had sent me to call the horses to water. I had called them: whether they came or not was another matter. I said nothing more to them and began to walk prudently and quietly home.

On the way I began to make up a story in which I lived far from Uncle and my family in a great city, in a luxurious house with a bath and a lavatory and a small garden and no horses. However, when I got back to the farm buildings a wonderful surprise awaited me: the horses were back. They had come back themselves by another way, round by the flax and the millet fields, and now they were drinking at the trough. They leered at me as I passed them into the yard. I made no mention of our dispute out on the land, and Uncle seemed pleased with me.

'Peggy brought the horses in while you boys were wasting time this afternoon,' he said at supper.

'Peggy's a regular cowgirl,' said Joe nastily.

'Get her some silver-plated spurs,' agreed Ernest.

'You boys can do the mending,' said Uncle, pleased with

the conversation. 'There's a button off my overalls you can start on and a hole in the sheet big enough for my two feet. Peter can do that while Peggy mends the tractor he busted this morning.'

'I fixed it,' said Peter dourly.

'Fix my button too,' returned Uncle Arthur. 'Everyone on a farm needs to be handy at everything.'

'Agile and smart!' said Peter, beginning to gaze at me malevolently across the table. 'And active and brave! Peggy's so brave, isn't she, Dad?' he went on innocently.

'Women are never all that brave,' replied Uncle Arthur, 'but Peggy'll do.'

'I must teach her to swim,' said Peter. 'Say, Dad, we could take a holiday, couldn't we, go to the lake for a couple of days, and I'll teach Peggy to swim.'

'We might manage to drive over again one Sunday,' said Uncle.

'I'll teach her,' said Peter. 'I'll push her in the deep end, and then she'll find herself swimming right away.'

Fortunately, we did not take another holiday at the little lake Peter was talking about. And while he was speaking, I did very much hope that it would be a long time before Uncle could find the time to drive us over again. But I let him go on about it, and show off the knowledge of swimming that he had picked up, because it got him off the subject of horses; and he was so astute that of all the family he was the most likely to uncover the truth, and then there would have been no peace from him.

Some time after this episode, when there had been time for Peter to forget about it, all four of us spent a week at a real lake, to the north, Lake Winnipeg, not a little piece of water that you could easily see across, but a vast sheet that stretched for miles, nearly three hundred miles altogether. We stayed near the southern end of the lake with some friends of Auntie's, and their children, and the beach below the house was flat and sandy and there was no place where anyone could push you in suddenly, so I managed to practise a little swimming at the edge with the other children while Peter contorted about in the canoe. The children had a raft made of logs nailed roughly together, which floated aimlessly on the water and could be directed by a paddle, or, near the edge of the lake, by a long pole. When we all stood on it at once, though, it sank quietly out of sight, and submerged us again.

After we had been swimming, we walked up and down the beach, and picked up the tiny shells off the sand, and took them to the cottage and made pictures by sticking them onto cards, painting them all to show the different patterns, tiny whorled shells and minute flat shells that you could make into miniature roses and violets with sprays of buds and leaves. We used to go out, too, looking for birds, the bright waxwings and orioles, and the little humming-birds that hovered over the foliage. And when all the boys had gone away for a day, picnicking, we collected wild flowers, touch-me-not and monkey flower and Blackeyed Susan, wild tiger lilies and wild cucumber and fringed gentians and Solomon's seal, and arrowhead from the edges of the stream that ran down to the lake.

The holiday was a great adventure — especially the day we all went to Winnipeg Beach and rode on the roundabouts — with only one discordant note, the fishflies. They were flies like Daddy-long-legs with the legs cut a little short, with fine long-veined wings. They kept quiet during the day and you might forget about them, unless you walked too far into the long grass, and then they would awake and whir above you and become entangled in your hair, and they landed on your arms and legs and struggled desperately just inside your collar, and hours later fell out half-dead from the folds of your clothing. The rest of the day they slept. Then when evening came they awoke and soared up in clouds above the vegetation, and they whirred out over the lake and rose and fell above the water like a dark drift of smoke between the land and the sunset.

In the course of their dance hundreds of them died, I don't know why, perhaps they fell into the waves, and thereafter the lake washed them up in sluggish bundles, gathering ever more thickly in ridges on the sand like patches of grey seaweed, and they lay there amid the whitened driftwood and the shells of crabs and skeletons of fish. They decayed slowly, and then they stank like dead fish. I complained about the smell; but the boys began to twit me, so I said nothing more about it.

But this gave Peter some ideas, and he and the other boys, Joe and Ernest and Tommy, went away and collected a number of little frogs from the lake edge, and popped them into our beds just before we came along from the kitchen sink all washed and ready to get into bed.

We were sleeping, myself and the other two girls, on a verandah at one side of the house, whose outer door opened onto the lawn outside, and the inner door into the main part of the cottage. It had been pleasant to lie there at night and look at the trees outside, and the pale sky over the lake. We used to lie awake until late at night and whisper to each other, telling wonderful stories of excitement and adventure, and peering out from our beds through the mosquito netting towards the trees and bushes, wondering what little animals might be moving about in the night.

But when we got into bed that evening and found these little creatures in our beds, we did not lie there for one half minute, but popped out again squeaking and twittering to each other, and ran in our pyjamas through the cottage to the many-windowed room on the other side of the house, looking over the lake, where the grown-ups were sitting having a drink and reading detective stories. The father of the family, in great wrath, went to look for the boys, but under Peter's direction they had climbed onto the roof of the outhouse where their sleeping-bunks were and they sat there safely while Mr. Savage shouted at them. In the zeal of his high spirits Peter suddenly got to his feet and jumped aloft and grabbed the long branches of the tree that hung over the cabin, and having seized a branch in both hands he took to the air and swung to and fro over our heads, yelling aloud as he zoomed past. Then he dropped back onto the roof and bounced up and down until the little house shook. Mr. Savage was now so far beyond self-control that he simply went back to the house and had another drink, and nothing much was said about the matter afterwards, because it was so obvious that Peter's behaviour was abominably bold and bad that nobody thought it worth mentioning it to him again.

But his blood was now up and he planned a whole campaign. He did not tell us about it until it was completed. Ernest came up to us two or three mornings later when we were sitting in some deckchairs under the trees.

'Peter says youse is to come to the beach,' he said.

'Your brother talks in an awful ignorant way,' said Betty Savage.

'I know,' I agreed. 'It's a desperation to me.'

'He'll be mad if you never come,' said little Ernest.

'Tell him we're occupied,' I replied. Ernest ran away. In a little while Joe came swinging up the path between the bushes and crossed the grass.

'He wants you-all on the beach,' he said.

'So we heard,' replied Jane Savage.

'You're hearing it again,' said Joe.

'We're not interested,' I said.

16

'He'll come himself, then,' said Joe. He moved off quietly and went away through the bushes. Very shortly afterwards Peter came up, his hands stuck in his belt where his two knives hung. He came to us and jerked his thumb over his shoulder towards the beach.

'Git!' he said.

We got up at once and went down to the lake with him. Here the other three boys were squatting round a little driftwood fire, built in the hollow of the sand behind the shelter of some rocks. We sat down on an old grey weathered tree-trunk while Peter stood with his back to the lake.

'This is a ritual we've got here,' he said. 'This is a little tribal fire we've lit for you to celebrate the return of Big Chief Running Bulge. Now see what the Big Chief has here.'

He picked up the satchel he used to carry his schoolbooks in. 'What's in there?' asked Betty.

'Wampum,' said Peter. 'Heap big Wampum.' He unbuckled it while the other boys covered their mouths with their hands and began to snigger. Peter tilted the satchel up and to our amazement there fell onto the sand, in pink, white and blue, a number of brassières.

'Peter!' I cried. 'You've been robbing the store!'

'No, my little chickabidee,' he replied, squatting down on his haunches and thoughtfully sifting the garments through his hands, 'I didn't get them from any ole store. I got them in a well-planned raid.'

'Where *did* you get them?' asked Jane.

'He got them from the Girl Guide camp!' Ernest burst out. Peter shot out his hand to strike him, but Ernest jumped aside.

'Well, as this ill-fated brave has told you,' Peter went on calmly, 'we have carried out a grand raid on the squaws.' He sat back comfortably in the sand and told us the story.

17

In the night, he and the other boys had got up and tramped the five miles up the road to the Girl Guide camp, situated in a field near the shore. Here Peter had crawled into every single tent, combed through every pile of clothing, and abstracted every single brassière he could find.

'And did you do all that without them hearing you?' I asked.

'I have such patience,' he said. 'And now we're going to burn them all on our ritual fire and sing a song. But first of all, tell me, what is the meaning of this?'

He picked up one of the garments and dangled it before us, gazing at it quizzically. It was a smart white padded brassière. Jane and Betty and I began to giggle loudly.

'What is the meaning of this?' asked Peter.

'He means what has it got them lumps on it for?' said Joe.

'To make it stick out right,' said Betty.

'Carry me away!' said Peter. 'You mean when you meet a girl and she sticks out nice in front——'

'Like a well-shaped cow,' added Joe thoughtfully.

'You keep quiet,' said Peter. 'Girls is all of one piece, not in bits like a cow. But here's this girl and she sticks out and it's all lumps she bought at the store?'

Betty and Jane and I rolled about on the log laughing and would not answer him. He gazed at us hard. 'I'm shocked!' he said. 'I'm shocked at you women!' He stripped off his shirt and amid our merriment he put on the brassière and pulled his shirt back over it; and to our horror he wore it for the rest of the day, obtaining some very sharp glances from the adults. Then he and the other boys burnt the other trophies on the fire and danced round it, singing a hideous song. And for the rest of the visit, Peter carried the bra in his pocket, with his compass and his other bits and pieces, as a memorial to his own resolution.

The end of our holiday came too soon and we stood reluctantly at the tiny station by a rank of fir trees and waited for the train. That is, the rest of us stood and Peter pranced about over the tracks — for the platform was almost level with the ground — and even stood on his hands on the wooden sleepers. We shouted to him that the train would suddenly come round the corner out of the dark wood and kill him, and he rerighted himself and began to collect some of the leaves that were already beginning to fall and to pick the willow-herb that grew by the tracks. He was the most restless and annoying boy. But you had to give in to him and let him do as he wished, because he was determined to have his own way and there would be no peace until he had it. In fact the best thing to do with Peter seemed to be just to let him do everything he wanted, and make no comment on it. This produced a good effect, until anyone came along who was as stubborn as himself. Grandma, for instance, was fonder of Peter than of any of her other grandchildren, and so she was always correcting and advising him and making him annoyed. Her visit to us after our holiday at the lake was typical. We all sat in the parlour, as Grandma liked to be honoured, and she dominated the scene from the largest armchair. She asked Uncle about the cows and the horses and the chickens, and told Auntie that she didn't like the pattern of her new curtains. And Joe's boots looked too small for him, she said: Auntie should put them aside for Ernest and buy Joe a new pair at the store. 'Or maybe you've got a good pair of Peter's laid aside?' she asked.

'Joe's boots will do,' said Auntie. 'He has small neat feet.'

'Not at all,' said Grandma. 'He's a big ungainly lad and he's outgrowing all his clothes. Ernest will never grow much, though — he reminds me of your brother Roger,' she added. 'Now don't giggle, Ernest! Sit up and don't scuff your feet about.' She turned to Peter. 'You've never yet learnt to brush your hair,' she said to him.

'I brush it,' said Peter. 'But it curls.'

'Nonsense!' replied Grandma. 'Any hair can be made tidy by a careful man. Yours is a terrible sight. It's even worse since you went on holiday. Bring me a brush and I'll brush it now.'

'Go fetch your brush, Peter,' said Uncle, smiling nastily as he wadded tobacco into his pipe.

'I don't want to,' said Peter loudly.

'Nobody cares what you want, Master Donovan,' replied Grandma. 'Fetch me your hairbrush.'

'The truth is, I lost it,' said Peter.

'I'll bring a new one for you from the store,' said Grandma, 'and your dad shall pay me out of your pocket money. Then we'll see about your hair, young man.'

Uncle smiled away to himself and Peter sniffed loudly in contempt. In the fondness of her pride in him Grandma overheard the sound.

'Sniffing now!' she cried. 'Where's your handkerchief? Blow your nose.'

'Ain't got a handkerchief,' said Peter.

'There's a handkerchief in your pocket,' she said.

'That ain't a handkerchief,' replied Peter, carefully tucking away the little white corner that showed in his pocket. 'That's my new necktie.'

'A white necktie! I never heard of such a thing! Show it to me!' cried Grandma.

Peter refused and Grandma persisted, until at last Uncle, losing patience with the argument, put down his pipe and said in the short black voice he used when he was getting angry:

'Bring out that necktie before I knock the samhell out of you, Peter.'

Peter put his hand in his pocket and brought out his well-thumbed treasure, the padded brassière. Grandma's dismay on that occasion was a joyful thing to witness. She accepted Peter's story that he had picked it up on the sand by the lake, but his vulgarity in carrying it around with him quite overcame her. And when she had examined the garment, her eyes glowing with interest, she expounded on the sinfulness of young women who wore such things, and then made a slow procession to the kitchen range and stuffed it in. Peter kicked the kitchen table angrily; and then he went away into the scrub and did not come back until everyone had gone to bed. I expected him to plan some form of revenge: but instead he only redoubled his vendetta with Benjamin, as he seemed to realise that in Grandma he had met an equal.

Because I, on the other hand, practised a diplomatic and yielding approach to Peter, the result in the end was that he particularly sought me out. He would keep an eye on me at school, and if any of the boys teased me in the playground he came over and knocked them hard. But if I had started to whimper and cry, he knocked me too. And at home if he had any special expedition to go on, an extra visit to Merrilee perhaps, or a journey to one of the other farms, he would tell me to come. He liked, for instance, to take me with him when he mended the fences. This was a pastime that belonged particularly to spring. Now the weather would become warmer after the winter, and the snow turned to slush and the birds began to sing, and Peter would stick his head into the kitchen in the spring vacation and yell to me to help him with the fences. He would take one of the big horses, doing some work for once in its life, and a flat cart and a sledgehammer and some wire, and drive round the wire fences that marked off some of Uncle's fields, and lift up the fallen wire and hammer in the loose posts.

He prattled to me as we rattled along, telling me his plans and how Uncle Arthur would send him to college (with some help from Grandma) because he was so clever, and how he would study agriculture and become a rich farmer and grow more wheat than anyone else. If he stopped talking he had to sing, or whistle the songs of the birds and tell me their names, or he stood upright on the cart and forced the horse to go at a really fast amble, nearly a canter, showing off how he could stand even when we lurched over the ruts.

'You make too much noise, Peter,' I used to say. 'Oh, I spend so much of the day silent!' he replied. 'You'll never make a farmer if you have to be always talking,' I said. 'I tell you, I'm not always talking,' he said. 'Only now and then. Perhaps I will make a farmer, perhaps I won't. We'll see' — and he danced about from one leg to another and flapped the reins.

For myself, I said to myself, I will not make a farmer or a farmer's wife either. Farm life had too many dangers for me, and at the same time, too much drabness. There was this old cart, for instance, where I was sitting on the boards and leaning against one low side and bumping along just talking to my cousin, nothing better to do in all this empty land except sit in a cart and talk to a cousin I knew far too well. And when I got home there was still cooking waiting to be done, there was always so much cooking; and sometimes at harvest time we even cooked on the second stove in the back kitchen, and whenever it rained the raindrops fell through the unmended roof and sang and danced in the smoking fat of the frying-pan; and then the fat spat out and hit the hot iron of the stove and suddenly evaporated into tiny sticky patches that all had to be wiped away later. And maybe then, if I moved away suddenly, I might tread on a cat with her new kittens, or a hen that had got in by mistake, or trip on Uncle's bales of wire and rope: it was drab, definitely.

As I got older I used to brood sometimes about how drab it was. I sat on a stool in the larder by the tin of honey, by a little window that opened onto a view of the barn and the fields past it, and piled butter and honey onto pieces of bread or fresh scones, and ate them up, and brooded horribly. Or escaping again, I brooded on top of one of the stacks of straw, flat on my stomach with the straw making criss-cross red ridges on my bare folded arms as I lay under the hot afternoon sun; and late at night on my bed, swinging my bare toes, I sat and looked at the fantastic spectacle of the Northern Lights with their curtains of colour hanging in the sky, and continued my soliloquy. It was difficult to tell, exactly, what I was thinking about, it was difficult to put words or sentences to one's thoughts then, questions that never quite took shape, appreciations that never really crystallised; it was difficult to know why one had to think so or what one really wanted, or what might be the answers to questions one did not know how to ask. Then suddenly I would swing right round again and become very active and busy; and sometimes would even believe that I was enjoying farm life. It seemed happy enough, sometimes, with all the different things that lay at hand for us to do; and even the boys managed to be pleasant sometimes, especially in the evenings when we sat together lounging about on the couches in the verandah, and sang songs, and they played their tin whistles and their old guitar; and in the twilight a sort of peace settled over the land, while we sang and played to the accompaniment of the frogs, and the crickets that lived behind the walls of the house.

Thus time passed away over the eternal plain without bringing us much change, until I had just turned fourteen and my uncle inadvertently burnt the farm down. Uncle Arthur was a true Irishman and he had taken to drink. Well may Grandma have subscribed to temperance societies and read us extracts from their monthly papers: the old Serpent was preparing a relevant surprise for her in her very bosom.

Uncle Arthur was always fond of a glass, if not two, three, or even more glasses. He kept his supply of bottles down in the basement where the beetles played, affixed to a rope so that he might haul it up speedily. Especially in the winter, when the snow piled up around the windows again and work was no longer so pressing, he liked to have two or three of his friends come stamping in and sit around the kitchen table, and they passed the bottle around and told improbable stories. The farmers round about us were mostly Scots or Norwegians, not noisy men, but able to take a quiet amusement in a little convivial company. My cousins sat cross-legged on the floor around the range with sharp eyes and ears and drank in every word. I sat at the back of the room wedged down on the floor between two armchairs; I played with the cat and stared at the men's faces. I learnt with precision every shade in the transition of a face from a weather-beaten, hardbitten Canadian farmer into another Benjamin.

Sometimes we were forgotten and were allowed to stay up late, and then at length I would see the Benjamins rise to their feet and put Benjamin hats over Benjamin faces, and they lingered awhile at the door and then made their way into the frosty, sparkling night, shouting Benjamin cries at each other. At first we would all go to bed after their departure. Later on, however, Uncle Arthur took to staying behind to clear up. I crept out of bed one night — crocodiles forgotten — and picked my way delicately to the bend in the stairs, where I crouched and listened. The linoleum on the stairs was painfully cold to my feet. Uncle Arthur was chatting away to himself, and pouring out an extra glass or two. I did not like to go to bed again while this strange person sat chatting in the kitchen; but at last my cold feet drove me away, and I left him there to murmur to himself.

Wartime came and Uncle Arthur grew very morose in the evenings. His younger brother had left his job in Winnipeg and joined the army; he had been killed quite soon, and I think my uncle felt it bitterly. He sat up late at night, enjoying the soft light of a lamp and thinking of the bad state of the world. And, quite simply, when he stood up late one night he knocked against the table and sent the lamp flying. Consequently, the farm burnt down. What a bustle there was then! With what haste we leapt out of the windows into the six-foot drifts of snow! What a roasting there must have been of the beetles and crickets left behind! What a riding and driving the farmers round about made towards us over the snow. And what a flame poured up with consuming heat, waving defiant red hands at the bright Northern Lights. In one crackling rage, the security of fourteen years of life disappeared to ashes in a few hours.

And now, the question was, what to do? Here we were in the snow, sparks raining around us and the house disintegrating: what to do next? Joe was gasping, Ernest was whimpering, Peter was loving it. He hurried to and fro with buckets of water pumped up from the well, and whenever he had emptied them towards the flames he would stand for a moment and stare, passionately drinking in the spectacle. Then when further effort was obviously useless he stood and stamped his feet, thrust into unlaced boots, and stared with a set, unsmiling, fascinated face. I think it was at that moment that it became finally clear to Peter that the farm was too dull for him. He began to see the vision of a wider world. Meanwhile, everyone else was discussing the question 'What to do?' They sorted it out between themselves in their slow determined voices. Someone had a bed to spare for Benjamin, and one of the elder farmers whose children had grown up and left his house could take Uncle, Auntie, and the three boys. No room there for me, so I was to stay the night with someone else and in the morning go to Grandma. This tied things up nicely for a while. Then insurance could be claimed, the farm rebuilt, and life start as it was again. That was that, and, still bundled up in my borrowed coat, I was driven away in the back of a car to Merrilee, where a number of people were awakened and out in the streets having a good look at the red glow in the sky. When we had gone into the house several of them came knocking at the door with parcels for me and promises of more to come for my family, and they sat around in the kitchen watching me drink soup and planning to call on Uncle and Auntie and offer their help at the earliest opportunity. And so to bed, and to prepare myself to meet Grandma in the morning.

Chapter Two

GREAT was the encounter with Grandma in the morning. First the knocking at the door, then the long wait, then the appearance of the old lady, then the explanation.

'But what started the fire?'

'Uncle started it, Grandma. He knocked down the lamp.'

'What did he need the lamp for when he's got good electric light?'

'He likes the lamp to sit up with, Grandma.'

'And what should he have to sit up for?'

'He sits and takes a beer, Grandma.'

'What?'

'He takes a beer, Grandma.'

'Don't mumble at me.'

'Uncle takes a beer at night, Grandma.'

'Nonsense!'

'Yes, Grandma, it's true, Uncle often has a beer.'

Marvellous understatement! It was not beer he drank.

'You're just telling me lies. None of my children ever took a drink.'

'It's true, Mrs. Donovan,' said the farmer with me. 'The farm's clean burnt out. Shall we go take a look at it?'

'No thank you! I'll not go to see the Devil's handiwork.'

She stumped away into the house. I followed her.

'Grandma, I've come to stay with you,' I shouted.

'What?'

'I'm here to stay with you!'

'Who sent you to stay with me?'

I began to feel unwanted.

'Uncle Arthur sent me to stay with you!'

'I'll not take any of his children into my house, bringing the drink in with them,' she said.

'Grandma, Uncle Arthur is not *my* father!'

'And who was your father but a drinking man too?'

The farmer began to shift about at the door.

'Mrs. Donovan, will you take the girl or shall she come right back with me?'

'No, no, I'll not be beholden to you,' she said. 'Bring in your parcels, don't stand blocking up my door.'

So I moved into Grandma's little house. Later in the morning someone brought round the pony and stabled it in the shed in her little field, explaining to me that Uncle had thought that I would like its company. The long morning passed. Grandma and I held conversations.

'Don't do this,' she said.

'No Grandma.'

'Don't do that.'

'No Grandma.'

Grandma had her house all arranged. Everything had its own appointed place, and to move anything was accounted a mortal sin. Grandma showed me all her contrivances. Meanwhile, she gave me moral instruction.

'Strong drink is raging,' she said.

'Yes Grandma.'

'Woe unto them that rise up early in the morning,' she said, 'that they may drink strong drink.'

'Uncle Arthur don't *rise up* early, Grandma. He stays up all night.'

'Don't interrupt me when I tell you God's Word.'

'No Grandma.'

One of the farmers called near lunch-time with some clothes from his wife. Grandma addressed him on drink for a while. 'Well, Peggy,' he said to me at the gate, 'I guess this is a life-giving blow to your Grandma.'

It was a blow all right, but I don't know that it was strictly life-giving. As the days went by it merely seemed to reanimate the old lady into a more adamant prejudice. Drink hovered perpetually on her vision. To her it was the one great evil and she mentioned it constantly. But I made myself as snug as could be managed in the range of such inspiring company. I had a little bedroom at the top of the house, and at the side of it where the roof sloped I had my bed, and had to be careful not to sit up too rapidly or I would bang my head. The bed was a small one, with a pretty flowered cover on it, made by Grandma. The floor was covered with old-fashioned linoleum patterned with flowers, with a rag rug, made by Grandma. Grandma was a most industrious old lady. The larger window, hung with chintz curtains, looked out to the front of the house, and a smaller one oversaw the rear garden and the field. I had hooks on the back of the door on which to hang my clothes, a chest of drawers, enamelled green, with a small mirror on it, and a window seat at the front window, with coloured cushions, made by Grandma. This was all the furniture, but it sufficed. To wash, I went to the kitchen sink. But who wanted to wash?

I arranged the room to suit my taste, put the rag rug at an angle, pinned up a few coloured postcards, and made another cushion. I was really happy to be alone at last. Now at last, provided I kept out of sight of Grandma, I could go my own way.

Avoiding Grandma was not such an easy task. It required a good deal of subtlety and foresight. I was at school still, but when I returned in the afternoons Grandma would have plans all ready for me. Of course I was used to housekeeping: in fact when it came to harvest time on Uncle's farm we used to feed as many as fifteen to twenty big men at once when the team came round with the thresher. They would all come into the kitchen and pack in around the table with its bright oilcloth cover, and would expect something significant in the way of beef, scones and apple pie. I had peeled a mountain of potatoes for them, sitting on the doorstep with the black-and-white collie dog lying beside me and the hens pecking nearer and nearer and then skipping away rapidly when I slapped at a mosquito. But Grandma was so fussy. Everything must be done exactly her way. I used to curse her behind her back. 'You old bag, you,' I used to say. 'Go jump in the creek, Grandma!' Everything must be done exactly as Grandma appointed. If you decided to wash the steps for her, why, one *never* washed steps. If you didn't wash the steps, well, why hadn't you washed the steps and whitened them? If you sliced the vegetables for pickles thin, she had meant to tell you to slice them thick. If thick, they would never cook through properly. I determined not to grow up into a prejudiced old lady like her. *I* would be a reasonable old lady.

She was a stout, determined, courageous old woman, and she kept her home in perfect order. She had the most lovely pieces of china saved from the course of her lifetime and arranged in a big black dresser in the front room. I used to look at them one by one. There were plain and fluted cups and saucers, plates and jugs, decorated with birds and flowers. They were beautiful. Everywhere there were evidences of her industry — rugs, patchwork quilts, pillows and sheets edged with crochet-work, embroidered cloths, chair-covers, footstools. The whole place had been decorated up to the nines by Grandma, in the intervals of producing a flow of the same goods for church sales. She was a living example of what tenacity of purpose can do for a human being.

When the warm weather came and the snow began to melt away into dreary pools and a high wind sang in the treetops, and when the blazing heat of summer opened over us, Grandma worked in her garden. She watered it laboriously from her pump. At the back she kept chickens and grew vegetables, tomatoes, sweet corn (among the tall leafy rows of which I used to hide while I surreptitiously ate some of the smaller cobs), cucumbers and others. At the front she planted flowers. Her rows of sweet peas were like nothing I have seen before or since. In the evening I used to look out at them from my high window, while the tobacco flowers and the tall yellow evening primrose, which she thought a weed, were opening, and the sweet peas shone in the late day like so many puffs of coloured light, wine, red, pink, white, blue and mauve. They were utterly desirable. I could have eaten them all, if it could have been done without altering or destroying them.

Grandma liked social affairs too, church meetings particularly or Conservative suppers: and she liked to entertain her own personal friends to tea. On these occasions there was a great baking of scones and cake and even bread. With a nice bun mixture, Grandma used to make cinnamon rolls. You rolled the dough out flat, sprinkled it with soft brown sugar, cinnamon and sultanas, rolled it up, cut it off into alluring little buns, baked it, and ate it hot with butter. It was delicious. At tea-parties Grandma also brought out her best home-made jam and provided blueberry pie. She allowed everyone a boiled egg, used her finest china and her silver teapot covered with an embroidered tea-cosy, and supplied coloured paper serviettes.

She had one friend in particular whom she liked to invite,

but I did not care for her so much. Her name was Mrs. Ransom and she kept the general store. Her appearance was unusual: she was a thin, stooping woman, with a nose and teeth that wandered away from her face out into the open air, rambling, as it were, in search of adventure: but it was not her appearance that chiefly discomforted me, it was the unfortunate fact that in earlier days my cousins and I had often carried out small raids on her store.

On our journeys to and fro, the boys and I often used to come upon the main road, and would follow along it, myself usually riding the pony, Peter, Joe and Ernest walking alongside picking up and dropping stones and sticks, and jumping to and fro over the ditches and chasing occasional insects. Eventually we would reach Merrilee. Near the general store there stood a tank. Here I would dismount and the boys would water the horse: it was now my task to enter the store in a noncommittal manner, buy some chewing-gum, and on the way out steal a few handfuls of candies. How those candies burnt in my memory whenever I saw Mrs. Ransom! I felt she could read my action on my brow whenever she looked at me. At times I almost wished I had not done it. But it was the boys' fault, of course, for leading me into uncivilised actions. In the future, I decided, I would find company that did not drag me down and cumber me with remorse.

In the meantime, I made do in the vacation with Grandma's visitors. In the school term there had been plenty of company at school, but it was company that I did not wish to pursue in the holidays. I accepted Grandma's friends, and took as well to exploring and making visits of my own, beyond the reach of our usual social circle. I ranged around an odd collection of farms and shacks. One day I paid a visit further afield than I had ever ridden before. I came into a part of the countryside that undulated gently; there were small dips and elevations that passed for valleys and hills, with little knots of trees here and there and one or two shallow ponds edged thickly with water weeds. As we came past one of the small hills and the land opened out again before us level to the horizon, I saw a small cottage beneath some trees. I walked the horse towards it and reined in in the small front yard. An old black-and-white collie was lying by the front step with his nose on his paws, crushing down a patch of long coarse grass; he thumped his tail on the ground but made no sound, and I had a moment or two to study the house while the hens came gently returning.

It was a little tarred wooden building containing two or three rooms. To the left were the hen-houses, and to the right a small garden. The curtains at the windows were clean and bright, but the whole cottage had the appearance of having settled down year by year more eagerly towards the ground and of hovering now on the edge of the final crumble which would scatter its planks among the brambles and wild oats. As I sat in the saddle and stared at it a face appeared at the window, wavering and indistinct like a reflection in our water-trough, a patch of yellowy-white fragmented together with blue lights from the sky. In a moment or two the door was pushed open and an old, old lady appeared. She stood on the step in her wrinkled grey stockings and battered slippers and the hard summer sun illuminated the dust motes in her hair, which lay coarse and tangled around her head like the tufts of pale winter grass which rise out of the huddled snow.

'Have ye business?' she croaked.

'I'm visiting,' I replied.

'Come away in!' she said.

I hitched up my pony in the shade of the hen-houses and walked in through the door. Inside it seemed to be as dark

33

as night. Through the gloom I perceived an old man sitting in a basket chair.

'Wha's there?' he exclaimed.

'A visitor!' said his wife.

'Sit ye doon!' he cried.

I sat down. She took an old black kettle, already filled with water, and put it on the round black stove, pushing aside a covered saucepan. This had been boiling over all around, and now it began happily to boil over on one side only.

'Wha's this, Jeannie?' asked the old man.

'A visitor!' she croaked.

'Aye, aye,' he said.

We sat in sombre silence. A dirty ginger cat came from the corner of the room and sat down meditatively in front of the stove. In a passing breeze, almost the only breath of wind in the day, the outside door of mosquito netting, unlatched, creaked idly to and fro.

'Wha's there?' asked the old man.

'Naebody,' said his wife.

'There's some folk at the door,' he said.

'There's naebody,' she replied. ''Tis your sins coming in at the door, more likely.'

She made a pitch black brew of tea and served it to us. As we drank I remembered a packet of candy in my pocket, and drew it out, now rather warm.

'A present!' I said.

'I'm grateful,' said the old man. 'Ye'll be the new nurse?'

'A visitor!' cried the old woman.

'Aye, aye,' said the old man.

Tea proceeded in this slow fashion, timeless and deliberate. We sat drinking from our cups while outside the Redskins fought, the French explorers came, the settlers followed, the herds of buffalo and the Indians were driven back, vast wheat farms spread out, roads were laid, towns sprang up, cities grew, industries flourished and fell, aeroplanes passed overhead, wars were waged again, and the great Day of Judgment drew at hand. The mosquito door still creaked in the tailend of the purposeless breeze, spent from its journey across the plains.

'I must be going,' I said at last.

'Grand to have seen ye!' said the old man. 'Ye'll be the Minister's wife?'

'Aye, aye!' I said. 'Good day to ye!'

'Every blessing to ye!' he said.

I mounted my pony and turned him home, kicking him into a fast amble for the pleasure of hearing the rattle of his hooves on the hard ground and feeling the saddle leather creaking under me. I was depressed, and was glad when we reached the open ground past the little hills and could see the long sunlight lying across the countryside.

I came home as fast as the pony could comfortably go, happy to see the town coming into sight, and as we went I brooded in my heart on my little visit, profoundly sorry for the old couple living their monotonous and unsuccessful life, which above all things I was eager to avoid. The gloom of this aimless ending to an aimless life hovered over my spirits for a long time after this visit. The prospect of such a future haunted me. Then, as it seemed to be the only way to escape it, I decided to work harder and do well at school, and to win a scholarship. With a scholarship one could proceed to do something useful, something at present rather vague, the form of which could be decided later, but something which would at least take me away from Merrilee and the farming districts.

There were two years of school left, long enough for study, but I began right away, even in the summer vacation, to read the books for Grade X. Peter had finished Grade XII and in the fall he would be leaving for college. Perhaps, I thought vaguely, I would leave for college too. The situation was not altogether clear to me.

Peter, however, was clear enough. He was going into Second Year, because he had finished Grade XII, and he was going to study engineering at college in Ontario. He was not going to be a farmer. This did not matter, as Joe was so obviously going to be a farmer: he was so good at farming, for one thing, and so completely unsuited to everything else, for another. Ernest was too young to have to decide yet, but ever since two R.A.F. pilots had come out to the farm for Christmas, he had been besotted with aeroplanes and it looked as if he would take up something to do with flying. I was not sure quite what I would be: except that it would be a great success.

As the fall approached I was really beginning to enjoy my efforts at studying hard. But an ill wind blew up with the autumn. I had gone over many times to visit Uncle and Auntie and to help Auntie all I could, and now that the fall was at hand and the farmhouse had been rebuilt, and they were ready to move in from their temporary shelter, it appeared that they expected me to go back and live with them.

The news was very unpleasant to me, for though it might scarcely be believed I really liked living with Grandma. There was something about her, annoying as she was, that secretly appealed to me. And if I was to go back to running continuous errands around the farmhouse, to say nothing of the longer walk to catch the bus that took us to the High School in the next town, when would it be possible to study as hard as I had planned? It was quite disconcerting: but after a long meditation at the back of Grandma's hen-houses a plan of campaign unfolded itself to me. I went into the house and found Grandma.

'Say, Grandma,' I shouted, 'here's welcome news for you.'

'News?' she said. 'Somebody dead?'

'No, Grandma,' I said. 'It's real pleasant news from Uncle and Auntie. They're ready to take me off your hands now.'

Grandma's mouth closed very firmly. She moved slowly, ponderous in her black print dress, out to the verandah at the front of the house, and sat down in her rocking-chair. I followed her and dropped onto the couch.

'Uncle and Auntie are all ready to come with the car and pick up my things any time now,' I went on. 'They've not just fixed the date yet, but they'll soon pick on one that suits them. And they thank you very much for looking after me, they know it's been a great burden to you.'

Grandma rocked to and fro deliberately.

'Maybe it doesn't suit me,' she said.

'Oh well, Grandma,' I said, 'that would be just too bad, because Uncle and Auntie are dead set on it.'

She rocked away. 'It doesn't suit me at all,' she said.

'Well, Grandma, that's too bad,' I said. 'I wish you'd said something earlier on. Maybe if you'd put it to Uncle Arthur nicely he might have thought about it and seen if he could suit you a little. *Maybe!* My!' I added to the ceiling. 'How Uncle and Auntie do like their own way. Especially Auntie. My, there's a real determined woman there! Two of a kind! Oh no, we'll have to do as they say.'

I was becoming hoarse so I closed down and lay back on the cushions.

'She's got my Arthur,' said Grandma; 'she shan't have my only granddaughter too.'

The interview was going admirably. I helped it on.

'But I'm such a help to Auntie!' I bellowed from the depth of the cushions. 'It would be cruel to deprive her!'

37

'You're a help to *me*,' retorted Grandma. 'And sit up. You look downright indecent sprawling there. Go and tell your uncle to bring his wife to tea on Sunday.'

I went out and borrowed the neighbour's telephone and issued the invitation. On Sunday Auntie and Uncle came to tea. Auntie, the busy little woman, lost no time at all in telling Grandma that she and Uncle would soon come to fetch me. 'And thanks for your help, Mother,' she said. 'It's been most kind of you.'

'Peggy is my own flesh and blood,' replied Grandma deliberately. 'I'm not looking for thanks. I'm happy to look after her. And I'm going to go on doing it.'

There was a very lively little argument. Auntie got quite annoyed and pointed out — as I had expected — what a necessity to her I was.

'With what you'll save on all her keep and her school-books,' replied Grandma, 'you can get a hired girl for all the summer, which is the only time you need it.' Then she played her trump card. 'I gave you a bit of money towards Peter's college,' she said, 'and if Peggy stays with me I'm going to pay money to send her to college too. Peggy's really gifted. She's always studying. Peggy's a real scholar and she'll be a great credit to me.' She went on with her tea calmly.

Uncle and Auntie naturally looked stunned at this news about my love of study, but I rejoiced. With my scholarship and Grandma's money escape from Merrilee would be certain. Meanwhile Auntie tried to put in one last spoke.

'How about Joe and Ernest?' she enquired tartly.

'Neither Joe nor Ernest has any brains. They don't take after my side of the family at all,' replied Grandma. 'Peter and Peggy are the gifted ones. Money for Arthur's boy and money for Sheelagh's girl: that's right and proper. So that's settled.'

38

With a little more argument it was settled, and Uncle and Auntie drove away leaving the situation to go on just as it was. So the school session opened and I settled down to do some hard work. It caught my interest, and even seemed to make the days go by faster. And with visits to the farm, guests coming to our house, and all the business of Merrilee town, winter passed, and spring and summer seemed to come around in no time at all.

In the summer, at the beginning of his vacation, before going to stay with his parents and help them on the farm, Peter came to visit us for a few days. He had been home at Christmas but had been working somewhere else in the spring vacation, and so we had not seen him for several months.

Grandma was thrilled with the preparations for his visit. As we made all the arrangements she sang Peter's praises to me, and then in a reminiscent mood she began to tell me again about Grandad and how much Peter took after him. Grandma loved to tell me stories as we sat on the verandah; I think it was one of the reasons why she was not eager to part with me. You could catch a fine dream of Ireland from her, hilly and misty, and of the sea, whispering and beguiling on the coast, and of Grandma and Grandad setting forth stoutly to reach a new life.

As for Peter, I had always been contented to think that he took too much after Grandma, but she seemed to think he was like Grandad and there was no stopping her. But as Grandad sounded like a monument of business resolution combined with the astutest mercenary judgment, able to make ten dollars grow in the place of one and a horse fetch treble its value, I began to think that there were shades in his soul even deeper than Peter's, for Peter, though not very honest, was not apparently mercenary. It began to dawn on me as I listened to Grandma's tales, rather more frank than ever before, now that the glow of Peter's expected arrival warmed her ever more cheerily, that Grandma was probably very well able to send me to college and that her industrious life in the little house she had bought when Grandad died and Uncle Arthur took over the farm was entirely due to taste and not necessity. Fortified by the prospect of the support of her money, I became more than ever determined to win a scholarship and to gain her approval.

Meanwhile the days went by, and Peter arrived at last, in his city suit and a spotlessly clean white shirt such as I had never seen on him before. He came late after supper and after a talk on the verandah we all retired to bed. Standing in the half-light of the summer evening as I got ready for bed that night, I happened to glance at the wall between his bedroom and mine, made of pinewood planks, varnished, but still showing the grain and knots of the wood. There was something unusual about one of the knots: looking at it closely, I saw that the knot itself had been pushed out, and in its place was a round blue eye. I did not like to have this eye peeping at me joyfully, so I took out my chewing gum and with it I blocked up the merry little window. I could hear Peter's bed creaking as he rolled about on it trying to stifle his laughter.

Next morning, after the housework had been cleared away for the time being, he came down to the bottom of the garden where I was standing between the two rows of sweet corn, thinking about the summer. I felt a little afraid of him, as always, especially as he seemed to be even taller now. The sun blazed down on his black hair and I could see the colours of the garden reflected in his bright blue eyes.

'What are you doing?' he asked.

'Thinking,' I said.

'You should find something to do,' he said.

'What do you do all the time at college?' I asked.

'I study engineering, of course.'

'Is engineering a good job?'

'It's a wonderful job. I'll build things, big things, you know, dams and bridges and things. There's going to be any amount of building to do in Canada. And I'll be able to go anywhere I like, right up to the North, down to the States, anywhere. It's a marvellous job.'

'What do you do when you're not engineering?'

'I go out with girls.'

'College girls won't go out with *you*,' I said.

'College girls like me a lot,' he replied.

'But you're just a small-town boy.'

'Oh no, I'm not.' He smiled at me. 'I'm smart, you know, Peggy,' he said. 'I get around. And girls just love me. But you're a small-town girl, Peggy. Why do you always wear those awful old slacks? You should buy a pretty dress. You'd have a pretty figure in a dress. At least, you'll have a pretty figure when you grow a bit, but you should start and train it now.'

'Thank you, Peter Donovan,' I said, 'I know how to dress. But I only dress when there's company.'

'Aren't I company?'

'You're just my brother.'

'*Cousin*,' he said. 'Cousin's a different thing altogether. But even if I were your brother, I could still help you a lot. Brothers can tell you things. They give you advice. Now, for instance, I bet you never kissed anyone.'

'How could you tell?' I replied. 'People start kissing at ten years old. I know.'

'But I bet you never,' he said.

'Huh!' I said. 'I never saw anyone I wanted to kiss.'

'Well, you still ought to know how,' he said. 'I could give

41

you advice.' He bent his head suddenly and kissed me before I had seen what he was planning. It wasn't too bad, really. On the other hand, it wasn't very uplifting. 'There you are,' he went on: 'you don't do it right. You should shut your eyes and sort of lean against me. And then you should put an arm round my neck and run your hands through my hair.'

'Gee whiz!' I said. 'I'd as soon run my hands through a pile of brushwood.'

He twitched his black brows angrily together and suddenly he kissed me again, but I jerked away. 'You're doing it too hard,' I said. 'I don't like you, Peter. And you feel too hot. The sun's got into your skin.'

He started to laugh and I tried to seize the opportunity to dart away, but he shot out his hand and grabbed my wrist. His grip was terrible: I counted all the bruises in the evening.

'Don't tell my brothers,' he said. 'If you do, I'll beat you all up. You first. There'll be blood everywhere.'

'You're uncouth,' I said. 'And when you've done snapping my hand off, I want the bits back.'

He let go and I began to rub my arm. He bent down and leant his forehead gently against my shoulder and I could feel his mouth against the crook of my neck. There was something rather nice about the feeling.

'Don't tell my brothers,' he said, in the softest voice I had ever heard him use.

'Well, of course I won't,' I said. 'I promise.' Without thinking I put my hand up and patted his head. He straightened up at once and smiled at me wickedly.

'There you are,' he said, 'you're coming on.'

I was angry at him and I ran away. I ran up the garden as far as the hen-houses, and feeling safe there I turned round and shouted at him: 'Peter's a hick!' But he only laughed. 'Slacks don't suit you at all,' he called out. 'Especially when

you run. Buy yourself a dress' — and he walked away to
the field to see the little pony.

'Cousins are no use!' I said to myself, as I walked back
into the house. And the rest of his visit did not change my
mind. When we both escaped from Grandma, he lectured
me on every possible subject. Nothing that I thought was
right. I told him, for instance, about some of my long rides,
and about the old couple I had visited. 'So you see,' I said,
'how much better it is to get away from here and to get on
in life.'

'Why?' he said. It was nasty of him, because there was
nothing better he wanted than to get on in life; and he had
already succeeded in getting away.

'Well, what a dull old age,' I said.

'Maybe they've enjoyed their life,' he replied.

'But now they're old,' I said, 'and she's got nothing better
to do but look at him.'

'What better?' he said perversely.

'There's lots better,' I retorted. 'That's an awful life.
There's no enchantment in it at all.'

'What nonsense,' he said. 'Women don't need *enchantment.*'

'What do they need?' I asked.

'A woman needs to marry a satisfying man,' he said
grandly. 'Capable and active, with a good, useful job that
he likes doing.'

'And then what does she do all her life?' I asked.

'She looks after her family,' said Peter, 'and she loves it.'

'Mary and Joseph!' I said. 'What a future! I don't want
to live like that. I want something with a rainbow over
it.'

'You won't get married, anyway,' he replied. 'Not in
those old slacks. They don't show off your figure to advantage. You've got no idea of market value, my girl.'

'Well, I'll keep my slacks,' I said, 'and I won't get married at all, and I'll just settle for the rainbow.'

'You can settle for the rainbow,' he said, 'but you'll find it's composed entirely of rain.'

I got up and walked away. As I went through the door I paused for a moment. 'I'm so glad I'm not an engineer,' I said, 'made of waterproof cement.' He threw the paper at me, but I had already closed the mosquito door, and I went peacefully away to the garden.

After that I went for a walk. 'Cousins are no use!' I said to myself again. 'If there's one thing I've got to avoid, it's my cousins!' In some perfect and sunlit existence that was always ready to burst in on me, soon, soon, not this year and not quite the beginning of next year but soon, soon, soon, there were to be no cousins, no drunken men, no old clothes, no monotony and yet no disasters, no arguments, no irritations and hindrances at all, only a lavish and brilliant flowering of everything I cared for, sunshine and excitement and bright patterns of flowers. And in this summer that preceded my last year at school, when so many new experiences and such a spectacular new existence were waiting to descend fully developed upon me, I began to feel that I must prepare myself for the life that was coming. I must decide what I really wanted to do and what I really thought about things. Above all, I must decide who I really was. The problem was now beginning to worry me.

After Peter had gone and left us in peace, I used to sit by my window looking out and thinking, and used to peer carefully into my mind, hoping to find Margaret Talkative inside: but she never seemed to be at home. I peered carefully about in the interior, hoping to see some little active, kicking pink thing that one could grab hold of, crying out 'This is Me!', but the more I poked about the emptier and drearier the place seemed to be. Turning my back on the spectacle, I

44

would decide that it might be more practical to discover myself by establishing a definite course of action.

I used to saddle up my pony then and trot off through the scrub, turning over in my mind my plans for the future. I was to begin in a modest way by becoming the Premier of Canada; then by special request I would graduate to Prime Minister of Great Britain. I would write several novels which would easily be recognised as the greatest ever produced by the human mind, tossing off in the interval one or two astonishing pictures. In this way, I would come to know exactly who I was. Everyone else would, too. Having thus established myself as another and greater Winston Churchill, I used to idle along the paths by the fields, looking over their flat expanse, stretching away on either side as far as eye could see, and would watch the sun sinking on the horizon, and the red lamps of sunset lighting up in every small cloud scattered over the surface of the vast, uninterrupted sky. Coming home in the evening sometimes, I would see the evening train going past, and as it roared through the failing bars of sunlight its shadow used to fall on the smoke that drifted down beside it, and a real and a shadow train would speed to Winnipeg together. But which was real, and which would be the shadow? I used to watch them vanishing in the distance; and then the hooves of my pony would arouse me as they broke out a ploppety-plop on the main street of the town. Sometimes I would see Benjamin there, come into town on an errand. The children would shout after him: 'Benjamin! Benjamin! Benjamin's a hayseed!' I used to raise my hand as the pony trotted past him. 'Hiya, half-witted!' I would call; and he would be convulsed with laughter.

In the late evening, then, returned home from my ride, or on a warm Sunday afternoon, having struggled through church in the morning, wearing one of Grandma's old straw hats and concealing a great deal of boredom while the preacher addressed, alternately, the empty front seats and the rafters (it was a little wooden Canadian church and the fields came right up to the walls, and outside there lay such a vision of fresh air and cheerfulness), I would sit by my window and consider even more personal matters. I would think about love.

Love, I had noticed, was a frequent topic of conversation, a subject of obvious importance. Why, there was even Peter, as unromantic a figure as you could think of, talking about marriage and practising kissing down by the rows of sweet corn. Everybody was interested in love. It must, therefore, be fitted into my plans for the future. But in what form? Not, certainly, in the shape of any man *I* knew. I had often formed a temporary attachment to one or another feature of some man — somebody's black hair, for instance, or some other farmer's flashing smile — but closer acquaintance had soon dispelled the illusion of charm. In the future, therefore, I was to fall in love with some stranger. But how fall in love? This was the part I could not fathom. What came over you to make you fall in love? I finally decided that to fall in love one must fall for someone who represented perfection. Otherwise how could one feel such an overwhelming set of sensations? No, the man must be perfect or one would not fall in love with him. People who had not met someone faultless were not in love, they were just getting by.

In my mind's eye I saw my encounter with this adequate hero. I was no longer dressed in slacks, sandals, and a check shirt; I wore a gown strangely compounding all the various colours of the sweet peas outside in the garden. My hair was miraculously reordered into a fashionable style. My sunburn had faded into a perfect English complexion. Into a room I came, therefore, in a large, fashionable straw hat, astounding everyone with my elegance, that is to say, everyone who was not already knocked flat by my being Prime Minister of Great Britain. In that eventful room I met the last Prime Minister of the islands. Odd, I had not met him before. He had not been dispossessed of his position: he had resigned in order to pursue a career as a famous surgeon and a significantly audible musician. He had plenty of time ahead of him for these pursuits, for you could tell by a glance at his smooth face and rich black hair that he was not more than twenty-two, if that. We fell in love. Immediately, he began writing long letters. Page after page he covered with impassioned declarations. I kept them in a gold filigree box and wrote back to him. Subsequently all these letters were published together and outdid the very Brownings, of whom the interesting Robert figured in our Grade XI syllabus, which I had already begun to read. 'That's my last Duchess hanging on the wall' — I can remember her still. After that the picture ceased to be interesting. The subject of my future loves was temporarily exhausted.

I did, however, try to find out why Grandma had married Grandad. What reason had stood *her* instead of falling in love?

'Say, Grandma,' I shouted at her, favouring a direct approach, 'why didya marry Grandpa?'

'He asked me,' she said tersely.

'But why didya say, "Yes, Henry"?'

'What?'

'How did he hookya, Grandma?'

'He was a fine upstanding man with money laid by, and he had the biggest black beard in County Galway.'

A beard? No: I did not favour that; but still, every man to his own taste.

Looking for further material for thought, I began to devote my spare time to reading; real books, not school text-books and set works only, but proper complete books such as middle-aged people sometimes had in rows on their shelves simply because they liked to read. I borrowed everything it was possible to lay hands on. I soon learned to skip all those prefaces which at the beginning of some great work of literature set out to explain to us in analytical detail exactly how ill-constructed and lacking in real invention the story is going to be. I had met their kind before, for in my school Reader I used to see the vast rhinoceros: on his massive back he bore, ungrateful pensioners, a host of little pecking birds. I doubted if they felt a real concern for him. Come along a bigger and better and buggier rhinoceros, and they would soon transfer without a tear shed.

Brushing them aside, I devoured the books for myself, lying flat on my stomach on Grandma's verandah. When I had finished all I could obtain, I took up her enormous copy of the Bible and opened up in the New Testament. Brought up by cynical Uncle Arthur, I had never attended Sunday School, and as a straightforward narrative the story was new to me. I took in every word of it. I saw it all — the people, the lake, the storm, the angels; I trod along in very reality through Palestine in fascination at the back of a hero. But when we entered Jerusalem together and gave the dreadful answers to the Pharisees, I realised with a shock that I knew my companion already. It was my old friend the Devil in a new disguise. I recognised him by his aweful self-sufficiency, planted foursquare on two firm legs, the sufficiency that could subdue lions and crocodiles, disciples and Pharisees, the self-sufficiency of the being who knows exactly who he is. 'And you are not yet fifty years old and you have seen Abraham?' they said to him. 'Before Abraham was, I AM,' he answered. I fell in love with the man at that. Religion descended on me from heaven in a cloud; I became a disciple, my face shone with holy fervour. I rushed from the house in an ecstasy of imagination and saddled up the old pony, and with a long stirrup and short rein, as we always rode, trotted away sharply down the main street and out at an amble through the scrub. The horse's hooves rang out his name, the hawk overhead repeated it, the sun beat it down on me, the silver birches defied the Pharisees on every side. I was in love already!

I flung myself into my new life. I even managed to smile frequently at Grandma. I looked every hour into the mirror to admire the effect on my curly brown hair of the tight plaits into which I had drawn it, to mark my renunciation of vanity and worldly desires. As I went about doing the dishes, I sang hymns at the top of my voice. I practised them a little on Grandma's piano. On Sunday, I tried my best to listen to the preacher, as he addressed first one wall and then another. Failing to keep my attention on him, I learnt a few more hymns from the hymnbook. I recited them loudly as I paced about at night under the brilliant stars, in a bright darkness where stars and moon and hymns and I appeared to be all one radiant mixture. But when Ernest and Joe came to stay for a few days and I found them as provoking as ever, the glow seemed to fade: and under Grandma's ever vigilant, aggravating eye it departed quietly one evening for good. I was not in love any longer.

Now I began to seek a little more company. I even hung about the streets of an evening with some of the other young people: but I still could not manage to appreciate their conversation. It had none of the qualities I wished to cultivate. Everything they said was interlarded with the latest fashionable sayings; if a saying was the latest, then you had to say it. 'Hiya Cookie!' the boys would shout. 'Hiya Dogbiscuit!' you had to shout back. But the next week the boys shouted, 'Hiya Overdone Beef!' Well then, what was the answer? Or, if you wanted to tell a story, it must be this week's story. 'Did you hear the one about the Moron who made a hole in the carpet?' 'I don't believe you!' 'Yes, he wanted to see the Floor Show. Arf! Arf! Arf!' I could understand something about these stories: they were about a moron. But that was all. Once again I decided I did not fit in on the rural Canadian scene.

Chapter Three

WHEN the next summer term came, it was time to write the Grade XI exams, and to put on to paper all the knowledge we had gathered for this day, or as much of it as could be conveyed at a time during such and such a space of a summer's day. After this, there was a long, long wait for the results.

I looked daily for the envelope that would bring them to us, but it never seemed to arrive. Sometimes I felt afraid that it might have been misdirected, so I walked across the fields to the mailbox standing on a little white post at the head of the road leading to Uncle's farmhouse, and peeped in, unsuccessfully, which meant a long return across the hot fields for nothing, and then another aimless evening to while away. And in fact, the long suspense impressed my mind very much more than the celebrations Merrilee held for the end of the war.

But one afternoon when I had walked over to the farm itself, I saw Joe and Ernest on the verandah: and as they saw me coming they began to wave to me and jump about. I came up the verandah steps and through the netted door, and they continued their chorus, 'Look! Look!'

They thrust at me the newspaper they had been waving, which they had sat down to read after lunch. There I stood, top of the list, head of Manitoba Grade XI with an average of 94%.

'You cheated!' cried Ernest. 'You cheated in the test!'

I smacked his seat. 'I never did!' I said.

'You cheated for sure,' said Joe. '*You* never did this on your own. Ninety-four-hundred-per-cent! Just wait till Peter hears!' But Peter, mercifully, was away at a summer job in Ontario, and Joe was not a letter-writer. Meanwhile Uncle and Auntie came out to the verandah. 'Well done!' said Uncle, kissing me. 'Well done!' echoed Auntie, but not kissing me. She never liked me quite as well as Uncle did.

'What did Mother say?' asked Uncle Arthur after we had discussed the news.

'She doesn't know,' I said. 'We don't take this paper. I'll go back and tell her, I think. See you again!'

I walked home rapidly, full of excitement, and hardly able to wait until I had hurried home and found Grandma. She was gardening, and straightened up when I tugged at her sleeve. As I shouted the news at her her face glowed. She made off into the house, beaming proudly, and there to my amazement she gave me a present of a silver tea-set.

'This is my mother's,' she said. 'It's my second set, for I had my wedding set too. I've been rubbing it up for the day when you got your scholarship.'

'But supposing I didn't get it?' I asked.

'But you *have* got it,' she said. 'What are you arguing for? But don't use the tea-set. Keep it for best. And now go make some tea in the brown teapot.'

We took a cup of tea and some home-made fruit cake; and while we drank Grandma made plans to go visiting. She drew up a list of all her acquaintances who must hear and discuss the news, and after tea she started on her visits right away.

She went to her bedroom, downstairs at the back of the house, and put on her best black frock and an old black straw hat with a bunch of red roses attached to the front.

She got out a pair of black gloves and a black leather hand-bag; and savouring her deep satisfaction, she stepped into the sunshine and along the road, to begin her triumphal round. The visits lasted her many happy days, and they were enhanced by the arrival of reporters who took my photograph and made some notes about our family. The picture of me standing (in a dress) by the dogwood bush duly appeared in the papers with a column of print about me; and thereafter Grandma carried some copies with her on her visits. Mrs. Ransom also pinned up the cuttings by her counter, and enjoyed telling her customers how she had always known I would make my mark. My progress to the heights was evidently well begun.

Then Grandma presented me with a cheque with which to open a bank account. 'This is not your allowance,' she said. 'I'll pay you that every fall. This is to set you up with a few useful things.' It was amazing that Grandma, who appeared so thrifty, could suddenly be so generous. I went over to the big town where our High School stood, and started an account at Grandma's bank there. Then I made a list of all the things I thought I needed to buy. Grandma contributed some ideas towards it as well, mostly suggestions for plain wholesome garments I did not intend to get.

Joe and Ernest found out about my list, and then they tormented me about it. 'Say, Peggy,' Joe would say, waving a rusty old tin can, 'here's a swell object I found for you. You could use it for sure.'

'What would I do with an old tin can?' I asked.

'Boil up your coffee,' said Ernest. 'The rust'll give it a flavour, maybe. And Peggy,' he said sweetly, 'I ferreted out an old cartwheel down by the creek. Could you use it for a pillow, Peggy, Peggy, couldn't you use it?'

These little conversations convinced me that I had done very rightly in labouring to make my way to go to college and leave my family far behind me. And when I passed Benjamin, with his dank brown hair hanging over his forehead, and his sweaty check shirt, when he leered at me and still perpetually wagged his head, my rejoicing was reinforced. So in pride and honour I bought a number of things at the general store, under the flash of Mrs. Ransom's teeth and the bright perception of her eye. There was no need to steal anything now, no, I had good Canadian dollars in my pocket. Or rather, I had good Canadian dollars in my fist, being counted and recounted every few minutes.

I bought a number of things from her; but my clothes I got in Winnipeg because I wanted them to be right. The farmers gave me lifts to and from the city. We had driven to Winnipeg before, now and then, but this summer I went there more often than ever before, taking a number of opportunities for a lift. The drive to and fro hardly seemed to take any time at all in the farmers' big cars that whirred along the straight road, flinging up the pebbles with a rattle on either side half the way.

Of course it wasn't the *best* Canadian road. There were roads, so we had heard, that ran dead straight for hundreds of miles, with scarcely any cross-roads or intersections at all, and you could get up a magnificent speed on them, leaving the surface behind you — Canada's best — plastered with the flat skins of surprised chipmunks and hedgehogs and frogs, and even, if you had been speedy enough, of the grey squirrels. However, we made do with sixty miles an hour; and then I did my shopping on Portage Avenue and took time off at every visit to stop at the Hudson's Bay store and drink a frosted malted milk, trickling coldly down the back of my throat. And then I went and stayed on the farm for a while, and Auntie gave me some cushion covers and ornaments for my room at college, and then, back in Merrilee, Grandma's friends came round with little presents too. And

Peter wrote to me, briefly, and sent me some ash-trays and a beer-bottle opener, which all had to be hidden from Grandma. So by the end of the summer, I was very well stocked.

I spent some time too in preparing my mind for my college career. I visualised scenes and situations in which I would star. Though I had already begun to modify my rather large-scale plans for my future, I still felt it possible that while at university I might be involved in incidents of importance. One might, for instance, be chosen to be the Freshie Queen. I walked to and fro about my room practising to be the Freshie Queen. Then I hoped I might be Ophelia in the Varsity Drama Festival, and I also thought about Lady Macbeth. After this I went outside into the fresh air and tore down the garden path, in an heroic attempt to win the Ladies' Five Hundred Yards.

I saw Grandma's face, globular and amazed, pressed against the panes of the kitchen window. I was afraid that she would begin to tap maddeningly on the window-pane and call out 'Yoohoo!', so I walked in sedately and rushed upstairs and began to compose a sonnet. What with one thing and another, the days were far too short for all the preparations I had to make. But at last there came the fall; and a fresh air began to blow over the land, and the trees began to die around us, yellow and red and orange, and the sumac and dogwood flamed scarlet. I made a last round of farewell visits, packed my belongings in my new suitcases, was duly escorted to the station, embarked amid pomp, and lo, I was on the road to college.

A cousin of ours met me at Winnipeg's vast station, and drove me to the women's residence of the college at which I was going to study. This residence was near the college itself, which was built, in fine decorated sandy-brown stone, near the Red River. Near at hand stood the men's residence as well; for although the college had many day students, at least a third of its members lived on the spot. So I unpacked my clothes and my possessions and settled down in my little room, and then went out to wander around the city.

It was lovely weather in Winnipeg then. There was a bright clear air about us, a bright blue sky, a bright sun, a flurry of red and golden leaves. It was weather for adventure, weather for mounting your horse and riding somewhere. Where, I don't know. It would have taken a whole heap of riding to get anywhere in Manitoba. Still, it was the weather in which to begin living: time for new thoughts, new friend-ships, new loves, new sensations. And in my little room I arranged and rearranged my things, and put my rug in different places on the floor, and my cushions here and there, with a sense of excitement. Anything might happen now! I might meet Anybody! I counted the few remaining days one by one: until at last there only remained, Tomorrow!

As I had some knowledge of social etiquette (for perhaps Peter's words had not gone unheeded), I dressed in my very best on the day when the college classes started. I wore nylon stockings, high-heeled shoes, a blue cardigan, and a pale blue skirt. Round my left ankle I wore a gold chain: around my right ankle, six red bangles. I brushed up my hair into as many curls as I could manage, and did myself up nicely with lipstick and nail-polish; and thus prepared for higher learning, I went very early to the classroom.

The students came lounging in by twos and threes, and as the young men appeared they took a quick look around to see what girls awaited them. A tall boy of about eighteen, with red hair, gave a long stare at me, and then he came across and sat down beside me.

'Hiya, Repulsive,' he said to me.

'Hiya, Excruciating,' I replied.

'This is Don Macdonald. What's your ugly name?'

'Margaret Talkative.'

'I take to you,' he said.

He talked to me for a while. Then he said:

'You're a small-town girl?'

'I guess so.'

'Then you don't know anything about Life?'

'I guess not.'

'I'll teach you,' he said. He took a volume out of his pocket. 'Look at this!' he said. 'Hot stuff! You should get an earful of it. Let me read you something.'

He started to read me a poem. It was about some knight who was in love with some lady. Donald loved it: he read it juicily. Busy times they had together, too. Anyway, the knight turned out to be a leper, and she cast him off. I didn't blame her at all. I was right with her there; I would have done the same myself. It was a proper Benjamin of a situation.

The professor came in and interrupted our thoughts for a while. Quite what he was saying I don't know, for I was busy part of the time looking out of the window at a very fine view of the maple trees and of the grass lawn curving down to the river, and the other part of the time looking round the room at the other students; and now and again too I admired my new looseleaf exercise book with the stiff cloth cover and clean shiny paper, and my new fountain-pen. I had written a big heading and a date at the top of the first page of paper. I liked them a lot. When the professor had moved off, and another one had followed him, so that must have been two lectures, Donald took me down to the canteen to meet his friends. 'Hi!' we said all round, and sat down to drink Coca-Cola.

I fell in very well with Don's friends, and was quite happy to share the beginning of my college career with them. We spent most of our time together, reading and arguing. Thus began my education. We sprawled about in the canteen with our feet up on chairs, eating apple pie and ice-cream. We walked up and down beneath the trees, and then we sat on the steps in the sunshine, still at it. They would come into the residence too and sit on the tables, swinging their legs, and on walks we recited to each other, and we argued about everything until late into the night.

With them I did more reading than ever before. We would read anything printed; but the more lurid the work, the more we loved to read it. We trailed in the rearguard of the generation who despised the Victorians, and wagged our heads with merry looks over our great-grandfathers and grandmothers who did not understand the true mystery of love. No doubt we were mistaken and the Victorians knew exactly what was what and did not choose to say so; but then, we wallowed in the works of men who did choose to say so, men to whom life had taught nothing except that times are hard and sex is fascinating. Now, with such descriptive scenes sucked down for ever into the bogs of my unyielding memory, I am determined that there will be no passionate embraces in any work of mine. No limbs will quiver on beds, couches, bearskin rugs, sunroofs or pingpong tables; nor in gamekeepers' sheds, Arabian deserts or steaming tropical jungles. But still, those were happy times, and we shared happy experiences. We lingered tip-toe on yonder misty mountain top. We galloped down the road and knocked at the window, bellowing out, 'Is anybody there?' We lingered under the elms, slowly decaying, and said mournfully, 'Hello, out there.' We sat among the rocks, mysterious, diving for pearls. We sat on pots on the Western front. It was just amazing how we got around the place.

Everybody now seemed to be ready to educate me. One young man, short and thickset with coarse tumbled black hair, tried to make me understand the heart of a novel. He gave me a book to read by one James Joyce.

I looked through it. It was full of words falling like great oily gobbets through the recesses of somebody or other's mind. 'Isn't that great!' he said. 'That's a great novel: powerful, evocative, haunting.'

'I don't understand it,' I said. 'I thought you wrote a novel because you had a story to tell.'

'You're dead wrong!' he cried. 'Nobody wants a story. You write a novel to get across a Mood. A Mood, that's the important thing. Look at Sweat. You can get across a colossal mood with Sweat. Imagine a scene where everything is sweating. You play the piano. Sweat starts out of the piano keys. You look out of the window. The place is full of Africans, all of them sweating. You pick up a whisky glass. You find it sweating. You lay your hand on your mistress's bare arm. Sweat starts up under your collar and runs down your backbone. What does this all make you think of?'

'High time for a bath,' I said.

'You miss it!' he said. 'You miss the significance, the inner symbolism of it all! The sweat means Destiny. It means the thing that is Puzzling at the bottom of human affairs. It makes you wonder. Why is everything sweating? Why is the whisky glass sweating? Everything is not as it should be.'

'You don't mean it!' I said incredulously.

'I do!' he assured me. 'You need to grasp it, you see. Take Boredom. There's nothing so great a novel can do as get across to the reader a really gripping sense of boredom. Imagine this hut by the railway tracks. There's a guy sitting there, drinking a coke. In comes another guy. "Hi," he says, "I think I'll have a coke." He sits down. In comes a third guy. "Hiya, Charlie," they say to him, "why don't

E   59

you have a coke?" There they are all three of them, sitting having a coke. Nothing is happening. It makes you wonder. Is anything ever going to happen?'

'It is,' I said. 'There's a train going to come out of the night and hit them.'

'Hopeless,' he interrupted. 'That would be Action.'

'It would be reality,' I said.

'But you don't want Reality. You don't want Drama. You want to puzzle your readers. You want to depress them. You want to get across something they can't possibly understand. If you can't do it with a Mood, you must do it with a Vision.'

'Where does that come into a novel?' I asked, thinking he meant a new Easter hat.

'That's one of the biggest things for a novel. Vision! You start with some big experience. You have to have a fright. You have to be sombre. When you are a child, about six or seven, you get up early one morning and you go sit on a hill. The sun is coming up. The mist is going down. All at once, you see it! People are dying, everywhere, people dying! Earth is beating, thump, thump, thump. The sea is lashing, slosh, slosh, slosh. Time is moving by you, tick, tock, tick, tock. But there you are! You! You know it is *you!* Everywhere, people dying, earth thumping, sea crawling, time passing, but you are you! Well, you've struck lucky. This lets you off for the rest of your life. Everything you write, you mention the vision. You don't have to be sensible. You don't have to be kind. You don't have to be religious. Your God is now the sun, the wind, and of course, yourself. You're lucky: you had a vision. You're a genius. You feel things. You *know*. After all, you had that vision.'

'Seems to me,' I said, 'that you might be a woman in a small shack with six mangy children and one drunk husband and you would feel things too. Seems to me you might get to feel things so badly it would make you a genius as well.'

'But not if you weren't sitting on a hill!' he said. 'Not if the sun wasn't coming up! Not if there wasn't the mighty heart of the universe beating! And certainly not if you couldn't put it across. That's the real crux of the matter. Can you get it across? Can you fill several hundred pages with close even handwriting? Can you call up the resources of the entire dictionary? If not, you're out. You don't feel things. You don't even begin to *know*. No, for knowing things, and feeling things, and having first-hand information, and plumbing the depths of life, there's nothing that can beat a really wordy female writer who likes to get up early on a foggy morning.'

I didn't agree with him much. Somewhere, I felt, there was something unreasonable about it all. I didn't think much of it all as an occupation: myself, I decided, I would stick to men. Men were handier, they had cash in their pocket, they could buy you a Coca-Cola. Besides, they lasted.

But my acquaintance had begun to gaze at me intently. 'Say,' he said, 'why didn't we have this talk before? There's something about you that really sends me. I've got just a marvellous collection of etchings. Why don't you come up some time and look at them?'

'Thanks, but no,' I said. 'I wasn't brought up to appreciate art.'

So then I went and wrote another letter home to Grandma. 'Dear Grandma,' I said, 'You will be glad to know I am working hard and learning many new things. I am sure college will help to broaden my outlook and enable me to be a success in life. I shall always be grateful to you for your help. . . .' Back came a neat little note from Grandma, in round handwriting on lined notepaper, saying that she didn't know about my outlook, but as long as I got good marks in tests that would be very satisfactory.

This made me feel a bit conscious for an hour or two, but I soon shook the feeling off, and returned to my social life. This was very busy, for I was not such a fool as to refuse all the invitations that came my way, only those that seemed too suspicious. If I had refused them, it would have put an end to any chance there was of my playing any part in university life: accordingly, I went to dances and parties and picnics, and plays and debates and films, like all the other women there. The curious thing about these girls was that they lived under rules as strict as those which governed any old-time Hindu lady. I recognised some of these rules myself — was I not soon wearing no gold chain, three green bangles on my left ankle and a necklace of gilt hazelnuts? — but their whole life was bound to them by a horrifying extent.

Every Friday and Saturday night, for instance, you must have a date. If there was a big dance, you had to be at it or else pretend to be ill. If there was a special outing, you must go on it plus date. If the latest fashion for date-catching feminine glamour had been six ponderous coconuts hung from each ear, the girls would have worn it. If it had been for pale blue pyjama trousers and a blouse made of holly leaves, they would have donned it unprotestingly.

They lived under the pressure of a relentless tyranny, to be lifted only when their children were born and *their* social life became the centre of existence. And meantime, like ants scuttling about under a magnifying glass — oh, the urgency and busyness with which we prepared for a date. I soon learnt the way of it. You started from the skin out.

First, the night before (if you were not going out) a hair-wash: then on the day, a bubble bath, and a rub and scrub with this and that and a dab of hand lotion all over, and a bit of talcum powder here and a bit of New York perfume there, and ten red toe-nails, and ten red finger-nails, and one big red mouth, and two of the latest ear-rings or ear-clusters or ear-blossoms or whatever it was now, and face lotion, and face cream and face powder, and rub it all off again to get that natural look, and add a lot of mascara to get that *madly* natural look. Then brush up your hair style and don the merest suggestion of underclothes, something in the way of a forward-looking bra, and some lace very properly called brief, and something to keep your stockings up, and stockings that did their best to look as though they were not there, and a mere suggestion of a petticoat, and a useful little frock, and a colossal fur coat to keep the whole outfit together, borrow it if you had to. And of course a generous use of Lxxxxxxx Soap and Cxxxxxx's Toothpaste. Nobody could miss them out, for had we not all heard the immortal advertisement:

> 'Ring. Ring. Ring.
> I'm Sad Sadie, the B.O. Lady.
> Every time the telephone rings, it's the Wrong Number.'

No, when the telephone rang there must be a Date on the end of it. So you got all dolled up, and out you went — with what? Just with some guy with a crew cut and a wad of chewing gum in his cheek and no new conversation: but still, he was a Date, and the very breath and stuff of life.

And then, of course, there was always the occupation of exploring Winnipeg, this notable collection of buildings, standing up bold and independent all over the place until I thought it was almost time to push them down and have a look at the sky again. Our favourite place, as students, was the Glory of the Prairie, or Portage Avenue, which stretched, more or less, from Eaton's store at one end to the Hudson's

Bay store at the other. On the map it maybe protruded a little way south-west of the Bay, but this was not important. Here you could always buy Coca-Cola, and ice-cream, and roasted peanuts; and at night Portage Avenue took on a resplendent magnificence, for advertisements lit up everywhere overhead, and decorated the night with their brilliant colours.

A little way south of Portage Avenue there was a hall called the Auditorium, where there was sometimes a concert; and as if this was not sufficient excitement, there was another small place farther east where a play would be held now and again, or an exhibition of ballet dancing. And far out to the west was the Assiniboine Park, and it had a bear pit with bears in it. The bears looked ill at ease ambling around the concrete pit and I did not go to this park again, though regretting my single view of the buffalo — or bison — or buffalo. And we went through Chinatown to the Chinese restaurant too, and sometimes we explored the back streets of Winnipeg, and went dancing late at night in halls where the other dancers scarcely spoke English. And we went skating on the ice-rinks, under the bright arc lights with a gramophone broadcasting waltzes all evening, and in the day we piled into cars with our skis and ran down the sides of the Red River, shooting out over the ice. And we took part, of course, in all the observances of the Christian Year: Hallowe'en first of all, and Eaton's Santa Claus Parade in November, where the clowns skipped and tumbled along the pavement while we encouraged them loudly, and the Christmas Carol Service in the Auditorium, and the Grand Ice Carnival, and all the other events leading on through Christmas to Easter.

Thus the first year of college passed easily by, spent in going about in search of excitement, arguing with Don and his friends, looking over my clothes and getting on with the other girls. I weekly wrote a letter to Grandma, to be read

64

by her in a loud monotonous voice to the rest of the family; but except for this and the Christmas vacation I gave as little thought to Merrilee as possible. I was too busy at college.

In excitement and variety, it certainly lived up to my expectations. And yet for all that, it seemed for some time that I was not going to find that touch of real splendour for which I had been hoping. It was all very exciting, and yet never entirely satisfying. And in particular, and this worried me, that desirable and romantic personage with whom I was going to fall in love seemed to be absent. I was often disappointed about this.

But then, at the end of my first year, I thought I had found him. We went to watch a baseball match against another college — and there I saw a most distinguished person. This person was the Grand Cheer Leader of Mackinawack College, near Portage Avenue. It was his duty to raise the morale of his team before the game began.

After our cheer leader had done his bit, having been allowed to perform first as a courtesy to ourselves, the visiting team, the Mackinawack Grand Cheer Leader and three lovely Mackinawack dames came out and pranced up and down in shorts and sweatshirts, and shouted the Mackinawack Cheer:

'M — Marvellous!
A — Astonishing!
C — Colossal!
K — Mackinawack!
        Rah! Rah! Rah!

No other College like Mackinawack!
No Greater Team than Mackinawack!
Victory sure for Mackinawack!

> Here we are, Fighting-Fit,
>   Spick and Spack,
>   Job and Lot,
>   Bric-à-Brac,
>   Knick-Knack,
>   Paddy-Wack,
>   Mackinawack!'

I was fairly bowled over by him. I thought about him all through the game and dreamt about him for days afterwards. A distinguished, muscular, chesty personage! Now at last I felt sure I had met my fate. I imagined many a scene where he saved me from danger and warded off lions and tigers, and the violence of my emotions and the supercompetence and sizeable chest expansion of my hero confirmed to me that I was indeed in love. But the pressing problem was how to meet him *personally*. Let me do that, I thought, and all life's problems would be solved at a blow, and woman's monotonous date-hungry existence would be lifted at once into the realm of pure glamour: for the thought of a Steady Date and a front garden wedding with catering by Eaton's or the Bay became much more satisfying when imagined for oneself with the Mackinawack Grand Cheer Leader, than with any other Date I had had.

At last, I had a great stroke of luck. I was at a University Dance and wearing a peculiarly becoming rose-pink frock, when I saw him sitting at a table with some other people.

'Introduce me,' I said to Don.

'Who to?' he asked.

'That guy with the red shirt.'

'Archie Belvedere? The Mackinawack Grand Cheer Leader?'

'The very same. I want to meet him.'

'You don't want to meet any old Mackinawack bigmouth,' he said.

'I do,' I said.

'You asked for it,' he replied, and he led me across the floor.

'Hi, Archie!' he said. 'Meet Margaret! How's the swimming, Archie? Who's going to win the four-hundred yards?'

Archie rose to his feet and gave me a long look.

'You and I could dance like one,' he said. 'Just like one long sweet lingering thought.'

He swept me into his muscular arms and pushed me off across the floor. I should have been in heaven, but I didn't quite seem to achieve it. There was a certain element of non-sequitur about Archie's conversation which had not been present whenever I had imagined meeting him; as the dance progressed I even began to wonder if he was not slightly foolish. When the music stopped I discovered the reason.

'Swell!' he said. 'And now let's have some refreshment.'

Out of his pocket he took a hip flask.

'Have a nip,' he said.

'Not me!' I said.

'What's the matter? Don't you like it?'

'Not at all.'

'Don't be dowdy,' he said. 'Don't be old-fashioned.'

'I don't like it,' I said, 'and I don't like men who like it.'

'Snakes!' he said. 'There's no woman going to come between me and a drink.'

I left him to it and went back to Don, who smiled at me nastily. Thus ended the second time I was in love.

So at the end of my first year my affairs were still not quite in order. However, I was not yet eighteen: and there was still hope.

Chapter Four

AT the beginning of the first summer vacation, I took a job in the Hudson's Bay store for a month, living in a bedsitting-room with a friend of mine and going out with Don and his friends in the evenings. Then I stayed for a while with some college friends whose home was in Tuxedo, at the outskirts of Winnipeg. By the end of my stay the weather had become brilliantly hot, and it was time for all who could afford it to leave Winnipeg and retire to the lakes to refresh themselves in the waters. I returned to Merrilee and spent a week or two with Uncle and Auntie, mercifully missing Peter, whom I had not seen since Christmas. After this visit at the farm, I spent the rest of the vacation with Grandma: and I set out to see if I could write a novel myself.

A readiness to take part in the creative arts was an essential part of life at our college, and with a mind full of new impressions and restless feelings I had plenty to say in my novel which spread all around my little bedroom on separate sheets of paper. It was difficult to write this novel properly because all parts of it occurred to me at once: but at last I learnt to write the different scenes on different sheets of paper, and laid them down in different places, one scene on my bed, one on the chest of drawers, one on the rug, and so on, and I perambulated to and fro among the different departments and added here a descriptive paragraph, there a piece of dialogue, sometimes writing as I stood, sometimes sitting, sometimes on all fours.

The theme of my novel dealt with a young Canadian soldier in war-torn Europe during the last year. Since peace had come, he was faced with the prospect of leaving his mistress in Paris, and returning to his fiancée in Canada. The novel was full of conflict: and I trotted happily around my room adding to the piles of paper with descriptions of ruined and starving Europe, life in the army, love scenes in bed at dawn, agonized farewells, and other subjects with which I was not familiar. But when all the highlights were written, it seemed impossible to connect them up.

For one thing, working under the pressure of a burning inspiration, I had written a number of scenes and descriptions for which there could be no possible connection: and for another, although I felt good at doing highlights and could readily rattle off sharp stark dialogue or moving and eloquent descriptions of scenery, houses, the state of the sky, etc., I seemed to lack a plain narrative style of the type that trudges steadily forward through the main part of a novel, and can be depended on to make one hundred pages into four hundred and fifty. I had one hundred pages, but not a novel. So I adapted myself, and wrote a play about life in a submarine during the war.

This was not completed before the beginning of the next college term: but all this intellectual activity had inspired me to try to take things more seriously in second year. After all, life was going by! I still did not know who I was or what I really wanted to do: and as for love — evidently I had not plumbed the depths of that yet. If I did not look out, I would grow old without ever expressing myself adequately, or realising anything of the spirit of the happy dreams that had hung round me as I trotted on my pony through the Manitoba countryside.

69

Looking out of my window at the garden and at the fields in the distance, I remembered those dreams — happy echoes of childhood, I said to myself — and the fear that life might go by without my ever having discovered how to live began to grip me by the throat. Stagnation and a dull old age loomed acutely before me once again. But in second year, I determined, I would make amends. In second year I was not going to miss a thing.

We started off well by taking to drama: and these were happy times again. Donald was President of Drama for our college that year, and he ordered us all around, and we spent many a long winter afternoon rehearsing while the snow came drifting down past the windows in thick flat flakes, or whirled in eddying circles, tracing the pattern of the wind in the air. That was a lovely little play, *Hamlet in Texas*: full of dust, and violence, and mooing cattle, and lowering clouds, and indescribable significance and tension. When, eventually, we had put it on and had held a little party afterwards, we all felt we had been in on something really big, something really worth being in on. We couldn't for the life of us have told you what it was; but never mind, we felt big.

For a while, too, I fell in with some geology students. They seemed very eager about their work; and when I asked them what they were learning, they said they were studying the Truth. I was interested in this, and felt almost inclined now to become a geologist, and I asked them what they had learnt about the Truth. So they told me what they could let me know within a hundred million years or so how old the earth was, and within a hundred thousand years or so how old mankind was, and if they had his toenail handy they could tell you what the horse looked like in the dawn of the world; and they worked it all out from the order of the rocks and fossils underfoot, but sometimes a wiggle of the earth's crust had disturbed the whole affair, and they had to start again from the top downwards instead of the bottom up. They did not seem to be able to say, however, whom you would do best to marry or how to grow into a reasonable old lady, so I concluded that it was not the truth they had discovered as yet, but only some old rocks and stones.

Leaving them to it, I turned my attention to the newspaper world. I accepted an invitation to go with one character to help produce the students' newspaper. This was called *The Assiniboine Weekly Groan*. A young man of about nineteen, a tall, pale, brown-haired young man called Joe McVie, invited me to accompany him to the office. He was a young man of affairs, versed in politics, often at meetings, loud in debates. To him, life was simply a chain of events. First something happened, a situation arose, and then you did something about it: you denounced it, and you began a revolution to set it right, or, on the other hand, it was satisfactory, so you took all the credit for it to yourself, and started to work tooth and nail on the next event. This was all there was to living, he told me as we walked to the office, manipulating events. What you were like, or your friends or enemies were like, did not come into it at all.

'The trouble with events,' I pointed out, 'is that they don't manipulate so very easy.'

'That's because you're a woman,' he told me. 'You're frightened of Life. You need to step out into things, get a grip on them, start things rolling. You want to meet clever guys, see important Events, learn to think big.'

I don't want to learn any such thing, I thought. I only want to find out what is controlling events already, and get my mind in step with it. But I said nothing, and talking animatedly, he led me to our destination. It was a winter's evening and the lights were shining on the freshly heaped snow. Small diamonds of snow glinted past us. We reached a tall, grey building and descended some stone steps into a small yard. Here we knocked at the basement door. Someone called out loudly in one of the Red Indian languages and Joe answered in the same, and we were admitted and went along a narrow passage and entered the room where the paper was edited. Here was a scene of indescribable confusion: never have I seen so many people being so busy in one small room. Students were milling everywhere. One student was sitting at a table, hammering out, on a typewriter, notes on Sport. Another at another table was covering American News. A third, European News. A fourth, fifth and sixth, Russian News. A seventh, Some First-Year Lovelies of Manitoba University. An eighth, What is Missing in Our Professors? A ninth, Why My University Course Does Not Suit Me. A tenth, How I Would Run Manitoba University. An eleventh, Where is the Best Joint for Hamburgers after Twelve Midnight?

'This is going to be a colossal issue of the *Groan*,' they all chorused as we strolled from table to table.

Every single student seated at a typewriter had a cigarette hanging from his mouth at precisely the same precarious angle. How it balanced there, I did not know. It was not glued on, for every now and then he would take it out, puff out some smoke, spit out some tobacco, and hang it back at the very same angle. If he left it there long enough, the ash would grow longer and longer, the cigarette shorter and shorter, and my nerves became tenser and tenser with dismal foreboding. But they were all gloriously happy and busy. They were convinced they were helping to make the world go round. It reminded me of a scene I had seen in a film where four chimpanzees in the zoo in London, England, had a convivial tea-party, assisted by their keeper. 'See, Ma,' said the small child sitting next to me, 'see, Ma, five big monkeys.'

Suddenly a dishevelled personage emerged through the

smoke of battle and accosted Joe and myself. 'Look,' he cried, 'we've nothing ready for our column on Big Times Around the City.'

'What were you aiming at this week?' asked Joe.

'We were lined up to have Brother Trombone tonight, but nobody's covered him yet. Could you two go hear him for us?'

'Sure!' said Joe. We emerged together into the fresh air, and clambered onto a street-car. In about ten minutes, we arrived at the haunts of Brother Trombone. He performed in a large building north of Portage Avenue. Here he held a really live religious meeting; and in the intervals of his sermons, he played to us on the trombone.

This was all very well: but when we got back to the office of the *Groan*, which was just as busy and as full as when we left it, Joe fell into a political argument with three other students on whether the Eventful State would allow anything but events to be worshipped. If Brother Trombone was to be written up, then, it looked as if I would have to write him.

To this end I found a vacant typewriter and sat down before it rather diffidently. I put in a sheet of paper and stared at it. When it came to writing up news, I did not know how to begin. Finally I decided simply to take a brave plunge. I shut my mental eyes and began to hammer at the typewriter. Words flowed forth. 'Why,' I thought, 'it's as easy as talking.'

My article on Brother Trombone was a great success: and I became a newspaper personage. After this I spent a good deal of time at the *Groan* office, and a good deal more of it arguing about the *Groan* when it appeared. And when I went home for my second Christmas vacation, I even had a project for the *Groan* with me: I had to write an article on Socialism in Britain.

This made me very proud. All the same, it did not get finished as quickly as I would have liked; and when, after Christmas, I spent a couple of nights at the farm, I decided to get on with it one evening. We were sitting in the kitchen. The range was open and the fire burning brightly within, and outside the house the snow was falling over the fields, now great Antarcticas of snow. I put my papers on the striped oilcloth of the kitchen table, and settled down to write.

I wrote quite loudly, as I was not averse to being noticed. For some time, however, I did not get any notice. Uncle Arthur was reading the paper and also talking to Benjamin, who was sitting near the range looking in, just doing nothing but sitting by the fire looking at it. Every now and then Uncle Arthur said something to his back, about feed or about shovelling the snow tomorrow or something, and Benjamin replied 'Uh-huh.' The other people were sitting around completely silent.

After a while, realising that the whole group were in the grip of a sort of mental paralysis, I tried to help them on. I spoke to them about the Welfare State. I spoke, seeing that they seemed to be listening, about nationalised industries, state-owned public services, the great principles of social security, and, in particular, about the idea of the National Health Service. With this last topic, we were successful. Benjamin looked up and contributed something to the discussion.

'A man near my dad's house,' he said, 'used to say chopped adders was the very thing for fut-rot.'

Peter, who was home for Christmas, looked up at him from the book with which he sat on the other side of the range. 'Who was to eat them?' he asked with real interest. 'The beast or the farmer?'

'Don't be silly, Peter,' I said. 'That's not scientific.'

74

'Scientific!' said Peter. 'This is the spirit of the settlers Benjamin is telling us about.'

'That's right,' said Ernest: 'better than socialism any day. Who was to eat the snakes, Benjamin?'

Benjamin looked hard at them, intelligence gradually making its way into his brown eyes like a frog rising in a pool. He opened his mouth and then shut it again. Then he made a big effort. 'Put it on for a poultice,' he said. He looked intently into the fire, his hands clasped limply between his legs, and then he essayed speech again. 'Guess I'll go and count the cattle,' he said.

'Coming with you!' said the boys. They put their books down and went out with him. 'They want a breath of fresh air,' said Uncle Arthur, as he refolded his paper. 'That was interesting, what you were telling us, Peggy,' he added as he started reading again. 'I'm glad you're learning things.'

I abandoned the idea of getting any better response out of this family. 'That's farm life for you,' I said to myself, back at Grandma's. 'Impenetrable. Absolutely.'

But fortunately I had — so wisely — escaped and arrived at college: and had stepped into my true métier. Or had I? If so, just what was it, precisely? Well, at least, I went on, evading that question, I had arrived at college and my true métier was just around the corner, ready for me to lay hands on in a moment. So into the train and back across the flat farmlands, with the depths of innumerable shadows lying across the snow and the cry of the train breaking into the night, and back to Winnipeg, and to lights and traffic flashing everywhere once more, and time for the second term of second year.

This term I was even busier than before. All the projects I had already taken up needed attending to: and as well it seemed to be a very sociable time in Winnipeg too, and there were several important Winnipeg dances, and a special season of plays put on by the Little Theatre. And for the first time I went over to Mackinawack College and attended their Mock Parliament. Don came too, and stood up in the middle of the floor and made a speech, and then was thrown out as an enemy alien, but broke away and came running triumphantly in again, and the Mock Parliament broke up for the day in a free fight between Don and his friends and the members of Mackinawack. And the university held a week of debates with an American college, and I went to it and made notes for the *Groan*. I went about Winnipeg too, and made notes on Community Projects, clinics for babies and plans for Aid to Europe and things like that. Going about in this way, I met a great many new people that term, until my head almost swam with them. But one acquaintance I made, which managed to have some effect on me, began at the *Groan* office.

At this office one often encountered students with marked political outlooks. One evening, in February, I met the arch-Bolshevist of them all, in a haphazard pair of trousers and long shaggy lightish-brown hair.

It was Don who had introduced us, as he had come in for a while with a bunch of cartoons about the postwar world, a thing that the sort of men who wrote for the *Groan* were always very eager to talk about. He probably thought the acquaintance would be an education for me. He called me over and introduced me to the man, whom I already knew by sight. But when I asked him if he was a Bolshevist, he said he was an anarchist.

'That's more profound,' he said. 'That goes more straightly to the centre. To the heart of things immediately, cutting through the rotten flesh.'

'Yes,' I said. The patient would be dead by now, I supposed. I wasn't sure what he meant to do with the remains. 'What happens next?' I asked.

'The fresh blood of life spurts out,' he cried: 'reviving everything!'

'So true,' I said.

He was thoroughly taken with me. That was the trouble with dressing well; all kinds of men took to you, whether you took to them or not. I made a note to put this problem to Peter one day and see what advice Smarty could think of now. Meanwhile the anarchist — whose name was Van de Behof — began pestering me for a date every time he met me. I warded him off as long as possible, and in the end we settled for coffee. We met at the *Groan* office one evening and walked to a coffee bar. He talked the whole way. It was the strangest thing: he talked about contraceptives all the way from the *Groan* office to the coffee bar.

Why such a field of skill, requiring a fairly exact mind and some methodical attention to detail to make it work, should be part of the anarchist way of life, shrouded itself in a dark mystery to me, but he talked about it without cessation even in a non-stop stream of words as we threaded in and out of the traffic and he went on as he hung up his scarf and coat and sat down and picked up the menu. I dearly hoped he would stop in time to give the order in an aura of decency. Or if there was a slip in his mental machinery and he ordered a supply of some useful contraceptive device with two cups of black coffee, we might be arrested, I thought. It had to be stopped.

'What do you think of these coffee bars?' I interrupted brutally. 'Bourgeois, aren't they?'

'My God!' he cried. 'I've never met a woman like you, with such an eager, understanding mind! Bourgeois! It isn't the word for them!' He told me the words for them. This was fine. It kept him occupied for the next hour or two; and meanwhile almost unobserved I ate a double strawberry ice, some chicken sandwiches, and a dish of peanuts that happened to be on the table, and drank a Coca-Cola and a chocolate milk-shake. But when the day of reckoning came I took pity on him and suggested I halve the check with him, which he accepted as a sisterly gesture. He insisted on taking me out to coffee again, and, although I took care thereafter only to drink coffee, he always allowed me to pay a sisterly share of the bill.

Later on in the year, when our acquaintance had ripened, he made a big effort, and invited me to a cultural jazz party, and I made an effort, too, and fitted the engagement into my crowded programme. 'Jazz is classical music now,' he told me as we went along, 'part of the beautiful past.'

'I thought the past was to be destroyed,' I said.

'Ah, but jazz can never be destroyed. It is the very note of destruction itself, the sublime logos of the essential chaos.'

He really had me there, so I gave up, and let him talk about jazz. The jazz party was crowded and incredibly erudite. A student in glasses gave us an analytical lecture on jazz, illustrated with excerpts from records. Then we had coffee, passed to us in our crowded positions, and a serious analytical discussion on jazz.

I returned to the fresh air with interest. Van de Behof however was just getting warmed up. 'What an evening!' he cried, pacing along on the grass verge between the pavement and the road. 'Don't let's stop. Let's have an orgy! Let's go to Maria Slinks' place. There's a little group that meets there every Tuesday night to read free verse. Come on!'

'Poetry!' I said. 'I couldn't.'

'Well then,' he said in quite the most natural voice he had ever used, 'come up to my rooms. By God, I do want to kiss you.'

I was ready to refuse this invitation, in spite of his extremely adequate knowledge of contraceptives. 'But Maria

Slinks!' I cried, recollecting myself rapidly. 'Haven't I heard of her?'

'In third year,' he said.

'A genius,' I said. 'I can't miss hearing *her.*'

'I might read some poetry myself,' he said enthusiastically. As he walked along he began to recite to me. It sounded like that poem about the leper again; there were bits in that poem I was beginning to know rather well by now.

We went along rapidly, deep into the city, down streets I had never been through before. The whole atmosphere of the place was becoming more and more decayed; the wooden houses seemed to be slipping down at all angles, the dead grass hung in sombre bunches by the doorsteps, only the maple trees preserved their dignity in the bright moonlight. At last we turned up a side street and went into a dark doorway — smelling suspiciously like a barn to me — belonging to a grey stone house; and went all the way up the bare stone stairs to rooms at the top.

The situation here was much the same as the one we had left, except that instead of hearing jazz, we were hearing poetry. I sat down on the floor and leant my head against a chair. Someone was reading some translations from the Arabic. They were, of course, about sex. An ineffable dreariness stole over me, a deep weariness of the spirit; or perhaps just the languor of the advancing night.

These people in the Arab poem were making good use of the night hours before dawn was going to break with its one star. I thought I knew the poem; I must have heard it, or several like it, from Don in first year. I half fell asleep, and woke up again. Dawn would be breaking over Winnipeg in a while. Surely, I thought, there must be some real Canadian poets? Why did we never read their poems? And what did they write about nowadays? Very likely, I supposed, about sex.

I fell partly asleep again: and now another picture began to form in my mind. It was Christmas Eve on the farm several years before, and I was crossing the snow to the barn.

The boys were milking and the yellow light fell from the windows and coloured the rough surface of the snow; and Peter was standing in the open doorway, holding a bucket, watching me come. And the air was so fresh and clear, and the infinite night so still and quiet, so still and quiet that I could remember, now, how clearly the barking of a dog for a few moments, miles away across the land, rang over the snow. I became obsessed with this picture and the thought of the cool quiet air and the lighted barn: the whole scene became more and more beautiful, and the city seemed more and more dreary and sordid, falling into bits as it was, and a voice in it that would not stop talking.

I fell asleep completely then; and woke up again at about half-past two, feeling quite ill, to find the party over and coffee being handed round once more. And I remembered that when signing for a key to the residence, I had certainly made no mention of two or three o'clock. But perhaps, I hoped, no one would hear me coming in.

Mercifully, one of Van de Behof's friends at the poetry reading had a car, and he drove us both home, which saved me both from walking and from Van de Behof. And so, after a full evening, I got into bed, at about three forty-five in the morning.

Chapter Five

A<small>T</small> classes next morning, I confided in the friend I always sat beside, an excellent girl called Sarah Ann Whiting, who lived in River Heights, that my plans for the fully rewarding life were somehow failing me.

'I hurried away from the farm because it was such a dead end,' I told her, 'and today, do you know what, I feel as if city life were all kinda pointless. Things keep happening all right, but just where is it all heading to? What is the purpose of all this confusion?'

'You should learn to be contented with things as they are, like my folks,' she said.

'You can't be contented with things as they are until you've got what you want,' I said. 'But as fast as I seize hold of one thing I wanted it seems it was something else I really wanted after all. Or even if it does feel like the right thing at first, after a little while it doesn't seem to be so valuable any longer. And last night I even wondered if I didn't like the farm better after all! Imagine it! So now what?'

She did not say anything more about it, but took me home for supper that night. I had been to her home several times before. The Whitings lived quite near the Assiniboine River, in one of the streets running from Wellington Crescent across Academy Road. They had a square, unornamented house, covered with what I supposed might be called a putty-coloured pebbledash, though its neighbours were painted white.

It was set, with the others, in a continuous piece of open grassy ground. Beyond the pavement the grass continued to the road, with maple trees growing solemnly at regular intervals. Here and there stood a little flowerbed or flowering shrub, but the chief part of each garden was the open lawn, and the children bicycled up and down the grass for the whole length of the field, and the dogs played beside them.

Inside, the Whitings' house was quite plain and simply furnished, even though Mr. Whiting was doing well at business. In parts, the decoration looked positively old-fashioned, especially the pots of trailing ivy and geraniums standing along the window-sills. Mr. and Mrs. Whiting never went anywhere exciting that one could notice: after business Mr. Whiting simply worked in his garden or did his carpentry, and Mrs. Whiting, when she had finished the housework and the cooking, sat and sewed or knitted or read, or visited her relatives. Sarah Ann and her sister preferred staying at home to going out. They used to play the piano and sing, or play records of classical music, and they made up little plays together or read books aloud to each other. For city life, it was all quite remarkable.

Mr. and Mrs. Whiting were very well satisfied with each other. They had met at Gordon Bell High School, gone steady together after that, married after graduating from college, and moved into the house where they stayed now. And in the summer, Mrs. Whiting went to their cottage at the Lake of the Woods with her children, and Mr. Whiting joined them whenever he could, even if he could only manage to fly to Ontario for the weekend. They carried out this routine contentedly every year.

I was forced to admit that it suited them. But I knew it

would not suit me: it was just another avenue of stagnation to me. To my mind Mrs. Whiting had let life go by when she made the mistake of marrying a fellow she met at High School. That was something I would certainly never do!

I chuckled to myself at the thought of marrying anyone at our High School or of getting anyone from that district for my mother-in-law. Those school-days were fast fading out of mind, thank goodness! I looked at Mrs. Whiting a little pityingly as she knitted in her big armchair, the geraniums in a row behind her. Mrs. Whiting went to bed at ten-thirty every night, I knew. It boggled the mind. She even asked me, after supper that day, what time I went to bed. Of course, I did not tell her. I just said, 'Twelve o'clock.'

'It's too late,' she said. 'You're looking a little pale and depressed. Why don't you spend a weekend with us and get a good sleep?'

I thanked her politely and refused. She could not be expected to understand, of course, that sleep would not cure the trouble that had crept up on me, which was a deep malaise of the spirit arising from the frustration of the essential Me that life was always inflicting on me. So though I was grateful to Sarah Ann for her helpfulness, I did not take her mother's advice. But over a Coca-Cola the next day I discussed things with Don.

'I feel kinda nauseated just now,' I said. 'I'm beginning to think there's nothing in life really suits me at all. And perhaps living in the city isn't quite as wonderful as I thought it would be. Its net effect on me is beginning to be depression.'

'What you need,' he said, 'is psychological integration.'

'Honey,' I said, 'I've been looking for that ever since I moved in with my grandma. But I'm nearly middle-aged now and I still haven't got it.'

'You should read some good books,' he said.

'Thank you!' I replied smartly. 'I know your books! The reading you've made me do! Look at all those volumes of Havelock Ellis. I read them, but I wasn't integrated, just exhausted.'

'Not that kind of book, you dope,' he answered. 'Books about psycho-analysis and the Id.'

'The Id?' I said. 'That sounds mighty rude to me.'

'The Id is fundamental, thoroughly fundamental,' said Don. 'You need to understand your Id better. And about repression and symbolism and all that, all the rest of it you know, I can't remember it right now. I'll get you some books.' He got me a pile of books and carried them to the door of the women's residence. I thanked him cordially. 'Not at all,' he replied, pushing back the locks of red hair that were always falling forward over his forehead: 'I like to do things for you, Peggy. You're a friend.' I took his books upstairs and added them to a small collection I was beginning to make myself, quite wide in its scope, embracing subjects like pragmatism and rationalism and humanism, and even Moral Re-Armament. I felt too busy just then to read them, but they would keep.

At the end of the college year, which was hard at hand, I went to stay for two or three weeks with friends in Tuxedo; and then I worked in Eaton's store, selling sportswear. Then, later in the summer, I went back to Merrilee. I took all my books with me, for this was the time when I was ready to study them.

I was determined that this summer vacation should mark a real step forward in my development. Here, with all these good books, I would surely come upon some resounding discovery, the evidence of that good thing in search of which I had come to college and Winnipeg. My books, it seemed, covered nearly every department of thought: somewhere within them the truth must surely be lurking, waiting for me to encounter it. As I had come back to Merrilee in fairly good time this summer, there would be plenty of opportunity for me to read and think. Auntie had a girl to help her; Joe and Ernest were busy on the farm too; and Peter had not arrived home yet. He would arrive later, but I felt sure that my studies would protect me from him. I should be immersed in books every time he came by. At present, then, my way was clear.

So I began well, by taking a pile of psychology books and going to the verandah at the front of Grandma's house. I put the books in one of the armchairs, and sat down in Grandma's rocking-chair, and I sat there rocking and looking out towards the road, with one of the books open in my lap, watching the cars that came by now and then, and the children playing about, and the birds in the sky.

In a little while Grandma came pottering out, and at her long baleful look I got up and moved into another chair: and she sat down contentedly in the rocker, and prepared to take an interest in things.

'What's that you're reading?' she asked. 'Part of your course?'

'No, Grandma,' I shouted.

'I hope you're not wasting time reading trash. You should be studying.'

'I am studying, Grandma, kind of. I'm doing a little extra-curricular reading.'

Grandma looked amazed. She picked up one of the books and read the title aloud.

'What is there to learn from this?' she enquired.

'It helps me understand myself, Grandma,' I replied, perhaps somewhat hopefully. 'It gives me an insight into things. It helps me find the key to my personality.'

'When I was a girl we didn't have any Personality,' replied Grandma, unabashed.

'You must have had something to keep you going,' I said.

'We had Charm,' said Grandma. 'A little clear cooking fat in a bowl with some sugar mixed in it and it kept your skin smooth. And an extra ribbon to wear on Holy Days.'

'Well, the world's moved on since then, Grandma,' I said.

'It had no need to move on,' replied Grandma. 'But never mind about wasting time with these books. You've ample to do keeping up with your course.'

'Well, this one,' I said, lying boldly, '*is* on my course,' and I picked it up and put it open on my knee in place of the other one. Grandma was satisfied. 'I like to see you industrious,' she said.

Very shortly afterwards she invited Mrs. Ransom to supper, and told her my news. The two of them sat together in the warm evening and enjoyed themselves in a glow, moral and righteous, full of vicarious merit and understanding, derived from their vision of my behaviour at college, one of stern application to study and avoidance of all idle pleasures. At their interpretation of my college career, exchanged with much satisfaction over the supper table, my own mind quite reeled, but I kept my composure by tucking heartily into some blueberry muffin, well laced with butter. Grandma went on revelling in my zeal for learning, and reminded Mrs. Ransom every now and then that of course I held the top scholarship of my year in Manitoba, while Mrs. Ransom clucked merrily as she relived that moment of triumph for Merrilee.

'Gee whiz,' I thought, re-establishing contact with the blueberry muffins, 'they haven't an idea what college is like. Oh dear no,' I thought, piling on the butter again, 'these two old folk just haven't *lived*.' I polished off the blueberry muffins and turned my attention to Grandma's pumpkin pie. 'Why,' I exclaimed to myself, 'Grandma wouldn't know how to talk to a man intelligently. Even,' I added, as the pie melted away gently within, 'even if old Grandad *did* have the biggest beard in County Galway. No, no, beards and pie and stuff like that isn't Life: not life like it's lived nowadays. Not psychology and all that — all . . . well, TV and all that.' However I was quite drowsy by now with the muffins and pie and the heat of the summer evening; and I let the talk flow on without attempting to guide the thinking of these two old people. My plans for spending the summer in profitable study warmed me gently, hand in hand with the efforts of the very cosy lining I had just put into my tum. The prospects looked fair.

Grandma was happy, too; and as the days went by she cheerfully invited several different friends to visit her, and took me to visit them too. Or sometimes we sat in the front verandah by ourselves, and she told me the news. She announced to me, one evening, that Joe had a girl-friend now. Her name, said Grandma, was Mary Lou, and she had been at High School with us. I said I didn't think she had, for I could not remember one single Mary Lou. But Grandma insisted, and she even described her. 'Mary Lou,' she repeated: 'with long brown hair, Joe says.'

'Sounds a bit out of date,' I said.

'It's becoming, even if it's not fashionable,' she replied. 'I expect she'll be a grand wife for Joe. And now if Peter would get a suitable wife, I'd be really happy.'

'Peter!' I exclaimed. 'She'd be a tough woman who'd marry *him*! Oh no! Spinsterhood would be a pleasure compared to *that*!' But I muttered most of it to myself, as I knew Grandma would be annoyed if she heard.

She prattled on about Mary Lou, and promised me a visit from her very soon when she came to stay for a little while on the farm. But when we next had a visitor from that family, it was Auntie by herself. I made some tea and we all sat down together in the verandah.

'Well, Mother,' cried Aunt Mary smartly, 'you'll be startled to hear my news.'

'I'll see about that when I hear it,' replied Grandma.

'Well, I'll waste no time about it,' said Auntie. 'It turns out Mary Lou's going to have a baby.'

I choked sharply into my tea and set down the delicate china cup and saucer, painted with roses, with shaking hands, though whether through laughter or amazement I was not sure. Grandma, meanwhile, had begun to rock to and fro with a horrible stateliness, fixing Auntie with her round grey-blue eyes, hard and quiet and remorseless. At last she spoke.

'Joe!' she said.

Auntie put her cup and saucer down with a bang.

'How dare you, Mrs. Donovan!' she cried. I was amazed at her: she was shaking. 'How dare you speak like that about one of my sons!'

'They're my grandsons too,' said Grandma. 'I may speak about them as I wish.'

'Maybe they are,' said Auntie, getting to her feet and gathering up her bag and gloves, 'and I'm very sorry about it too, but as long as they have their mother no one shall speak about them like that.'

'You might have thought of that long ago and brought them up right,' returned Grandma, rocking diabolically.

'Goodbye!' said Auntie. 'There's no use in my staying here. I'll go and find Arthur right away!' She hurried away, slamming the front gate, and set off down the road in the direction of the general store, where Uncle was doing his ordering. Grandma sat in her rocking-chair still.

'This is a terrible thing,' she said.

'Oh, Grandma,' I said to her, 'maybe it wasn't Joe at all. Mary Lou must know hundreds of guys.'

'But she will still say it is Joe,' replied Grandma. 'And probably it is Joe. And there will be a hasty wedding and the baby will be born soon afterwards, and everyone will know. Of course it is Joe. Well, Peggy,' she concluded, 'you and I will never visit with that family again.'

This startled me, but it hardly seemed likely that she meant it, so I did not say anything more at the moment. But when I suggested to her two or three days later that it might be a good idea to go and hear more about the affair, she forbade me to go at all. I was annoyed with her. In the evening, I walked round to the family who were keeping our pony now and asked if I could borrow it, and I saddled it up and rode over to the farm.

When we had arrived, I hitched the pony up near the gate of the field where the barn stood, crossed the yard and went in through the back kitchen and through the main kitchen into the verandah, which ran all along one side of the house. There was no one there except a very pretty brown-haired girl who was embroidering a supper-cloth. She didn't look very pregnant to me.

'Hi!' I said, switching on the light, though the single bulb in it did not make much difference, except to show up the brighter light of the descending sun. 'I'm Peggy. Are you Mary Lou?'

'No,' she said, looking at me, I thought, a little sharply. 'Certainly not.'

I sat down in an armchair.

'Well, excuse my asking you, but who are you?' I said.

'I'm Wilma,' she said.

Of course, she must be the hired girl. She seemed to be very much at home. 'Where does she fit in?' I wondered. 'How do you like it here?' I asked.

'Fine, thank you,' she said.

'How do you like Ernest?' I asked.

'Fine,' she said.

'And Peter?'

'I haven't met Peter yet.'

I felt quite glad about that, somehow. 'Well, well,' I continued, 'too bad about Mary Lou.'

'It is,' she agreed.

'Oh, goodness me,' I said, 'Joe is in for it when Grandma gets him.'

'Joe?' she exclaimed, staring at me. 'What's it to do with Joe?'

'Well, Mary Lou's his girl, isn't she?'

'Mary Lou!' she cried. 'Mary Lou!' She looked as if she were going to cry. 'What's Joe to do with Mary Lou?' The poor girl was quite scarlet.

'Mary Lou's Joe's girl, isn't she?' I said. I was getting quite annoyed at the way any mention of Mary Lou seemed to produce a General Post. 'She's come to stay with him, hasn't she? And Grandma's out to kill him because she's going to have a baby. So that's it.'

Wilma's eyes were quite round by now.

'Mary Lou's the hired girl,' she said.

'Well then, who the heck are you?' I asked.

'I'm Joe's girl-friend Wilma,' she said.

I recognized her then; she was one Wilma Mackenzie, who came to the High School just before I left it, when her father moved into that district. I told her I was Joe's Cousin Peggy, and was happy at this successful end to the incident. But it turned out that it was not ended. When I tried to explain things to Auntie, she simply told me that she wanted to hear nothing about Grandma. Grandma equally did not wish to hear a word about Auntie, though she did not mind saying a few. The situation seemed impassable. 'If it drags on,' I thought, 'with insults flying on both sides, it will build itself up into a real family row.'

I thought and thought about it, and wondered if I ought to write a note to Uncle Arthur. But then I remembered that Peter would be home soon for a short holiday. Repulsive though he was, he was also resourceful. I decided to ask him about it.

When he was expected home, I gave an excuse to Grandma, made my way to the farm, and waited on the verandah, by myself, for Uncle and Auntie had gone to the station, and Wilma had left now. Soon I saw the car come along the track, and then in a minute Peter came bouncing in and crashed down into one of the armchairs and clasped his hands behind his head.

'Well, sweetheart,' he said, staring at me, 'you've got a dress on.'

I prickled all over. 'Go away, go away, Peter,' I said.

'Such a welcome!' he replied. 'And I haven't seen you since Christmas. Surely you're pleased to see me?'

'Sure, I'm pleased to see you,' I said, 'and I hate you like poison ivy too.'

'You keep the last half of that sentence and I'll keep the first,' he replied: 'like those old folks that broke a ring in half and each had a bit. That was a cheap way out, wasn't it?'

'Peter, I hope you're working,' I said, ignoring him. 'Getting on with your practical training or whatever it is now.'

'You bet your life I'm working,' he answered. 'There'll be nothing of Canada left when I've done working, but just one big magnificent concrete construction from sea to sea.'

'Where'll we farm?' I asked.

'I don't know, dear,' he said. 'Fortunately I'm not a farmer. You can all worry about that. I just want places where I can build.'

I decided to introduce our problem to him now. 'I've something to tell you,' I said; and explained the situation to him.

'Why don't you just tell them?' he asked.

'I've tried and they won't listen to me,' I said. 'And even if they understood about the names, they'd still be angry with each other.'

'But why?'

'Just because. Because they are both wrong. Women are like that.'

'I see. It needs a peace-offering,' he said. 'Well, I'll come over tomorrow and settle things.'

He drove over the next morning in Uncle Arthur's car, and came in and kissed Grandma, and sat down and told her all his news over a cup of coffee. Then he leant back and addressed her carefully in the deep clear voice in which he always spoke to her.

'Grandma, you know Ma's hired girl Mary Lou was sent away because she was to have a baby soon and Joe's Wilma went a couple of days ago?' he said.

Grandma looked at him keenly.

'I didn't hear you,' she said. 'Speak up.'

He repeated himself slowly in exactly the same tone of voice. Grandma listened, with her acute old eyes narrowed.

'Yes,' she said.

'Well,' said Peter, 'I know you want me to tell Ma how sorry you are her plans are all gone wrong, and you're sending Peggy to help her out.'

'Yes,' said Grandma thoughtfully. She rocked a bit, tapping the table with her finger-tips. 'Peggy can stay for a little while and she'll still have some time with me before college starts.'

'Grandma,' said Peter, 'I don't know what Ma would do without you.'

Grandma smiled at him wickedly. 'It's lucky there's *one* wise woman in the family,' she replied.

'Well, so long, then,' said Peter, rising. 'I'll go and tell Ma. See you tomorrow.'

'Stay to lunch tomorrow,' said Grandma.

'O.K.,' he said. I walked with him to the gate. 'And what'll you tell Auntie?' I asked.

'I'll just tell her straight out about the names,' he said. 'And I'll say I told Grandma she must learn to put Ma first, because Ma has such a burden on her shoulders with the farmhouse and all. And I'll say Grandma said, "Yes, son, you're quite right, your mother keeps everything going and we must help her out".' He smiled at me, an exact imitation of his grandmother.

'You're a skunk, Peter,' I went on. 'Why should *I* be the peace-offering?'

'The place will be more like home with you there,' he said.

'I've so much work to do,' I complained.

'Work?' he said. 'What work do you and Grandma do except sit and knit on the verandah?'

'I've all my vacation task to do.'

'What vacation task have *you* got?'

'I'm busy, Peter,' I began. 'I'm studying psychological adjustment.' But he opened his eyes so wide at that, and raised his black eyebrows so high, that I decided not to go on; and still shaking his head in a bemused sort of way, he got into Uncle Arthur's car and drove away.

Soon after I had arrived at the farm to stay, I sat on the verandah with Auntie and heard about Mary Lou. As she had only arrived at the farm in April and was expecting the baby in October, it obviously could not belong to Joe or Ernest, as Grandma would have heard, if she had waited a bit longer.

It could not belong to Benjamin either, which was something I had been wondering about; for I had been thinking that perhaps Benjamin still enjoyed his love of the barn, and had lured Mary Lou into it for pleasures and pastimes he had not been able to achieve with me. But I did not tell Auntie this, as it had never been my habit to confide in her. Auntie was pleased with herself over her alertness in noticing the baby and sending Mary Lou away, though it did seem to me that, since the damage was done, she might as well have kept her.

I asked how she had acquired it. No doubt, said my aunt, at one of the dances in the town near her own home. There was a big black-haired man who used to drive over and take her out on Saturdays and Auntie gathered that Mary Lou loved dancing, and always had a boy-friend to take her out.

'And of course they go off in a car afterwards and you know what happens then!' she said. I had not actually realised that you could acquire a baby in a car — perhaps for want of thinking the matter out — but still, that was something new learnt. 'And what will she do now?' I asked. 'I expect she will marry the black-haired man,' said Auntie. 'I believe he had already asked her, but she preferred to work and have her own pay.' 'Then it must be his?' I said. 'Oh no,' she replied, 'I don't think so. In fact I don't think she really knows *whose* it is.'

'Quite a little packet of goods,' I said.

'Oh yes,' agreed Auntie. 'I'm so glad I got her out of the way of my boys. Oh dear!' she sighed. 'These hired girls are such a nuisance. They are always lazy or dirty, or not honest; and Mary Lou was downright immoral, it's all such a worry. I'll be glad when Joe's married.'

I went out shortly after this and wandered about under the bluff of trees, looking out into the sunny fields. 'Aggravating little thing, Auntie,' I thought spitefully, 'always trying to get other people to work!' I picked a stalk of grass and chewed it and thought about Winnipeg. Suddenly Peter came up behind me and put his arm around me. He kissed me on the cheek.

'Well, dear,' he said. 'How's the relentless pursuit of adjustment?'

'It takes time, that,' I said. 'It can't be done in a day. It's a major line of study, that.'

'I can believe that,' he said, 'but it's so much helped, of course, by the taste of grass.' He took my long grass stalk and threw it away, and suddenly he made a dive at me as though he really meant to kiss me properly. I put both my hands on his chest and shoved him away.

'You think you're just a big farm bull,' I said, 'going about and doing all the females good; but leave us alone, we like our quiet life.'

For once in his life he looked a little modest and abashed. 'I don't know what it is about you,' he said. 'I just don't know.' He looked thoughtfully across the fields, and I watched him staring into the sunshine with his eyes narrowed. 'Of course, Peter is a man,' I thought. 'A man, a man. All sorts of thoughts go on in him I don't know about. It's odd.' He looked at me suddenly and smiled. 'I just don't know,' he said.

'I don't know anything much,' I replied, 'but I'm planning to find it out.'

'Always triumphantly hoping!' he said. 'I don't know if it's a gift or not.'

He stood meditating for a minute or two longer, and then he went away to finish the piece of work he was doing. I went back to the house to go on helping Auntie. I had brought some of my books with me, too, and whenever it was possible I went and sat on a fallen trunk just at the edge of the bluff of trees, half overgrown by the thick coarse grass, and read them. What they said was very interesting, like reading some old fairy book full of creatures that excited the imagination, but because it was difficult sometimes to discover the creatures under the words, like a thick criss-cross of briars and dead branches keeping you out, I could only take the enjoyment in small doses.

I read a paragraph full of strange and wild ideas, and then put the book down and blinked a bit, and looked at the sun, and wished I were going to a dance that evening. Then I pushed at the grass with my feet, and picked a dandelion and looked closely at all the separate yellow teeth. Then I read a bit more.

Then sometimes, when I was really getting a grip on what the book said, I would get excited and my heart would begin to pound, and I had to lay it down. Then I shut my eyes and opened them again and wondered if it was all really true, because something else might be truer after all, and my heart stopped beating so fast.

Then it felt like time to go indoors for a piece of bread and honey. Then it was time to roam around eating the bread and honey and another piece of bread and jam and peanut butter, and to wander in and out of the cold dining-room and the shady parlour with its slatted blinds drawn right down, and to pick up the ornaments and look at them once again, and put them down and play three notes on the piano. Then perhaps I would go onto the verandah and lick my fingers and wonder what the boys were doing. I was not sure if I was bored or not. Sometimes it seemed as if life were going by too fast, and if only I were in the city I could be using up time better by going to a dance this evening; and sometimes I decided this was a fruitful period of creative meditation, here where there was only the flat grain on one side and the curved blue sky on the other and nothing — except a mere handful of objects, a house, a barn, and a few trees — in between to distract you. In mid-afternoon, before it was time for tea, when Auntie was resting for an hour on her bed, the burning sun produced a perfect silence everywhere, reducing movement to nothing. At this time, sitting on my tree-trunk, I achieved a state of complete nonentity. I read in my books that this was the ideal end of Yogi or Nirvana, or have I got it wrong? It was the ideal of something anyway. Sitting on my tree-trunk, I achieved, except for a slight stiffness in the bottom, an ideal state of nothing altogether.

We received, however, a rude jolt. Benjamin fell in the creek and got drowned. 'But what was he doing by the creek?' asked Grandma afterwards.

'We don't know, Grandma,' shouted the boys, who had found him.

'What did you do?'

'We pulled him out, Grandma. And tried to revive him.'

'You should have got the doctor.'

'Joe went for the doctor. But he was out. And Benjamin was dead anyway.'

'Really dead,' said Ernest. 'Like the mouse that fell in the soup. Do you remember that mouse, Peggy? Its ears were all wet.'

I could remember that particular mouse; its back was damp and shining, rising out of the good soup that supported the little creature, floating like a big black water-beetle, and its ears were crumpled like the thin bloody petals of a poppy-bud. I was going to remember Benjamin too, when Peter and Ernest had finally carried him in. Auntie and I were sitting on the verandah sewing the sheets and we saw the two of them carrying the corpse. They took it to the milk-shed and put it on the floor, while we ran out to see what was happening. Auntie, of course, began to flutter. I simply stood still and stared and stared, I could not help it; it seemed

97

essential to stare and take it all in, the wet clothes and livid face and fearful seaweed hair. Then Peter, who had been talking to Auntie, turned away to go indoors and fetch a blanket, and realised that I was there. He grabbed my wrist and jerked me out of the shed and, holding me tightly, made me come across the yard with him and into the house.

'You little fool!' he said. 'Deliberately making yourself ill!'

'What do you mean?' I cried.

'Now you'll be terrified for ever. You silly little fool!'

'Why should I be terrified more than you?' I asked.

'Don't think I don't know,' he said. 'Don't think I don't notice.'

'Don't get too conceited, Peter,' I said nastily.

'Don't think I don't know,' he repeated. 'Why, even of the horses——'

'Oh, the dead horses!' I exclaimed.

'There you are,' he said triumphantly. 'I had forgotten them. But *you* remember. I meant the horses you didn't bring in to water. I was in the fields. I was watching you.'

'So what, then?' I asked. 'What did you care?'

He spoke more gently. 'Well, I care now,' he said. He began to go upstairs slowly, and then he stopped and looked over the banisters. 'I wish you could go back to Grandma's,' he said.

'Auntie would never have it just at this moment,' I said.

'I know,' he replied. 'But I wish—— Oh well. At least you can stay in the house.' He looked at me fiercely. 'If I see you near the milkshed,' he said, 'I'll knock you into pieces.'

'So gentle and kind!' I said. I went into the kitchen and switched on the radio and sat down by the range. I felt cold and sick, and even when I propped my toes on the ledge of the stove, to warm them gently, I still felt like crying. It was a dreary and depressing day, and by the evening I felt out of tune with the world.

At bedtime I crawled thankfully into my bed. The moonlight was bright and I lay awake; and after a while I actually started to cry. I was beginning to settle down to it when the door creaked open, and someone came in. I looked up and saw that it was Peter. I sat up a bit and took my cardigan from the chair and pulled it round my shoulders. He came across the room and sat down on the bed.

'You need to stop crying,' he said. 'You'll get a headache.'

'How did you know?' I asked.

'I heard you as I came up the stairs. Everyone else is in bed.'

'Is Auntie asleep?'

'I think so.'

'Good,' I said.

'She needn't suspect me,' he said.

He leant on his elbow and remained silent for a while. 'What are you going to do tomorrow?' he asked at last, just to make conversation.

'I don't know,' I said. 'And I don't care!' I added, beginning to cry again. 'Everything is so horrible.'

'It's horrible, but not irredeemably so,' said Peter. 'I can't say he was a happy man.'

'I can't say we helped,' I said.

'No.' He took my hand. 'There's a lesson for us. Or for me, perhaps.' He sat silently holding my hand, and after a while I cheered up.

'Are the Northern Lights up yet?' I asked him, seeing him glance out of the window.

'No.'

'I wonder what makes them,' I said.

'I'll tell you,' he said. He did. I still didn't feel I knew what made the Northern Lights. But it was very comfortable holding his hand and listening to him talking softly, and the solid feeling of him sitting on the bed was pleasant too; and for once I felt as if one could have been quite fond of Peter, if only he hadn't been such a bad boy and if only he had not become such an arrogant man. He was the bossiest man for his age I had ever met. But still, his hand was very comfortable, and his voice was very soothing: so in a little while I reached out and stroked his hair.

'Aha,' he said, bending his head down so that I could reach it better, 'a truce!' He turned his head about, rubbing it against my hand. 'Well,' he said suddenly, 'shall I go?'

I did not answer. I wanted him to go away and I wanted him to stay; and I was amazed that I wanted him to stay, and sorry that he had come. But I did not reply. Then he sighed, and he leant forward, and pushed my cardigan aside, and kissed the hollow of my neck. I did not do anything about it. Then he laid his head down and slid his arms tightly around me. And there was something nice about it, very nice, a sort of warmth and unexpectedness. Acting on an overwhelming desire, I put my hands on his head and burrowed my fingers into his hair. He took a good grip on me then, and that was very nice too. I was pleased and happy with the situation. But then he suddenly took his arms away, and stood up.

'I must go,' he said.

'I hate you, Peter!' I said, pulling my cardigan around me again.

'Don't misunderstand me,' he said. 'I would prefer to stay. So I think I'll say good-night.'

He went to the door. 'I'll tell you something, Peter,' I said.

'What?'

'The less I see of you, the better.'

I could see that he was smiling at me. 'You said it!' he replied. He opened the door with infinite softness, and went away.

After that I kept out of his way a bit; and at night I locked my door. And then I got up and unlocked it, because I was ashamed to insult him by thinking he would come. And then I got up and locked it in case he did. And then, I got up and unlocked it. And it was coming to the turn of the summer and sometimes at night the north wind came rushing across the plain; and the trees outside bent and whispered so dismally, and looked so painfully clear and bright in the moonlight, waving their long dishevelled branches, I was distracted at night with the wind and the moonlight and the creaking floorboards and all this tiptoeing to the door. So that when at last he went away, I was delighted; and then I was sorry; and then I was pleased.

But it was the end of the summer, and the sun seemed a little less bright now, and the leaves of the trees a little tired; and often there were clouds, and their grey shadows lay across the farm. So I was glad to go back to Grandma's and gather her little house around me. The wind was blowing, and some of the leaves were falling, so we left the verandah and used to sit in her parlour with the log fire burning; and we would drink a cup of coffee together, and she would talk to me and tell me her stories. I liked that, it made the whole place seem less empty. And then life still went by too fast: and once more it was time to return to college.

Chapter Six

Now the same wind was blowing through Winnipeg, and handfuls of brilliantly coloured leaves gathered together at the roadsides and around the trunks of the maple trees, and conversed together for a while; and scattered and met other leaves, and went along with them, and rested and walked and ran and somersaulted in the gutters.

Airborne high overhead, some of them even managed to tumble over the rooftops. 'Like the wild geese,' I thought, 'travelling!' A terrible restlessness stirred in me. Benjamin's death had upset me. 'Too fast,' I said, 'too fast! It all goes by too fast!' Too fast, too quickly ended.

But I must discover it, I thought, catching at some of the leaves that blew past me: I must know what it means. What is precious, what is valuable, what needs keeping. What cannot be destroyed, what remains. A great gust of red and yellow swirled around me. 'What cannot be blown away?' I asked. 'What will not go away? What is really precious?' There seemed to be no answer. But I shall find it, I thought, I shall find it.

The wind appeared within the very college buildings too, pressing its way through the doors and windows if it could, and catching pieces of paper and blowing the curtains: and making do when it was thoroughly shut out by throwing reflections everywhere.

At night in the dark the maple leaves in front of the lamps

danced solemnly hour by hour across the bright patches on my bedroom ceiling. There were true shadows and false reflected shadows, the true shadows black and white, the false shadows and false patches of light grey and hazy, but all thrashing and moving together. In the day-time the whipping patterns disturbed the stark bare patches of sunlight on the classroom walls, attracting your attention, making you see that the paint needed renewing, that it was all a little dusty, that it was too cold and still, that life was going on somewhere else than this place which was now a prison. It was time to rush outside, but outside, the hands of discontent waited to seize you.

I felt very ill at ease. Then I had a talk with Don about it one day, when we were in the office of the *Groan*. I was sitting on a table reading through some old numbers of the *Groan* that someone had brought out of a back room and dumped in a corner. In the middle of the war there had been a lot of sombre poems by one of the students. I was trying to decide if he was a really good poet or not. There was such a lot of language lying about his poems. If you tidied it up, had he really got anything to say? Or was he just another of these people in the grip of a Mood?

I called to Don. 'Listen to this,' I said, and read him some of it. 'Now,' I asked, 'is that a poem or just a Mood?'

'Just a Mood,' said Don.

'Will he make a poet?' I asked.

'*Has* he made a poet?' said Don, looking at the date. 'I don't know. I've never heard of him. He's got the gift, but he needs to clean up his thinking. Feelings won't do by themselves. You have to be observant too and do some real thinking. Analyse things, you know.'

'I like it, though,' I said. 'All these wet leaves and wet winds and all that. Death waiting round the corner. That's the mood I'm in too.'

'That's a good old Winnipeg autumn Mood,' said Don.
'It won't get you anywhere. This man wants to know why
he feels so melancholy, but he hasn't thought it out. He
worries about destiny and talks about dead leaves. It won't
do. He needs a course of metaphysical thinking.'

'Oh dear!' I said. 'Psychological integration hasn't got
me anywhere yet: and now it's to be metaphysics! I can't
keep up with you.'

'Metaphysics!' said Don. 'That's the very thing for
autumn. Who is man? Why is man? The wind compels
you to think about it. Who are we all, anyway? It matters.
Tremendously.'

I sighed. But there was no escaping it, the wind had
started Don off on the new subject. Now Don and his friends
and I talked about metaphysics. Once we got started it was
quite entertaining, because I did want to know the answers
to the questions we raised. Having failed to understand my
own affairs yet, I was ready now to try to understand the
affairs of the whole world.

'Who is man?' we began to say to each other. '*What* is
man?' we asked, in a more brutal mood. Someone, braver
than the rest, read to us out of a book by one Kant. This
produced a sort of stupefied silence, in which it was possible
for him to hold the floor much longer than he would otherwise have done. We read some other books too; and then
we started talking about Being and Becoming and the Good
and the Real and I and Thou. We looked at each other
over our bottles of Coca-Cola and we said, 'But what does
it all *mean*?' 'Who am I?' we used to say when we met:
'and who are You?' We fidgeted through our college lectures because, as we said to each other, they were not grasp-
ing the Essential. 'They are not dealing with the *real*,' we
said: 'they do not tell you *who* or *why*.'

We longed to escape, to rush out, to embrace the night

sky. We strode rapidly out of cafés and flung our arms wide, and looked at the night sky, and said, 'But why?' And then we strolled away to the edge of the city, where habitation had thinned away; and stared at the immensity of the Canadian night as it stretched between us and the stars. If you stood at the edge of Winnipeg and turned northwards, you could know that there was not such a city again between you and the polar ice: and the very breath of that ice-cap seemed to blow in your face out of the prairie wind. We used to stand there at the rim of our world and look out; and I used to wonder, Is there any answer, out in that darkness: is there any answer? But the prairie grass would shiver back our questions disregarded.

So it seemed as if the wind was perpetually coming, over the prairie and over the city, and bringing handful upon handful of its own questions with it, until I was blown inside out with enquiry. But at the university, I thought, there must be some means to discover a better answer: or why have we come here? Why did we arrive here so hopefully, if there was nothing to be learnt?

But if private thinking or discussion with friends will not do it, I thought, I must try the effect of a real community. There must be somewhere, rooted deep down, groups of serious-minded persons, living out the answers to our questions in one way or another, like those people we read about who, on the edges of Swiss mountains or on islands deep in the Pacific, discover all sorts of mystical insights. I must find them, therefore. I began to look around more diligently than ever before: and after I had searched about a bit, not very fruitfully, my attention was attracted by the members of the College Christian Meeting.

These were not ordinary United Church or Episcopalian worshippers, nor even adherents of the meek and useful S.C.M., but followers of another movement altogether, imported into North America from the Old Country and much reinforced lately by a group that had begun to roam about the United States, with a party of trumpets and a choir that sang 'Come Softly to Me' so loud they said you could hear it in Britain on a windy night. And wherever the persons of this persuasion had managed to take root, they spread their tendrils hither and yon: for, like leaven, they designed to leaven the whole lump.

Quite a number of them had collected in Manitoba University and in our college. If there were ever as many as two or three of them anywhere at the same time, they would coalesce like lumps of quicksilver: and would stand right in the middle of wherever they happened to be, and perform a little primitive dance. To carry this out, you stood in a circle and clapped everyone else on the shoulder in turn, uttering their Christian name extremely loudly. As a religious ritual, I could never quite grasp it. At first, in fact, I did not realise it was religious at all, but thought it was some kind of fraternity or sorority greeting. But when it dawned on me that it was religious, I wanted to find out more about them, and to see whether any good thing lay behind their certainty; and I wondered if I should start by bursting into one of these little nodules myself and clapping everyone on the shoulder. Would I be accepted and received into the mystery: or would I be recognised, and shunned as an outsider?

Before essaying it, I made some enquiries among my friends, and they advised me to take a more moderate course, and one less blistering to the palms of the hands, and to attend the weekly meeting, disguised in some plain, old garment. I did this, and we prayed and sang hymns, quite loudly, and I was not very much enlightened: and would have been glad to let it be the end of the matter.

But I had made a mistake in allowing myself to be seen

in enemy territory. Spies began now to close in round about me. In the very heart of our residence there lived a good, Christian girl named Edith. She had red, wavy hair, pinned tightly back, a pale luminous skin, glasses, which made her tilt her chin up slightly, and for apparel an old brown sweater and skirt and low-heeled rubber-soled shoes. She informed me, now, that she was praying for me.

I think she spent all her spare time praying for me. Whenever I noticed her in the dining-hall or the street or college classes, her glasses would catch my eye and would signal me the message: 'Praying for *you*!' I began to feel quite persecuted by her. Whenever I saw her come trudging down the passage, her books stuffed under her arm, her toes turned out at right angles, and her glasses beaming out their heavenly semaphore, I would urgently recall another appointment. But she would track me down, and would come into my room in the evening, and over a cup of coffee she would tell me her religious convictions. We never arrived anywhere together, as we argued with completely different sets of ideas. 'Think of the Blood, Margaret,' she used to say. 'Think of the Blood that covers your sins!' 'Covers my sins in the eyes of WHOM?' I said to myself. Our conversations had as much consequence as the question and answer in the nursery rhyme:

'The man in the wilderness said to me,
How many strawberries grow in the sea?
I answered him as I thought good:
As many red herrings as grow in the wood.'

But she persevered — and laboured on — and every time she rose to leave my room her hair and her glasses and her very toes seemed to cry out to me: 'Praying for you! Praying for you! Praying for you!'

Early in my acquaintance with her, she pressed me to accompany the Christian Meeting on a Weiner Roast one Saturday afternoon. Unlike most of the people at college, they managed to go on an excursion without pairing off into loving couples, and so we trooped out carrying our little bundles, a sort of Noah's Ark gone wrong, the custodians of salvation but not walking two by two. Thus disporting ourselves, with many references to God's mighty workings displayed around us in the sky and the grass and the last few autumn leaves that blew down from the trees as we went along, but avoiding the poison ivy as well as we could as we went through the woods, we arrived at a convenient spot, and made a fire out of branches and twigs which we collected with our own hands.

Then we stuck the weiner sausages onto long sticks, and indulged in the old-time custom of roasting them in the fire. I enjoyed this. There were some marshmallows that we roasted too. After we had partaken, we gathered round the fire, some standing and some sitting on old gas cans or tree-stumps, and we sang what they called Choruses. Then a young student addressed us on religious matters for quite a time. The sky was dark and leaden and one or two of the early snowflakes of winter fell down to join the leaves now meek and quiet underfoot among all the debris of summer and the twisted brambles on the ground around us. I became very cold and had to clap my hands together a good many times. After this, we trooped off home again, discussing the religious talk; and when I got back I telephoned Don and we went to the pictures together.

Edith was disappointed at this, as evidently she had wanted to spend the evening with me. She missed me on Sunday too. On Monday evening she was able to gather me in, and to share with me her delight at the Weiner Roast we had attended together and her hopes for my spiritual future. She put all her heart into her talk and I was enchanted with the performance: and yet the more I watched and listened to her, the further away she seemed to recede, until she became like an animated figure on a screen far far away, speaking and moving on the other side of some great picture house. But like some film of strange tribes, Edith and the members of the Christian Meeting really fascinated me. I could not help returning again and again to have another look at them. Don was disgusted with me. 'Gee!' he said, one day near the end of term. 'Every time I ask you for a date on a Friday, you're at that Meeting.'

'Why don't you come too?' I asked.

'Me!' he exclaimed, his hair almost standing on end.

'You yourself,' I replied.

'Never!' he said. 'And I don't know why you go.'

'It has a strange hypnotic power,' I said. 'I don't understand it, but it seems to fascinate me. That's all the explanation I can give you.'

Don simply jeered at this and so did my other friends. I put the matter away quietly and went home for the Christmas vacation. I stayed with Grandma.

Now the snow was piled high outside her house and I shovelled it away, wearing my little fur-lined hood and big fur gloves. Grandma watched me through the window, looming solid in her black wool dress. Then she came to the door and called out to me. 'Make it nice,' she said; 'Joe and Wilma are coming to supper.'

Indoors, she made everything ready, and when I stepped in from shovelling she was sitting by the fire knitting. It was too early for supper, but we made ourselves an extra cup of tea and sat by the fire. Then later there came a knock at the front door, and there stood Joe and Wilma.

Joe had pulled Wilma all the way on our old sled. She was looking prettier than ever in her hood and her big fur mitts, and even Joe seemed to be rather animated, so I supposed they must be serious about each other. Joe hung up their coats and they came and sat down, and as they talked to Grandma I studied Wilma more closely, wanting to see who this person was that Joe was likely to marry.

Grandma, who seemed to think her charming, settled down to telling her a long story about Ireland. I watched them; and thought that Wilma looked agreeable and cheerful, just the sort of person who would love to make jam and pickles, and altogether a very suitable wife for Joe.

After supper Grandma and Wilma went on talking to each other; and Joe and I cleared away the dishes. When they were done we went back and sat down near each other: and Joe pulled a letter out of his pocket.

'This is from Peter,' he said.

He began to take the contents out of it, and then he separated them carefully and handed me a snapshot.

'That's Peter's girl-friend,' he said. 'I guess he must be staying with her this Christmas.'

I stared hard at the photograph. The girl was tall, taller than me, with very long legs and a big smile and a lot of hair. She was laughing in a big way and holding up one hand to shield off the sun.

'Her hair's red, he says,' Joe told me.

'Ginger, I think,' I replied.

'Peter says red,' said Joe. He turned Peter's letter over carefully. 'Here you are,' he said. '"Fine red hair."'

'Ginger,' I said.

'And her name is Annabelle,' said Joe.

'Mercy on us!' I said.

'She's grand at basketball and she loves fencing,' went on Joe, scanning the letter.

'And mad about men,' I added.

'She's mad about Peter, I guess,' said Joe.

I looked hard at the snapshot, and then I took a long shot. 'She wears a padded brassière,' I said.

Joe began to giggle and he took the photograph back and put it in the envelope with the letter, still snorting to himself. Then he stopped ho-ho-hoing, and said:

'Time for a double wedding, eh, Peggy?'

'You're too young to marry,' I said.

'Peter's not,' he said: 'and we may as well economise on the preacher and the cake, mayn't we?'

'Peter shouldn't marry,' I said. 'He's too bad-tempered. And if he did, it should be someone sensible, not a ginger-headed piece like that one.'

'Well, if he fancies her . . .' he said.

'He's got a wandering eye,' I said. 'He doesn't really fancy her.'

'Well, I admit he doesn't *say* anything about marrying her,' conceded Joe. 'Perhaps that's just my hopes.' He put the letter in his pocket and leant back in his chair and began to gaze appreciatively at Wilma. In a moment she looked up and smiled at him; and then Grandma turned her chair a little, and included us in the conversation for the rest of the evening.

The next day I sat for a while and looked at the snow lying over Grandma's garden. 'So everyone is getting married,' I thought. 'I ought to fall in love.' There were little icicles hanging from the top of the window frame outside, and I thought I felt something like that myself, slightly chill. It was time to fall in love and make a warm spring with flowers blowing. They danced, visionary, in yellow and red colours over the top of the snow. 'In love!' I sighed. 'I ought to fall in love!' There was a small excitement coiled around my heart, as though to fall in love was something really more stupendous than I had yet been able to imagine. Better even than to find the answers to our metaphysical questions? I was not sure. There were too many things altogether that needed finding out: they pressed too heavily. It's as bad as shovelling Grandma's front path, I said to myself: every time you clear a little way, the smooth snow fills it up again.

Opportunity for love turned out to be nearer than one might have expected. A few days later, after Christmas had passed, Don drew up at our gate, in his father's second car, a big blue one, with chains slung on the wheels to prevent it from skidding.

Grandma let him in at the front door, and I wondered how she would behave, but Don treated her with great politeness, shouting agreeably to her and looking at her with great earnestness from behind his locks of red hair. Out in the country, he looked a little pale and slender by comparison with our friends and neighbours, and Grandma saw an opportunity to do good to this polite visitor. She invited him to lunch and heaped up his plate, telling him how much better good home cooking was than stuff from tins. Don was always fond of food and he ate steadily, looking up very knowing and acute at Grandma as she talked to him, and nodded enthusiastically whenever she seemed to need a reply, but never pausing in his munch munch munch. After this he enjoyed some coffee, and it seemed the lunch party was a success. He helped me to wash the dishes; and then he suggested to Grandma that we might both like to go for a drive.

'No thank you,' said Grandma. 'Mrs. Ransom is coming to visit me. But Peggy would enjoy a drive.'

Don drove me off through the town and then out into the open countryside. The snow had been shovelled up in high banks on each side of the road, but beyond these walls we could see the bright unbroken whiteness of the fields, sparkling in the sun, too bright if you looked at them for long.

We drove on for a while until we came to a little rise in the road, and at the top of this Don stopped the car so that we could look at the view. It was an icy-cold day, with a cold breeze rustling over the top of the snow, so it was fortunate that his father's second-best car was a new one, with a good heater in the front.

'To tell you the truth, I'm glad the old lady didn't come,' said Don after a little while.

'But you like her,' I said.

'Oh sure!' he said. 'A great old woman. Full of personality and character. But I drove out because I wanted to talk to you.'

'What about?' I asked.

'Well, you know,' he said, 'a tremendous idea occurred to me at Christmas. I nearly rang you up, but you haven't got a phone.'

'What are we to discuss now?' I asked.

'Not just a discussion,' he said. 'Something new.'

'Let me know,' I said.

'Well, you know what,' he said, 'I thought we might get married.'

'!!' I said, looking at him amazed.

'Well, look how we get on,' he said. 'Always got something to talk about. And everybody seems to be getting married now. So I said to myself, why don't Peggy and I get married right away?'

I thanked him charmingly, and promised everlasting friendship, but said I wasn't thinking of marrying him. 'I'm sorry,' he said. 'It was a good idea. I take to you a lot.'

'And are you earning money?' I asked.

'I don't need to,' he replied, grinning. 'You know that. Dad has the biggest meat-packing business in Western Canada. I've told you that before.'

'But *you* haven't got a big meat-packing business,' I said.

'I've got a terrific allowance,' he said, 'and Dad gives me everything I ask. I'm his only child. You've missed a packet, refusing me.'

'It's funny that you like to think so much,' I said, 'when your Dad is a meat-packing man.'

'It's reaction,' he replied. 'I got tired of only hearing about beef at home. It kinda seemed to me there must be other topics in the world and I got avid to hear about them too. Oh well.'

He backed the car carefully, turned it, and began to drive me home. 'I feel cordially towards you, Don,' I said.

'I'm cordial to you too,' he said happily. He left me at Grandma's house and set off back to Winnipeg, seeming to be in quite good spirits in spite of my refusal. 'I've really enjoyed my visit to the country!' he bellowed to Grandma as he said goodbye. 'That's a nice young man,' Grandma said to me back in the house. 'What are his folks?'

'Meat-packers,' I shouted.

'Oh,' she said. 'In a big way?'

'A very big way,' I said.

Her eyes sparkled and she pursed her mouth and nodded gently. 'Very suitable!' she said. 'He will need a sensible, educated wife.' She went away back to the fireside to do her knitting, still with the same hopeful glow in her face. 'By the way, where is Mrs. Ransom?' I wondered. I saw no sign of her: so evidently Grandma had taken to Don right from the start. I did hope she would forget about it before I finished college: for I was not going to marry him.

But all the same, I still wanted to fall in love. After a few days in which I meditated warmly on his visit, the desire to fall in love came back and repossessed me. As Don said, everyone seemed to be getting married: and some of the ex-service students even had little children. It was time for falling in love and marrying. When the college term began, the idea was drumming within me. I was restless, disconcerted.

But life was still to be lived. I decided to go on with my quest for understanding. I would pursue our metaphysical speculations. And on Friday, I found, my feet even led me back to the Christian Meeting. No, I said to them, come away. Yes, they replied, plodding along, we are used to doing this on Fridays. But there was a notice. Our college Meeting was not being held at our college this term. It was to be held unitedly with the Meeting at another college. Well, said my feet, we'll take a street-car. No, I said, we'll go buy a Coca-Cola. This way to the street-car, said my feet. What is this strange necessity, this mass psychology? I asked myself on the street-car. Why this strange hypnosis? I asked, entering the dismal brown-and-green-painted halls of the other college. But it did not matter. My feet led me triumphantly into the joint Meeting: and there, very visible, was the leading light of the Christians in that college, young Mr. Alexander Mackintosh.

Young Mr. Alexander Mackintosh was a student renowned for his holiness. Every now and again he left Manitoba to preach for a week or two in other and presumably even more heathen Canadian universities, and the *Groan* would report to us on his doings. Young Alexander was six feet tall. He stood straight as a ramrod, if we may coin a phrase, the result, no doubt, of a year or two spent in the Cameron Highlanders, and in the Cameron Highlanders he had also acquired a kilt. Above the kilt there rose the splendid broad khaki-shirted chest and straight shoulders and handsome face and glowing blue-black hair of our Alexander. Below the kilt there emerged his knees and lower legs. I will speak about these later.

Young Mr. Mackintosh was the centre of the joint Meeting

and there was no doubt that he added to it a great deal of sparkle and excitement. His voice when he prayed! How warm, how glowing! His bass harmony added to the hymn-singing! The wit with which he gave out the notices! The earnestness with which he listened to the religious talk, despite the fact that, with his chin resting on his hand and his eyes narrowed thoughtfully, he looked very much like a pirate, dark and bold and romantic, too ardent to be really happily religious. But so earnest. And then, after the Meeting, the kindliness with which he shook hands with all the students who crowded round him, greeting them after the vacation and enquiring reverently how they spent their Christmas. The men he also clapped on the shoulder, but not the women. There were too many of them around him for him to clap them all, but instead he smiled at them, pouring into his smile all the tumult of his nature and making every woman think he was smiling at her alone. I felt the benefit of it myself. I was standing by the door and watching the scene, and hoping Edith would not see me and gather me in, when he finished his greetings, drew away from the others and collected his things, and came towards the door-way, evidently ready to leave. He saw me and stopped and smiled at me.

'How do you do!' he said, shaking my hand. Never was there such a handshake, it was all full of power and joyfulness. 'Are you from the other college?'

'Yes,' I said.

'I hope you enjoyed our Meeting.'

'Very much,' I said, 'but I must go now.'

'Oh, I'm going too,' he said. We walked out together. He was very attentive and polite to me. Of course, I was lucky; my hair was always naturally curly and my pink complexion never failed, it was a great advantage. And then he was a good deal taller than me and I could look up at him eagerly and he could look down and be tall and wise. He spoke to me a lot about religion even then; and then at the corner when he had to go one way and I another, he shook my hand heartily, and said he hoped I would faithfully attend the Meeting and witness to our Redeemer. On this point I was able to be quite clear: I assured him without loss of time that from now on I was very likely to be exceedingly faithful at the Meeting.

After this excellent beginning I looked forward to a fast-developing friendship between us, but I had reckoned without Alexander. His life was full and pressed down and running over. He was always busy. Every minute of his time was laid out in the service of what he called HIM. Alexander even got up at six in the morning and spent an hour reading the Bible and worshipping HIM. During this hour he planned out his day and he stuck to these plans. He made a list, and I am sure that on this list he even wrote down, 'So many minutes for greeting my brethren at the Meeting.' It was not possible, therefore, to charm him into attentiveness. If you got a chance to charm him at all, you might seem to be doing very well, and then he would suddenly glance at his watch and smile tremendously, displaying his perfect white teeth, and describe an appointment and shake your hand and suddenly disappear. So time went by without one getting to know him very much better or managing much conversation with him; and as for dates, they were plainly out of the question.

'Does Alec ever go on dates?' I asked Edith one day.

'With girls?' she said. 'No. He's not engaged, you know,' she added.

'But he can't do everything with men,' I said.

'He doesn't,' she replied. 'We all do things together. We go for rambles, you know. A lot of the fellows and girls together. Alec comes along too and makes a lot of jokes.'

'But never alone?' I asked.

'Why should he?' she said. 'I told you he's not engaged.'

But he must want to kiss someone sometimes, I thought, and if he's never alone how does he get to do it? This problem worried me so much that finally I had to ask Don about it.

'Gee whiz, Peggy,' he said, 'you are ignorant. These people that are saved never kiss each other unless they're going to get married.'

'But that's rude,' I said. 'You can't decide to marry someone you haven't even kissed. It would be like marrying your uncle or something.'

'I wouldn't care for it,' he agreed. 'To get all hooked up and kiss the girl and find her repulsive! No. But they do it.'

'But how do they resist kissing?' I persisted. 'I mean, you just hold hands, and then maybe you suddenly want to start kissing.'

'They don't hold hands either,' he said.

'But, Don,' I asked, 'how do they resist holding hands?'

'They don't get to hold hands, Peggy,' he said. 'They're never alone together.'

'But don't they *want* to be alone and hold hands and kiss each other?' I asked.

'Oh, Peggy, you do go on so,' he said. 'And you're so ignorant. They don't want to be alone *because* if they were alone they might want to hold hands——'

'And kiss each other,' I added.

' — and kiss each other,' he agreed. 'And then that would mean they had to get engaged. So you'll *never* get one of them alone——'

'Until he proposes?'

'Right,' he said.

'And if you get him alone and he holds hands, etc.,' I asked, 'you know he's going to propose?'

'Yes,' he replied.

'Good,' I said. 'That's all clear. Thank you very much, Don. I understand it all better now.'

I did feel I understood it better — until I began to wonder how any man so obviously full of sex as Alexander Mackintosh could manage to go on year by year without so much as holding hands once and how he didn't finally burst with the effort. What did he do, for instance, if, late at night, with the moon shining brightly, he found himself alone with someone inadvertently — perhaps, for instance, with a cousin. Sitting on a bed with someone, and the moon shining, did Alexander not hold hands? Not even a little? And did he not go any further? Just a little way further, nothing very much really, and yet all so splendidly satisfactory, and such a very happy memory afterwards? No? Well then, I worked out the answer, he was a real saint. When I had come to this conclusion, I was tremendously impressed. What a man! I thought, into his twenties and had never held hands with a woman yet, not even with one that was only a relative. Well, I decided at last, there really was something in this Meeting. Evidently I had not given it enough credit.

And then there were his legs. Now in speaking of them we must be humble and quiet for we approach a matter very sacred to me; we must sit quietly and keep our hands still and look back into the sunshine of this happy time, and reverently regard the legs of Mr. Alexander Mackintosh.

And it is a strange thing, as Mr. J. M. Synge would say, and me an old woman sitting by the road who once was the Queen of Old Ireland, though of course that does not really apply here, all the same, it is a strange thing that Alec hated lipstick and nail-polish and powder and slacks and immodest dressing in females, and would have wilted at the thought of a padded brassière had anyone been so horrible as to mention one in his presence, and never went to the pictures or watched the TV or read novels or even the newspapers, because they were all so lewd, as he had somehow discovered: and yet all the time, chaste and holy as he was, he openly displayed beneath that kilt a pair of legs that were simply pure and golden sex appeal. They were magnificent. Let us shut our eyes and remember them. They were like solid oak. And even when the weather was so exceedingly bitter that he reluctantly had to wear trousers, they still showed against the cloth, carved in their glory. And normally, in short woollen stockings with a *sgian dubh* at the side and shining black shoes, every curve of them was visible with the kilt swinging above them as he went along in the measured stride he had learnt in the Cameron Highlanders; and they were legs for bewitching you and making you water at the mouth. And as for evangelism, there never was argument like Alexander Mackintosh's legs and his appearance in that kilt. If I had any further doubts about the Meeting, they were dispelled most powerfully.

Under this stimulus, there flowered within me a whole rosebed of interests in religion. I attended every possible gathering of the Christian Meeting, Bible studies and prayer groups and all. I even tried to get up early in the morning to read the Bible. That was a very difficult practice and one that meant that every day started with a sensation of defeat — for usually one had not managed to rise early; and if one had, one had not managed to read the Bible.

I enquired one day of Edith whether or not one could read the Bible at night before going to bed, like having your breakfast the night before, but she said no, the Quiet Hour must come first thing in the morning. Evidently the Holy Spirit was more active in the mornings.

'And how could we call it the Morning Watch,' she asked me earnestly, 'if it didn't take place in the morning?' That was a very powerful piece of logic, powerful enough to convince me: though unfortunately, not enough to get me out of bed in the mornings.

When I went to the Whitings' for supper again, I spoke something about this matter: and also about my general new interest in religion. But to my surprise Mrs. Whiting frowned on my remarks. Sitting with her knitting, she counselled me to be contented with the United Church. She spoke with some feeling, as her brother had been a United Church Minister before he became the headmaster of one of Winnipeg's private schools. She recommended the habits of the United Church to me.

'But I like the Meeting!' I protested.

'Too much assurance is good for nobody,' she said. 'Moderate and modest ways are the best. In the long run, more gets achieved that way, you'll find. So why don't you join a church? Go and join the church nearest to the college.'

'The people at the Meeting,' I told her in my enthusiasm, 'say that most of the people in the United Church are certainly not saved — except for a very small and faithful remnant. Ninety-nine point nine per cent, they say, are chaff and tares only.'

Mrs. Whiting replied to that with unusual fluency: and she spoke again about patience, and, she said, quiet faithful endurance, and the absence of too much self-assurance. Well, I liked Mrs. Whiting very much indeed: but it never seemed to be possible to agree with her opinions. For assurance was one of the great charms of Alexander Mackintosh. It swung with his kilt and flashed with the quick turn of his black head and emboldened his smile. 'Rejoicing in HIM' was what he called it.

Assurance took Alexander Mackintosh deep into the worst quarters of Winnipeg, some of which were very bad;

and here he stood at the street corners and preached about HIM. We accompanied him sometimes and sang hymns, and regarded the attention he received from the poorer persons, the Ukrainians and the Slavs and the Chinese. In the earnestness and fire of his delivery, he almost grew wings and a halo as he stood on the dirty street. I observed then that it was of such that it was written, 'the zeal of Thine house hath eaten me up.'

In all our religious activities, Alexander took a foremost part; and when not leading some religious meeting, he engaged in spiritual talk with his friends. I could not but be moved by his earnestness. Daily his goodness increased in my eyes. In the charm of his holiness, there closed about him now an impenetrable mystery, deeper than the normal masculine mystery, an aloofness as of someone separate and different: whose ways were not ours, whose mind lived elsewhere, whose feet trod the way to Jerusalem, whose eyes beheld some other country, whose heart heard another language. Between us and him the Jordan rolled, brown and decaying, filthy river, separating us from his untarnished saintliness, his achievement we could never imitate. And as all the qualities of his character grew in my sight, I fastened my heart upon them, and I was ready to love these things.

I adapted myself therefore to the ways of the Meeting, otherwise strange to me: and in fact adaptability came easily to me, since I had long ago learnt it from Peter. Then a kind of tranquillity and happiness stole over me, as I had found someone to admire, and in pursuit of this admiration a regular way of life with a rule for every occasion. And then everything visible took on a new meaning, the thing lying behind it appeared to break through, pavements and sky and sun and trees had a new appearance. I saw them as made out of light, flexible, as alive, organic, hands screening the face of God who created them. I managed now to get out of bed and read the Bible in the morning, reading, that is, a few words here and there, and intermittently or rather mostly watching the first grey shadows and cold lights of dawn break beyond the dark untidy bushes and small trees along the banks of the river, and in this small still quiet time feeling there move and remove within me the waves of a great excitement. See, as the light spreads this way and that way it takes on opalescent colours, not yet daylight but promises of daytime practised out against the sky, and all these colours have a message do they not, a great writing on the sky like the names and titles appearing at the beginning of a film. See, they mean something, do they not; they promise some great story, some moment of history repeats itself today; Hannibal comes again across the Alps today; the king Alexander reaches the edge of the world today, it is a time that is already known and yet we are waiting for it. Then, after this too early morning, leading me on to a sense of despair and unreality at breakfast, I would begin to fall asleep in the college lectures: but awoke always in time to attend the daily activity of the Meeting.

This drew on me the fire of persecution, but I bore it nobly. It was a pity, though, that it led to a quarrel with Don. He was annoyed because I had time for the Meeting, but not to go dancing with him. I told him that even if I had time to go dancing, I was not in the mood for it now. This made him very cross; and after he had expressed himself rather well on the subject, we agreed not to meet again.

This was not the only argument, there were others. There was for instance the man who attacked me on political grounds. 'You should give up that Meeting,' he said. 'It's not an American activity.'

'But I am a Canadian,' I said to him.

'You live in North America, don't you?' he replied. 'So

you belong to the American way of life. Now that Meeting is not American.'

'But why not?' I asked.

'The American doctrine says that all men are equal,' he said firmly, 'but the Meeting doesn't agree. It says that some men are saved. So it isn't part of the American way of life — and so, it's wrong.'

He seemed very well satisfied with this argument, but it had little power over me. However, I paid more attention to Mrs. Whiting. 'But what do you do?' she asked. 'What do you *do*?'

I told her. 'But that's all talk in one form or another,' she said. 'What do you *do*?'

When I thought it over, I agreed with her, there did seem to be a lack of things to do; it seemed to be all thinking or conversation nowadays. So I thought a little more: and then I went down to one of the little clinics and nurseries that I had come across when I was working for the *Groan*. This was run by a guild of Winnipeg women; and in the nursery they looked after illegitimate babies while their mothers were out at work.

They said they needed help, so I started to go regularly twice a week in the afternoons. There were babies with fat tums of all shades of yellow, brown and pink: and if each separate shade had been a different note, you could have played quite a pretty variegated tune by tapping all the fat tums with a little hammer as the babies sat in a row on their pots. Except that unfortunately they did not sit, the male babies charged each other on their pots and crashed into each other all across the linoleum, while the female babies bounced up and down on the ring-lines. It was a mystery what magnetism it was that separated them out like this: the moment you popped a baby on a pot it decided at once, accurately, whether it was male or female and whether it should charge or should sit at the edge and bounce. And then we put them all back in their cots, and on each cot there was a little cardboard label, and every surname there hailed, in the past, from a different countryside — one from the Ukraine and one from Austria and one from China and one from the Red Indians of the Appalachian range: and so there was a brown face, and there was a yellow one, and there a pink.

I told Alexander Mackintosh, one day at a meeting, about this good work of mine, and about the different colours of the babies, though not about their behaviour. After looking a trifle austere, as suited one who was hearing about a sad and painful subject, he spoke somewhat about the brotherhood of man, all of whom might be one in Christ if only they were led to the fold. And he himself, he added, was going to be a missionary in India.

I admired him greatly for this. And after I had thought about it for a while, I thought I would like to do something really effective like that, into which one could put all one's energies. India, too, where so many brown babies lived, seemed to be the very place. I began to feel a definite leaning towards India. And this added very much to my happiness: it was nice to have made up one's mind at last. So I set to work, and got big books about India out of the library; and made friends with one or two people at college who had actually lived there, so that they might tell me about it in person. And now all my thoughts turned in this direction: and the clear visible springtime mornings with the light catching on the soft green leaves, which I now regarded over my morning Bible reading, spoke to me of a land beyond the horizon — India! And indeed it was a wonder that I ever pursued any other studies, or passed the end-of-term examinations at all, for having a mind so besieged and encaptured by the future that was now waiting for me in India.

At the end of third year, then, I had at last come to a definite decision about my career. I would be a missionary teacher, and work in India. So we dispersed for the summer vacation. Alexander was going to spend the vacation in evangelistic work and preaching. Every now and again he would send out a prayer letter to those who desired it, telling us how he and his brethren progressed, so that we could support him, before the Throne of Grace as he put it. I supplied my share of stamps towards these letters and was strengthened by the prospect of hearing about him in the long long months of the vacation. And after the long vacation, there would be the studies and the meetings of fourth year. And after that, stretching on perpetually, for both of us, glory in India.

Chapter Seven

INDIA now had to take a back place in my attention for a time, for it was early summer-time, and Joe and Wilma were getting married.

During the last few months their affairs had proceeded apace, and now the wedding plans were well under way. Uncle Arthur had had a little cabin built near his own house, where they could live, which he showed to me when I called at the farm; and when he and Auntie retired, he said, the cabin would come in useful for the hired man. The new hired man was not married, but if Joe's hired man married, the cabin would be handy, see, said Uncle Arthur. And they might have a second hired man in the house then, he added, the way things were thriving and expanding with all the new machinery.

In fact the outlook for Canada was a splendid one in every respect, said Uncle Arthur, whose mind seemed to be turning to optimism nowadays instead of to drink: and he began to talk to me about uranium and mineral resources. While he spoke I admired the cabin, which looked very smart, painted white, with a green door and green window frames. But I did not dally long. I had to get back to Grandma's. Grandma was preparing herself for the wedding. For some strange unfathomable reason this meant turning everything in the house inside out. 'We can't have a wedding,' said Grandma, 'unless everything is trim.' 'But Grandma,' I shouted, 'the wedding is to be held in Wilma's garden.'

'But we are going,' said Grandma.

'Yes, in our *clothes*, Grandma,' I argued. 'Not with these rugs and things.'

'Let's get on beating the rugs,' said Grandma firmly. I followed her obediently. When the rugs were beaten and laid out in the sun, we wiped the paintwork and the linoleum through the entire house and then I polished the linoleum. In the middle of this operation Mrs. Ransom arrived and saw me on my knees in my new blue jeans, polishing up the hall.

'Ah, here's your good Peggy!' she said to Grandma. 'And when is *she* going to get married?'

'Not before the end of her college course,' mandated Grandma. 'And *then* I'm going to be a missionary,' I said to myself, pausing on all fours with the polishing rag clutched in my right hand, and seeing for a minute the dusty (and altogether unpolished) highways of India along which Alexander Mackintosh must tread on his evangelistic way. 'Hurry up with that front hall, Peggy,' cried Grandma, 'and then the polishing will be done altogether.' I went on polishing to the glory of the Redeemer, and also to save argument.

Next day it was time for a grand wash. We seized on every available sheet, pillow-case, towel, tea-cloth, tray-cloth, and all the rest, and boiled the white things, as usual, in Grandma's big pan. I began to tell her about the different kinds of washing machines one could get, and how swiftly our wash would be done in one of them.

'Imagine it, Grandma,' I said. 'We would just put the things in for a couple of minutes, and then all the work would be over and we could sit and listen to the radio.'

'They wouldn't be white,' replied Grandma, stirring the wash with the long plain wooden stick she kept for the purpose, while the steam wandered impudently in little bluey puffs past her austere wrinkled face and her thick white hair. 'Some of the farmers have them and I never believe they make things white.'

'We would make them white,' I said, lolling against the kitchen wall for a minute and watching her, 'with one of the latest detergents.'

'What are they?' she asked. She plunged the stick into the centre of the pan and the wash rearranged itself tumultuously, glubbing and bubbling all around the edge of the pan.

'They are all the new thing in soap powders,' I said, getting on with my work again, which consisted of wringing out the cloths that had already been boiled. 'They make things whiter than white, you know, Grandma. Wouldn't that be nice for us?'

'I prefer old-fashioned household soap,' said Grandma stoutly, 'and not this useless modern stuff.'

'But Grandma!' I protested. 'Household soap is only a thing that used to be modern once.'

'What do you mean?' asked Grandma. 'Household soap is not modern. It is both cheap and lasting.'

'Not that,' I replied. 'I mean there must have been a day when the first ever packet of household soap appeared, and everyone thought it was modern.'

'No,' said Grandma. 'We have *always* been able to get a good supply of yellow household soap.'

'And even the settlers made their own in one grand communal soapboiling, and then sat around together and wove their own underwear,' I said, picking up my pile of washing and making off into the sunshine. In honour of the occasion I hung it all up with absolute symmetry, sheets first, pillow-cases next, towels next, all neat and orderly on Grandma's three zigzag lines. It made a fine show.

The next thing that entertained Grandma's mind was the

question of what to give Wilma to stock their house. She was going to give them some money for a wedding present; but she wanted Wilma to have a few useful things as well. In a tiny room, hardly ever used, that stood between the parlour and the kitchen, she opened a great dark wooden chest, and within I saw, arranged carefully in tissue paper, layers of fine embroidery.

We found a stool each and sat by the chest, and looked at the pieces together. Some of the very prettiest things she put aside, saying they would do for me when I married. This troubled my conscience, because I knew she was looking forward to a future of meat-packing elegance for me, whereas I was to go to India to be a missionary, and wear a sari, and sleep on an old Persian mat. I fingered the supper-cloths Grandma had laid on my lap. The top one was embroidered with apple blossom, in single threads laid carefully side by side, until each petal and leaf formed a little silky cushion, in graduated shades of pink or green. 'I think you should give it to Wilma, Grandma,' I said. 'It is one of the very nicest ones.'

'It will do for you,' she said positively. 'And *this* one is for Peter.' She opened it out. It was made of appliqué work on fine white linen, in a pattern of green shamrock leaves. The linen had been cut away almost breathtakingly around the leaves, so that it unfolded on her lap and spilled to the floor like a shower of loose petals. She sat and stroked it.

'This is for Peter,' she repeated. Her face was soft. She picked the cloth up again at each side and held it out and surveyed it. 'I hope he gets a good wife,' she said; and folded it carefully edge to edge, and laid it down. 'I don't care for city girls,' she continued, 'with all their paint. I see them in the magazines — it's disgusting.'

'Who will marry him, then?' I asked, prickling again as

somehow or other always happened when anyone tried to marry off Peter.

'I don't know,' she said. 'I hope the Lord provides him with a good wife. I think otherwise he'll be hard put to find one in a city.' She got some more things out of the chest, and we looked at them and assigned some of them to Wilma. Soon there was a satisfying pile ready for Wilma and Joe, and Grandma began to put the other things away in the chest. I spoke up suddenly.

'What about Peter's girl-friend?' I asked her bluntly. 'Annabelle? The one he stayed with at Christmas.'

'A nice girl with black hair,' said Grandma, 'but there's no plans to marry.'

'Ginger hair,' I said.

'Black,' replied Grandma. She felt in her pocket. 'This is Peter's letter,' she said. She opened it and took out a snapshot, and began to smile. 'He says in his letter, "This is my new girl, Grandma, but don't worry, I won't marry until you find me a wife." He is a good boy, you see, and ready to wait for the hand of Providence.'

I took the photograph, which showed a fine upstanding young wench with long legs and a lot of hair, justly to be described as pitch black. I looked at her big flashing smile, directed, one supposed, at Peter behind the camera, and felt an ice-cold surge of triumph. 'You come and go, all of you,' I thought, 'with your horrid long legs and hair, but he belongs to us.' 'Grandma,' I asked, 'is Peter coming to annoy us at the wedding?'

'Yes,' she said. 'He is working in Ontario this summer, but he'll be here for the wedding.'

'Good!' I said. 'The wedding will be more like home with Peter to quarrel with.'

There were others coming to the wedding too. Joe and Wilma had an evergrowing list of people who must be asked, and who would drive to the festival from all parts of the countryside. One day as I pottered about the cabin with her, trying out pieces of furniture here and there, Wilma told me about the relatives she would have to invite.

'There is Auntie Madge,' she said, 'and Uncle Glen, and he has three children. And Mum's best friend Mrs. Packington Lee is coming from Dauphin. They were girls together at the High School and Mum would be mad if I left her out. And then, of course,' she said with a faint down-dropping of her voice, as if something lay down in it like a small coil of summer dust subsiding once again in the track, after a brief moment of hope and rebellion, 'of course,' she said, as one defeated before she began, 'there are my ten cousins.'

'Your *ten* cousins,' I said, slightly dazed, and laying my hands firmly on the back of an armchair as I contemplated a triplicate row of Joes, Ernests and Peters.

'My eight Winnipeg cousins,' she said, 'and my two English cousins who have emigrated here with their parents.'

'Oh yes,' I agreed. 'Developing Canada's future prosperity. Building the backbone of our national greatness. I understand. So that makes *ten* cousins, you say.'

'Ten,' she assented, 'all aged from three to fifteen. Mum had several younger brothers and sisters,' she added apologetically.

'And I have second cousins, too,' I said, 'and these are not the only children *you* have mentioned. How many persons under eighteen do you reckon will be at this wedding?'

'About thirty,' she said faintly.

'Let us try out your new coffee-pot,' I suggested. We made some strong coffee and then sat down together by one of the front windows of the cabin. 'Tell me about your cousins,' I encouraged her.

'Well,' she said, 'there's one family of three boys. And

there's another family of three girls. And then there's a boy
and a girl.'

'And the English ones?' I asked.

'A girl and a boy.'

'Well, that's only four lots of children,' I said. 'The way
you said it, it sounded like one seething mass of ten.'

'They are all usually present together,' she said, scanning
my face anxiously.

'In a herd?' I asked.

'No. A herd of cows is quiet and obedient,' she said.

The subject was evidently painful, so I changed it to the
question of linen, and she brightened up as she recounted to
me, with some help from her fingers, the exact stock of linens
that had been given to her by different people. When she
had told me about them, we discussed catering and all the
things she and her mother and my aunt were to bake, and
the things Grandma and I would make too. I took away a
list, too, of flowers that might be brought from Grandma's
garden, since her mother, who was very busy, did not grow
many flowers. And there still remained our clothes to choose!
There was no end to this wedding.

Then, three days in advance of the great date, there came
Peter, looking very brown, and tall, and bursting out of
his city suit, I thought. I told him so.

'Can't help that,' he said. 'I can't afford another just
now. But this fall I'm coming to a regular job in Manitoba,
and I'll get good pay. I'll get a suit then.' He pulled his
jacket down and peered down at himself, his hands on his
hips. 'It's not too bad, I think,' he meditated.

'No, not really,' I agreed. 'It's not that the suit's too
small, Peter, but that you're getting too big.'

He flashed his smile at me. 'That's the result of hard
exercise,' he said. 'And what are you going to be doing this
vacation, my little one?'

'There's not going to be much left after this wedding,' I replied.

'Come now,' he said. 'Only three more days. Months stretch ahead of you after that. What are you going to do?'

'Well, for one thing, I'm going to stay with the Whitings at the Lake of the Woods,' I told him.

His eye lit up. 'Near me!' he said.

I changed the subject rapidly. However, there was not very much time to talk, as preparations for the wedding were hurrying on. I was to wear a green dress, with a full skirt, and a yellow hat. I practised in front of my mirror for a while to see if my hair looked better pinned up on top, but it did not, so I decided to leave it unpinned. And then, the day before the wedding, there arrived the first of Alexander Mackintosh's letters, stenographed on a sheet of foolscap, telling us how he was progressing with his evangelistic team.

They were in British Columbia, he said, bearing a mighty witness to the Lord. This letter flung me into a turmoil, because I wanted to follow their progress on the map and sit and dream about Alexander in his kilt among the tall hills of British Columbia, but every minute of the day was full of the wedding. For a while I felt a stubborn resentment that I was hurrying about preparing for someone else's wedding, and had no time to think about my own interests: but with all our busyness, it soon had to give way.

Then the wedding day dawned, and I got up early in the morning to be sure of being ready in time. It was a good thing I did this, as the morning was one of incident. Unable to let the occasion go by without marking it in some way, Uncle's horses broke out through the wire again. They hit the track to Merrilee, evidently, for suddenly Grandma and I, who were bustling about getting ready for an early lunch, saw them dashing past.

We went outside and watched them disappearing down a small road to the left which led back to the open countryside. They were followed, in good time, by Joe and Peter in the car, who stopped and asked us if we had seen them. We pointed happily to the west, and the two of them drove off. This was rather disconcerting: but still it did not dawn on us that the boys might put the horses before the wedding. But for a while it seemed as if this had happened.

A farmer gave us a lift after lunch, and drove us over to the Mackenzie's house. Wilma's father had a house that he cherished as being up-to-date and modern, and beside it he cultivated a large green lawn, encircled with trees, which was now full of people. Our arrival caused a little burst of excitement, but when we stepped out we found that there was disappointment.

'We thought you might be Peter and Joe,' said Uncle.

'Haven't they come?' I asked.

'No, we haven't seen them since before lunch,' replied Uncle. 'Where the devil are they gone?'

I smiled at him happily. 'They've gone to look for those horses, Uncle,' I said. 'They all broke out again.'

'Well, to heck with it,' said Uncle blackly. 'Must they look for the horses on Joe's wedding day?'

'Farmers first, Mr. Donovan, farmers first!' said Wilma's father heartily. 'It's nice to know the young man's real enthusiastic.'

'I'll be rid of those horses,' swore Uncle, ramming tobacco into his pipe. 'They don't pay their keep. Just a few odd jobs here and there, that's all. I'll be rid of them and get better machinery. They're just a survival, that's all. Two grown men searching the countryside for four useless animals! It's not economic.'

'Well, talking about something economic, and now that we've time on our hands, will you come and see the new hen-house I'm building?' asked Mr. Mackenzie. 'Willingly!' said Uncle, puffing fury out of his pipe. They disappeared. I mingled with the guests, taking time too to admire the flowery arch that had been set up to mark the spot of the wedding ceremony, and peeping at the long trestle tables, flanked by benches, standing under the trees, with white cloths covering all the baking we had done.

I was afraid that Wilma would be feeling unhappy, and indeed, whenever I came to windward of the house it seemed to me I could hear the sound of lamentation: so I decided to go inside and reassure her and her mother that Joe had, after all, only gone to look for the horses. But as I made my way across the yard, I was gladdened by the sight of Peter. He was riding one of the Percherons with no bit and bridle, but only a coil of rope twisted through its mouth and secured behind its ears. He looked a strange sight riding into the gathering wearing his old blue overalls, his legs astraddle across the animal's wide back and the rope reins held short in one hand. He joined me at the door of the house and jumped down and gave me the rope. The horse stood and puffed. Its flanks were dark with sweat, but it still had a bright gay look in its eye as one who had lived since the morning.

'Where did you catch them?' I asked.

'By the Petersens' farm,' he said. 'They came out and helped us, and we left the horses with them. No time to take them back today. Joe is off home in the car, and I cut across to let everyone know the wedding's still on.'

He went off into the house, and I could hear him shouting for Wilma. I took the horse to the barn, and then I circulated among the wedding guests and urged them not to flag or faint. In due time, then, Joe came screeching in at the gate, flinging up a shower of stones, and jumped out in his good suit, his sunburnt face glowing with its recent scrubbing.

But even now the wedding could not begin, for where was Wilma's father? Ever ready with my news, I pointed out that he and Uncle were to be found in the hen-house. But they were not. They had gone down to the edge of a little creek that ran through Mr. Mackenzie's land, and were knocking at the banks to see if they would stand another heavy storm. But we retrieved them, and we brushed them down, and we knocked the mud off their boots, and wiped the horse sweat off the back of Peter's overalls and blessed heaven that he was not to be the best man, and dried his hair, now full of a thousand black curls, which he had incontinently drowned in a Niagara under the Mackenzies' pump; and then we routed out the minister, a thin young man with large blue eyes, who had got obscured in the middle of a flowery bevy of young ladies: and after this interesting start Joe and Wilma were finally able to get married.

But now, to get to the point, I am happy to be able to report that the really memorable feature of this wedding was the behaviour of Wilma's ten cousins, the eight from Winnipeg, and the two young settlers from the Old Country. This solid phalanx of eight tough, unscrupulous-looking children had been noticeable, glowering in the rear, during the little ceremony: and I felt a little sorry for the two English ones standing near them, so much more fair-skinned and gentle-seeming than the others.

After the wedding a separate table, at one side, with ten places, was pointed out to these children, as belonging to them. The adults went their way to their own tables, and the preacher offered up a long grace. As I had offered to help to keep the tables supplied, I did not sit down at once at my own place: and so I was able to keep an eye on the cousins, for I was interested in them. Later on, when there were no reinforcements needed, I simply stood by frankly eating my ice-cream and watching them.

When the children were first shown to the table, I felt surprised that they should be left alone like that, without an adult to organise them. They stood in a little knot and I wondered if they were not glowering with shyness only, and whether they could really manage to arrange their own tea. The preacher then, as we have said, intoned the grace. The adults here and there around the lawn sank gracefully into their chairs, the women spreading out their pretty skirts and patting their hair, and everyone laughing and calling to each other.

Among the ten children whom I watched, there was a sudden wild convulsive flow, a thrashing May dance of arms and legs like Laocoön colliding with the serpents. It ceased abruptly, and the children were all seated. The English ones, not a hair out of place, were sitting opposite each other halfway down the table, at the most strategic places of all, commanding a clear arm's reach of all the provender.

And now I witnessed a piece of pure anthropology, a dumb instinctive tribal ritual. Before a single child put a piece of food on to its own plate, the three tallest counted every single article on the table, their long brown fingers shuffling the pieces like determined gamblers; and when they had finished, everything was completely rearranged, and I saw that every plate now carried its offering in little groups of ten.

On one plate with twenty sandwiches there were now ten groups of two sandwiches. On the next plate, with twenty-six sandwiches, there were ten groups of two and six-tenths sandwiches. And so on all over the table. The three monitors with their long lean fingers and quick glancing eyes now carried out a final recount, met each other's gaze, nodded briefly, and sat down. With one united movement, like English soldiers stepping out to drill, the ten began to eat. All conversation ceased among them. They simply sat and devoured. By now I was hovering near at hand, and looking on all the time. Watching them with a most observant eye, I came to the conclusion that the two English cousins, for all they had looked so courteous and aloof, and spoke in such sweet piping voices, were managing to eat as fast as any of the others. Indeed, I decided they were drawing ahead, for the fact that they ate with their mouths shut gave them an advantage, as nothing fell out or had to be grabbed and stuffed in again as it did with the others, hindering them considerably. Anyway, I suspected them of drawing ahead, and according to my count the English girl was already two sandwiches and three pieces of cake beyond the general apportionment. And in a minute or two a chorus of complaint broke out, for two of the Winnipeg cousins had found themselves faced with a plate empty of one kind of sandwich before they had had their fair allotted share.

There were now general recriminations and accusations of 'You took it!', 'I never did!', 'You did so!', 'I did not, you liar!' The two English children sat looking patient and surprised, politeness itself, except that I knew for certain that the English girl had had the two sandwiches, and that she knew it. The shrill twittering rose to such a height that people at other tables began to glance around. I dreaded to think what the noise would be when the loss of the cake was discovered. But justice was swift. The second tallest boy, a lad with curly brown hair, stood up.

He addressed each child in turn. 'You took it!' he said. They each denied it, while he watched them with his hard shiny brown eyes. When it came to the English girl, she denied it too, but under his stare she began to blush, and he cried out triumphantly, 'She did it! She did it!'

'She did it!' shouted all the children. The wedding party gazed around amazed. A brief silence fell on the little folk and their publicity passed away from them. 'What else did you take?' asked the curly-headed boy. 'Nothing,' she said. 'What did you take, what did you take, what did you take?' intoned the boy. 'Three pieces of cake,' she whispered. 'She took three pieces of cake!' shouted the children. 'Three — three cakes — she says it was her — three pieces — it was my piece I bet,' they cried. But now one of the fathers suddenly came over the lawn towards them.

'What's wrong?' he asked.

'Nothing, Dad,' said the boy.

'What are you standing for?'

'I'm telling them a story about Fu Manchu.'

'Sit down and keep your mouth shut. All the folk are looking at you.'

'Yes, Dad.' He sat down. 'Three cakes less every time for you from now to August,' he hissed.

'More for us! More for us! More for us!' sang the children *sotto voce*, drumming *pianissimo* on their table.

'You're a skunk,' said she in a perfect Oxford accent. 'You're a no-good skunk, see. I won't do it. I'll have my cake.'

'You'll have three pieces less every time,' he answered. 'Fu Manchu has spoken.' He picked up his half-eaten sandwich and they all began to eat simultaneously. I was a little dazed by now, so I went to the ice-cream freezer and had some more strawberry ice-cream. 'Hi!' said Peter, appearing suddenly: 'how's things?'

'Peter, do you like children?' I asked.

'Not much, except the ones I'm going to have myself,' he replied. 'They lead such disorganised lives nowadays. But I don't know: English children are O.K., I guess. I've met some, and their manners seemed very pretty.'

I shuddered faintly. We will pass over the rest of the children's wedding day: the faultless precision of the cartwheels they did up and down the lawn, their organised flight up one of the sloping willow trees near the barn, their sang-froid when the same tree fell down beneath them, having for a long time been finding life too much for it: and their strategic and brilliantly deployed capture of Mr. Mackenzie's flock of prize turkeys. Thankfully, we see them disappearing in their parents' cars, back to the startled city of Winnipeg. And Joe and Wilma were away now too, and some of the farmers went back to their work, while those of us who were left, one or two people from each farm, held a party and a dance on the lawn.

Uncle and Auntie and Ernest went away, but Peter, who went with them, came back, having changed into his suit. By the time he got back I was being very popular with the young farmers, and he did not have much time to dance with me: to say nothing of the girls who were trying to dance with him themselves. He managed to get the last dance, however; and then he drove me home in Uncle's car.

'This has been quite disappointing,' he announced, as we drove along.

'Disappointing!' I said. 'I never saw such a day full of incident.'

'That's just it,' he said. 'Far too many incidents. You know, I visualised this wedding time as a chance to talk to you. But you've been so busy: and now today you spent all the time hanging round that awful crew of children.'

'How about you,' I asked, 'hanging around the horses?'

'There you are,' he answered. 'Between horses and children and cooking and everything, there's been too much incident altogether these past three days. Well, it just means I'll have to come and see you at the lake.'

I tried hard to dissuade him from this idea. It did not appeal to me at all. But he remained firm. 'No, no,' he said, 'I won't be thwarted by animals and children. I want to talk to you, and I'm coming to the lake to do it.' But now we were home and he stopped the car by Grandma's gate. He moved around, and put his arm along the back of the seat.

'Make yourself comfortable,' I said.

'Certainly I will,' he said; 'I intend now to kiss you.' 'You will not,' I replied, opening the car door: and at that moment, unexpectedly, Grandma like the wrath of God appeared in the doorway in a red flannel dressing-gown, and that was that. I got out of the car. 'Good night,' I said haughtily. 'Just you wait,' Peter retorted from the car, 'wait till the next time we're alone. Wait till I get you at the lake!' And I walked in, very prim and straight and correct — and that was Joe and Wilma married.

And now to the Lake of the Woods, which lay a hundred miles or so eastwards, just inside the border of Ontario. I was heading for the lakeside town of Kenora, where the Whitings were to meet me.

I carried Alexander's letter with me in the train to read and consider. As I read it and thought about college, I could not help being sorry that I had parted with Don, who used to write me such interesting letters in the vacations, battered out on his typewriter with a variety of coloured ribbons, some-times even in two colours at once so that the tops of the separate letters were one colour and their little dangling tails something else altogether. I sat and thought about his letters now: but soon I stopped either pondering or reading, for the countryside was growing more craggy and interesting, and so now I sat looking out of the window.

The scenery became more rocky and more broken up into valleys and hills: beside the train the long grass was thick with brilliant patches of wild flowers, and the woods were full of pretty little silver birch trees, and aspens fluttering their leaves in the breeze. The Douglas firs seemed to be taller here; and the true pines grew more freely among them,

the long brown flakes of bark frilled and feathery at the edges
as they splintered from the trunks of the trees.

The loose rocks and stones cropped up everywhere, green
with their patches of moss and lichen: until sometimes the
whole side of a valley would look like an abandoned stretch
of quarry now half reconquered by bushes and trees, so
rough and rocky was it. I stared at it all fascinated as the
hours went by; and then at last we reached the lake and
Kenora, and I descended the little ladder from the train, and
found Mr. Whiting and Sarah Ann waiting for me. They had
brought their outboard motor-boat, and in it we set out
across the lake to the place where their cottage stood; and
here we landed, and went up the path to the cottage.

The Whitings' cottage was a single-story pinewood building, with a verandah on two sides, covered in, of course,
with mosquito netting. Because of the sloping ground, the
front part of the cottage stood on heavy wooden posts, leaving
a warm little cave beneath. We entered by climbing some
wooden steps, and went through the front verandah and past
an open doorway into the main room of the house, a square
room with an iron stove. From this one could reach the
bedrooms and the kitchen; and beyond the kitchen and the
back door there was a path leading to a little cabin with two
extra bunks, and another path running through the hazel
bushes to the plumbing.

My small bedroom was near the front of the cottage. There
was nothing much in this room: a bunk, a chest of drawers, a
washstand, some hooks on the door, and a blurred and
spotted mirror turning obscurely greenish in one corner.
The rest of the cottage was furnished with the same plain-
ness. It was meant to be a mere passageway, a place to
sleep, a roof against thunderstorms: the business of living was
to be done outside. The best seat in the vicinity, as I had
discovered by the middle of next morning, was a rock near

the house, which commanded a fine view of the lake. It was nicely warmed by the sun and surrounded by a close turf of grasses and trefoils; the air around it smelt sweetly of the fir trees, and near at hand hung the elegant branches of a pin cherry. This was the place to sit and think, to sit and confer with Sarah Ann, or to sit and drink milk and eat peanut butter cookies.

Sarah Ann and I had work to do each morning, washing the dishes, sweeping the cottage and preparing vegetables. Her sister was not with us now; she had gone to Banff in the Rockies for the summer, to work as a waitress; but their brother was there, and he helped us with the dishes, and then went out to chop wood for the stoves.

After this we all changed and ran down to the lake and went swimming. Sarah's brother Ross went swimming before breakfast as well, but she and I did not rise to this. Down by the water, there was a wooden dock, but it was too slippery and full of holes to be the best landing place for swimmers. It was more comfortable to dive in from one of the tall brown rocks and climb up again along the smaller rocks that stood like steps beside it. There were flat rocks, too, lying half in and out of the water, with branches tumbled and half-drowned beside them, but they were so green and slippery too they offered no advantage over the dock. The water, however, was perfectly clean and clear, offering a view below of a perfect world of stones and sand.

In this clear water, if we sat still on the rocks, we could see the crawfish moving about, waving their little bushy tails and opening their tiny lobster claws, and small shoals of minnows, and sometimes even the bigger fish which swam singly into view. And on the dry land, there were the squirrels going to and fro with a white squirrel among them; and there were chipmunks, and small frogs wishing they had not left the lake edge, and a hedgehog that made its way slowly under the bushes; and once we saw a porcupine, and sometimes caught sight of the deer watching us remotely from among the trees.

Leaving the others sometimes, I went even further up the hill: and then, with the cottage out of sight, silence closed in with the filtered sunlight among the dark evergreen of the firs. I used to imagine that if you pressed on you might walk one hundred miles, two, three or four, and never emerge from the firs that possessed Ontario. But turning aside, one could climb up yet another prominence, scrambling over the rocks and sometimes over the whitened body of a dead tree. The top of this other hill was made out of rock again: but with enough earth lying on it, drifted more thickly into the rifts and crevasses, to support a scattering of feathery grass and to hold the tiny blueberry bushes and the wild straw-berries and the bluebells, with their faint pencilled stems and petals like an afterthought of blue smoke. From this summit, which rose clear above the surrounding trees, one could see the islands and waterways of the lake.

Here on this hill I used to sit and gaze, and then I would dream about the explorers. The explorers were the best part of our history. There were the explorers, and the settlers with their quaint ways, and then the politicians. And now there was International Relations, but that was all in the newspapers still, and not history. And meanwhile the explorers were the best part of the lot.

I sat on the rocky summit of the hill and played at the explorers for the greater part of an afternoon at a time. And the view from the hill was such that it almost seemed that if I strained my eyes I could see them entering Canada along the Saint Lawrence, or disappearing southwards into the Gulf of Mexico. You could not believe that there was a place in the world you could not see from the hill. Or if there was such a place, it was not worth seeing.

And at other times, we would go out together and explore the lake in our little boats. We went in the canoe, and in the rowing-boat too, which was good for troll-fishing, when we trailed a line behind us and hoped to catch bass and perch. Or for a long journey we took the outboard.

The outboard, a Seagull, was necessary to go to Kenora to fetch the mail. When we had read our letters, we strolled around looking at the displays of Indian crafts, before travelling home again.

I enjoyed these journeys across the water to the little town. But my peace was disrupted one day. There was a letter from Peter.

On Friday, he announced, he was coming to stay for the weekend. Apparently he took it for granted that the Whitings or their neighbours would be able to find room for him. He took it for granted too that I wanted to see him, for now it was Thursday and too late to try to discourage him. I was not at all sure that I did want to see him. My hands were full already: I would like to see Peter, but some other time. But Peter was coming all the same.

So the journey was to be done again the next day in time to meet his train, and there was Peter, burnt dark brown with the sun, wearing a red shirt and an old pair of trousers. 'I've brought my sleeping-bag,' he said cheerfully, 'in case I have to sleep in the woods.'

'You can sleep in our cabin,' said Ross, who seemed to have taken a liking to him. 'I have one bunk and you can have the other. We can have great times out there.'

'My bag'll be handy for my bunk, then,' said Peter contentedly. He hummed to himself as we sped across the lake. He forbore to tease me, too, which pleased me, because I did not want my peace destroyed. And then back at the cottage, Mr. Whiting immediately took to him as well. After supper, they sat up late on the front verandah, with the rest of us sitting around or coming and going, and they contented their hearts with a long talk about Canada. Mr. Whiting talked about his building business and Peter talked about his engineering profession, and they found a hundred points of common interest and a dozen things to differ about, and one single united resolution that Canada was the best place in the world for an active, practical man to live in. Then, just before their jaws dropped off, talk suddenly seemed to run dry; and they hummed and hawed a bit and Mr. Whiting said, 'Well, yes, yes, yes,' and filled his pipe: and Mrs. Whiting turned on the electric light, and fetched us milk and cookies.

After this Peter and Ross went off to their cabin, and we began to get ready for bed. In a little while I went to pay a visit to the plumbing, and as I came back along the path through the hazel bushes, the grass delicate under my bare feet, I found Peter standing in the clear space of ground behind the cottage. He was rocking on his feet and humming to himself as he flicked his towel here and there. Out of doors, the night was perfectly clear, I could see him as though it were day and the soft white moths that fled past him.

'I didn't have much time to speak to you,' he said. This was not true, he had had time, but it had been necessary to his soul to talk about affairs with Mr. Whiting.

'I didn't have much time to speak to you at home either,' he said. 'You were always baking things and rushing round with Wilma. And as I said, the wedding day was frantic.'

'A wedding's a busy time,' I said.

'So I noticed,' he replied. 'You looked stunning, though, in that green dress. Did I tell you?'

'Maybe. I don't remember.'

'You remember I told you I would come and see you. I told you most carefully.'

'I didn't think you meant it, though,' I said.

'Sure, I meant it,' he said. 'Especially when you looked so alluring in that green dress. What do you think, Peggy,' he went on, 'will we get any time to ourselves?'

'I guess so,' I replied. 'Once the work is done in the morning we all do as we like.'

'We can't run away from Sarah Ann, though,' he said dubiously.

'Sarah Ann's got a boy-friend of hers coming tomorrow morning to stay in that house with the yellow boathouse, just along the lake: so she'll have company.'

'Good,' he said. 'Well, that's settled. We'll take a boat trip. We'll see the best day when it comes.' He looked at me for a moment, and then without saying anything more, walked back to the cabin, and I went to bed.

On Saturday Sarah Ann's friend, David Williams, called for her, and she went back to his house with him; but Ross was so busy showing Peter around that there was no time for his boat trip. On Sunday Sarah Ann, who had been swimming with David before breakfast, told us that his family were going to set out after lunch in their motor-boat, a large one with a proper deck and cabin, and that they would like all of us to come. Mr. and Mrs. Whiting, however, said they would not come, or else there would not be room for all of us. This disappointed Sarah Ann, who wanted her parents to take the outing: but Peter seized his chance and told them that he would like to take me out in the canoe, if they did not mind his borrowing it.

Mrs. Whiting, looking at him thoughtfully, decided to agree to this plan, and so it was settled. She asked if she should make sandwiches: but Sarah Ann told her that the Williamses would bring a picnic basket, and that they had a little stove and kettle with which they would make tea ashore on one of the islands.

'The Williamses have everything,' said Ross.

'I know,' she said, 'and perhaps it's a pity I'm not more keen about David. I know he's great fun, and I'm always pleased to see him; but...'

'Well, never mind,' answered Ross. 'You like him well enough for a boat ride, and that's fine by me.'

'His younger sister's coming too,' said Sarah Ann. 'She's very pretty.'

'Nerts,' replied Ross: but his eye gleamed, and he attacked his breakfast with greater energy.

During the morning I made some sandwiches for Peter and myself and some coffee to put in a Thermos flask; and then after lunch the Whitings set off in the outboard to travel round the point to the Williamses' house, and Peter and I waved goodbye to them, and took our food and went down to the canoe. Peter announced firmly that he was going to paddle all the way. He found me a cushion and I sat opposite him, leaning against the other seat, and admired his appearance in the bright blue shirt he had put on. He pushed off, and began to paddle, and the canoe slid away from the land and out into the open water.

We went on for a long way without saying anything much. Out on the open water, the lake always seemed smaller than it should, for the islands lay all around, and all the distances looked shorter, and the sounds rang clearly from far away. But it took a great deal of paddling to reach each island; and beyond it still another stretch of water would open out again. Whenever we came near one of the islands, Peter let the canoe drift on its own way, and then we stared at the holiday-makers going industriously about their own business, quite indifferent to us as we watched them sitting on their verandahs or cleaning their boats or plunging in and out of the lake.

'I would like a completely remote island,' said Peter, 'just a few rocks and trees where no one ever came past, and then

I could fish and sit and think and watch the sunset. Or I would like to go up to the North perhaps, and camp out in the forests.'

He sculled on meditatively. In an open piece of water ahead of us some yachts were racing, and as we came along they slid past us, running before the breeze at an angle to the water with the waves trilling at their bows. 'That's great!' said Peter. 'I could spend all day sailing. Especially in a high wind. I should take you out one day.'

'Not for me!' I said.

'No,' he replied, 'I guess you wouldn't like the wind. I should take you fishing instead.'

He paddled on. Then, he suddenly began to tell me about his job. He explained it all most seriously, so I set myself to listen, but I did not understand it very well.

The mathematical explanations were particularly difficult. What I chiefly wanted to know was: did he *like* the job?

Yes, he *liked* the job: it was a challenge, you see; now for instance take this problem . . . and there we were facing some obscure complication that I could not comprehend, but which Peter had been able to overcome by a display of real brilliance. 'And then when you work a thing out like that, you can save your firm thousands of dollars,' he said with satisfaction, starting to paddle along the other side of the canoe. 'You see what I mean?'

'I do, Peter,' I assured him. 'And you really *like* the job?'

'Yes,' he replied, 'it's a very happy and useful job. You can get great satisfaction out of it; for instance . . .' and there we were up to our necks again. However, he had steered the canoe slightly to one side, and had at last drawn near to the mainland again, and we were interrupted by sliding into the edge of a long fringe of bulrushes that grew in the shallow water; and he stopped talking for a while, and turned the canoe out of the reeds.

We slid slowly along past the bulrushes and the yellow flags, and the smaller rushes which were coming out into a sort of feathery bloom, and past the open patches of water where dark yellow lilies floated on the surface. We could see some of the lake water-fowl chugging in and out among the greenery: and over everything there was a perfect activity of insect life humming and buzzing and rising and dipping, or sculling on the water, with the dragonflies dancing victorious for size and beauty, while the sun blazed through their green and blue wings. The miniature water forest, with the sunlight broken up into lights and shadows in it, made a beautiful scene. Peter stared at it all, happy and absorbed. 'He is a child, really,' I thought suddenly. I splashed him with some water. He laughed at me, and began to get up speed as we left the rushes and journeyed on in and out of the mainland bays. As we went, he began to ask me how I was getting on at college. He put some questions here and there, and I told him a few stories.

'Your life sounds just a round of men,' he commented at length.

'Women's life so often is,' I said.

'Why do they go to college, then?' he asked.

'To see a better selection of men,' I suggested. 'And,' I added with feeling, 'to find one who is really interesting and romantic. Someone that will be a bit poetical to live with.'

'What nonsense,' he said. 'Women are satisfied best with housekeeping and children.'

'You can't get children without men,' I pointed out.

'I realise that,' he said, 'and it's very convenient for men. It's this daydreaming and poetry I don't like. Women shouldn't go to college and sit thinking about poetry. They should get on with their work, and if they have time to spare, they can learn dressmaking and cooking.'

'Peter, you're so uninteresting,' I said, annoyed. 'You've no romance in you. And you're so dogmatic, too. I must tell you frankly, Peter,' I added idly, wanting to annoy him for his disregard of poetry, 'you always were a beast. You were the most perfectly horrible boy I ever met.'

He scowled at me. 'What a tongue you have!' he replied. 'The place for you is in the stocks as a shrew. What a woman you'll grow into! And you were such a nice child. Even though you were such a cissy.'

'Perhaps so,' I said. 'But at least I wasn't a ruthless beast.'

He smiled at me. His annoyance seemed to have gone away. 'I was a brute,' he agreed, 'but most boys are. You thought I was the worst because you knew me best. But I've improved. You must admit that.'

'Maybe so,' I said. 'That's why we get on better.'

'I'm glad you recognise it,' he said. He went on for a little way without saying anything, often just letting the canoe drift quietly while he rested from paddling. But now, as we passed through the tranquil afternoon, I recollected myself. I had been passing the time in idle chatter, remembering stories from the past, and had given Peter a false impression of my outlook. I had failed to tell him of my new life. This must be remedied. I launched into it.

'My mind is not only on men now,' I spoke up and said to him. 'I have changed now. I am going to be a missionary, and go and live in India.'

'Jumping Jeremy!' said Peter, holding the paddle in the air for a moment as he stared at me. 'And which man did you get that from?'

'Well,' I conceded, 'the inspiration was actually Alec.'

'Alec who?'

'Alexander Mackintosh.'

'Mackintosh!' exclaimed Peter. 'The one that preaches! I know that man. There's a real pain for you.'

'Peter!' I said. 'How wicked of you!'

'I've heard him preach, Peggy,' replied Peter. 'He came to our college on a tour once, smiling like an old hen turkey. And that skirt he wears!'

'It's a good Scottish kilt,' I said.

'And is he a good Scottish man?' asked Peter, driving the canoe on with long sweeps of the paddle. 'No, he is not. So why wear a kilt?'

'The Cameron Highlanders wear the kilt,' I said.

'They are soldiers, and that's their walking-out dress,' he said. 'I've seen them on parade in the war, and it looked fine. And so many of them were killed!' he added bitterly. 'But Mackintosh is now just a humble Canadian student, and that is not Canadian student dress. In short, he wears it to show off, like his preaching. No, taking it all round,' he concluded, 'the man's an ape.'

'Your conversation is extremely illiterate,' I said furiously. 'You bore me horribly.'

'Well, you can't get away from it,' replied Peter darkly, 'unless you care to get out and walk.'

'I'd hate to go out on a date with you,' I added. 'You're so ill-informed.'

'You won't get the chance,' he retorted. He sculled the canoe along, and we sat in silence. We went on for some time like this, until he suddenly said, 'It's time to eat.'

'I guess it is,' I said. 'Shall we go ashore?'

'Let's just go past this point,' he agreed. He paddled past the dark outcrop of rock. As we went, I gradually decided to forgive him.

Peter did not understand Alec, and that was that. Peter was not religious, and people who were not religious never did understand Alec. I must be sorry for Peter. In the meantime, I was hungry. I said so.

'There's a little island right ahead,' said Peter reassuringly, 'just made for you and me.'

He paddled towards the island. As we went, we could hear the chugging of a motorboat. I saw Peter gazing ahead, and looked over my shoulder. The motorboat was now drifting in towards the little island for which we had been heading. Peter held the paddle sideways and slowed down the canoe.

'Perhaps not,' he said.

We drifted along and watched the boat disgorging its contents. 'What a lot of children!' he said.

I agreed. But a slight sensation of alarm had begun to take hold of me. I gazed more carefully at the figures of the children. My feelings were confirmed.

'Peter,' I said, 'you know, I believe it is——'

'Wilma's ten cousins!' he finished. 'It is!' With a few short strokes he turned the canoe around. 'We'll head back again and pick up an island on the way.' He drove the paddle into the water and we fled along the lake, the shrill sound of childish voices echoing towards us. As the menace fell behind us, Peter slowed down a little, and began to tell me some interesting news. Ernest, who had just left for his training camp, had written to Peter to tell him that on the way there he had stayed with some of Wilma's cousins in Winnipeg. Their father had invited him at the wedding. Ernest said, unbelievably, that he had enjoyed the stay, and was now friendly with one of the cousins, a girl of about fourteen. In fact, she had already posted him a box of cookies.

'Did she bake them?' I asked.

'She got them from her mother's cupboard,' he answered.

'Delightful,' I said. 'And now, they've all come to stay at the lake to keep it cheerful for us. But surely that was a very long letter for Ernest to write?'

'Ernest is quite a letter writer,' said Peter. 'He has a real gift for language. Anyway, you never know, in three or four years you might have this girl for your cousin-in-law.'

He smiled at me happily. I sat overcome at the prospect, and we continued in a state of solemn silence until at last Peter said, 'This'll do!' He had chosen a small neat island with a sharply pointed hill on it. We stepped ashore and pulled the canoe up onto a little stretch of sand between two rocks, and on the warm stones beyond we sat and ate our meal. Afterwards Peter lay down on his back in the sun and crooked his arms over his face and appeared to fall asleep. I sat beside him watching the birds, and plucking at the grass or throwing little stones into the lake. As it had been a very hot day, I was quite happy to sit and do nothing for a long long time.

Eventually, he moved gently and stretched out his arm, and took my hand.

'Let's go for a walk,' he said.

'O.K.'

He jumped to his feet. 'Ouf,' he said, 'I was half asleep.'

'You paddled a long way.'

'Any man should be able to paddle a long way.' He walked to the lake edge and knelt on a rock and splashed his face with the water. 'There we are,' he said, wiping his face conveniently on his bare sunburnt arms. 'Now we can get some exercise.' We set off gently to skirt the island, jumping sometimes from rock to rock in order to make our way along. After a while Peter began to look hopefully up the hill-side. 'Here's a convenient ascent, I think,' he said.

We started to mount the gentle slope, threading in and out among the bushes and large stones. Halfway up, we came to the beginning of a much more difficult climb. 'Let's look at the view for a minute,' he suggested. We stood and gazed, looking at the bright golden sun, now lower in the sky, and at the long, long stretches of blue water; and, nearer at hand, the joyful reflection of our own island upside-down beneath us in the lake.

We stood dreamily watching the scene, and while we looked, Peter put his hand out and took hold of mine. Then he ran his hand gently up my arm, and closed his fingers thoughtfully just above my elbow. I liked the sensation: but he kept moving his fingers about, and I realised that he was really enjoying himself and was attending to my arm much more than to the view. I suddenly recollected my allegiance to the Meeting.

'Peter,' I exclaimed, 'don't do that!'

'Why not?' he asked, tightening his grip and looking hard at me.

'It's not pureminded,' I said firmly.

'Pureminded?' he said to me. 'What is this nonsense?'

'We should be wholesome and pureminded,' I said, vividly remembering some of Alexander's talks on the subject, 'and put improper things out of our thoughts.'

'If you don't like it,' he said, 'just tell me. Then I might stop doing it. Or maybe I won't. But just tell me if you don't like it. I understand that. "Pureminded" is something I don't know anything about.'

'Now Alexander——' I began, but he jerked my arm sharply sideways. 'Shut up!' he said.

'I was going to tell you——' I said again.

'You tell me about that man and I'll throw you in the lake,' he replied. We both glanced down past the cliff of brown rock below us to the nice clear water beneath. 'See it!' he said. 'I'll pitch you in. Don't talk to me about that man.' He let go of my arm and took hold of my shoulder, holding it tight, and looked down at me a little more kindly. 'And don't imagine that he is pureminded either, Peggy. Men are not.'

'Well, you don't know any Christian men,' I replied.

'Oh dear,' he said. He let go and started to step up the rocks, and then he stretched out a hand to me. 'Come on,' he said, 'I'll help you over the rocks. I can surely help you, can't I?' I took his hand, and we went on upwards.

At the top of the hill, the small grasses were blowing and the sun, sinking gently, made them important with sunlight, and shone over the rough surface of the rocks, so that each stone was dotted with tiny lights and shadows. The flies and gnats hummed in the air, their little wings catching the light as they passed through it before us, and in the still evening we could even hear the faint ripple of the lake waters against the rocks below.

A motor-boat passed us, out in the open; and its wake came splashing against our island. As it died away, a sharper breeze sprang up across the lake, chasing the surface of the water here and there like handfuls of grey feathers blown into disorder. Gathering strength, it began to ruffle my hair, and I tried to smooth it down. Peter began watching me, scanning me intently with his eyes, his mouth shut hard. Suddenly he returned to the attack.

'I never once kissed you properly,' he said.

'You did!' I retorted.

'That!' said Peter. 'That's not kissing. Not properly. But it's a good idea, Peggy. We might never have another chance again.'

'Do we *need* the chance?' I asked.

'It makes things nice,' he said. 'Then you can remember it, the lake and the islands and the little boats, and a good opportunity made use of.'

'I don't want to,' I said. 'Don't let's talk about it. You seem to keep talking about it. Why do we always get back to this?'

He picked up some stones and began to throw them out

into the water and their plop-plop resounded in the evening air, and I could see by the quick flick of his arm as he threw them that he was angry. 'You are a fool, Peggy,' he said, throwing the stones rapidly one after another. 'Why don't you let me do these little things? Why should you resist me and get me worked up?' He turned to look at me. 'You only make it worse when you refuse the small things, you know,' he said; 'and in a minute, I'll get so aggravated, I'll set to work to do exactly as I like. The things I'd *really* like to do. And I'm so much bigger and stronger than you, you can't stop me.'

I hadn't any real idea what he was talking about; I seemed to have lost the thread somewhere and it had all become a jumble of words. I didn't know what he meant he would really like to do, except, as he had said, throw me into the lake, which didn't seem to be a practical idea. I walked away and began to climb down the rocks: and when I was halfway down the steepest part he left the summit of the hill and came down after me. By the time I had reached the spot where we had stood and watched the view, he had caught up with me; and he smiled and held out his hand and we went down together.

When we came back to the place where the canoe was beached, we watched the fish rising for a while, and I picked a few flowers to take home; and then as there did not seem to be anything left to do, we slid the canoe back into the lake, stepped in and pushed away. Peter settled down to paddling in earnest; and we made a rapid course through the water.

'Hope we don't meet Wilma's cousins,' he said suddenly. 'I hope they are well away from this end of the lake.'

'So do I.'

'It will be time enough to be intimate with them when Ernest gets married,' he said with a smile. We fell silent again and pursued our way. I sat back and watched the islands and their long shadows slide past us.

The sun had begun to provide the sunset, which stained the sky all over the compass with its blazing red and yellow. All the tranquil surface of the water picked up the colours, and reflected even the separate little wisps of flame-coloured cloud that hung here and there in the sky. The fir trees on the little islands took on a red light, and so did the edges of the little ripples running away from the paddle and the back of the canoe; and the sinking sunset outlined Peter in colour, and drifted its burning light across his head and his blue shirt and down the side of his face, and along the moving line of his arms. An almost unbelievable sensation of peace took possession of me: I would not have spoken for the world. I had never felt anything like it in my life; I had never seen such colours before, anything so clear, red that could never be redder, yellow as yellow as gold, black and purple moving in the shadows of the water. I began to trail my fingers carefully, delicately, on the surface of the lake, and as the water pressed gently against my finger-tips and the canoe ran and swung along, I decided that this was the first time in my life that I had ever felt perfectly happy. With such a sunset, never to be seen again, and such a silence, that should never be broken! And then even the sunlight began to die away entirely, and there was a dark blue half-light with pale images of red in the sky; and at last we came drifting like a shadow across the lake to our dock, Peter holding the wet paddle up while the drops of water fell off it small and quiet in the dusk, and the canoe glided on on its own way; and then we climbed ashore, and he put the boat away, and we went up to the cottage.

Now in the bare electric light the magic of the occasion seemed to have vanished. The others had not returned yet, and the evening seemed to have come to a loose end. I put my things away in my little room; and then I thought that this might be a good time to get everything ready for the night. I took the cover off the bed, and began to lay out my pyjamas. Peter had come to the doorway, and was standing watching me.

'Now is this a wise thing to do in front of me?' he said suddenly.

I looked round at him. 'Is what wise?'

'Getting your bed ready like that.'

'Why should you mind?' I asked.

'Oh, Peggy,' he said angrily, 'are you *wilfully* blind?'

I was going to go past him and out of the room, but he put his arm out and barred the door. I pressed against it, but it was all as hard as iron, so I gave up.

'Are you really a complete fool?' he asked.

I sat down on the edge of my bed and looked at him patiently, and he put his arm down again and stuck his hands in his pockets.

'May I fill my glass of water?' I asked.

'Oh, I suppose so,' he said. I went past him to the kitchen, and he came along behind me.

'I wonder about you girls, sometimes,' he said. 'You're supposed to know so much but sometimes I wonder if you understand a thing about it. Sometimes I look at married women too and I think, My God, I don't believe you understand anything at all.'

'What are you talking about?' I asked, filling my glass at the watertank.

'I'm talking about sex,' he said.

I was about to say, 'Again!' but decided not to, and I took my glass into my room. Peter sat on the living-room table and waited for me.

'Tell me something?' he asked when I came back.

'Perhaps,' I said.

'Did you never want anyone so badly you didn't know what to do about it?'

I decided to give him some attention. 'Well,' I answered, thinking it over, 'only when they weren't there. When they're there it puts me off.'

'That's funny,' he said. 'But when they weren't there, you did?'

'I guess so,' I said.

'So that you had to walk up and down your room?' he asked.

I looked at him with a slightly glazed expression. 'You're always talking, Peter,' I said, 'and you say so many words.'

'There you are!' he replied. 'You don't know what I mean. You don't know anything about it all.'

I walked around the room, trailing my fingers from one piece of furniture to the next. 'Peter Donovan talks so,' I said, 'I don't know what he's saying.'

'All right,' he said, standing up: 'I feel better now. Get me something to eat.'

'You want a drink?'

'I want some coffee.' He went into the front verandah and stood looking out and began to whistle. I heated some coffee and found some apples and took them to the verandah. Peter thanked me politely. As we ate, he asked me about college again, in a polite and noncommittal tone of voice: I could not see in the darkness, for he had turned the lights out, whether he was interested in my replies or not. When we had finished I took the cups away, and went back to find him looking out again. I stood a little way along the verandah and gazed out too. Looking beyond the hazel and sumac that grew, below us, at the lake edge, we could see the pale reflections of the moon beginning to shimmer on the water, and the moon herself which had now appeared on the far side of the lake, all neatly framed between the black zigzag of the branches of the two Douglas firs that grew, one at each side, in front of the cottage. The night was quite silent: but after a while we heard the sound of an outboard motor.

'Is that the Whitings' boat?' asked Peter.

'Sounds to me like it,' I said.

'So here they come,' he said. There was a sort of disappointment and regret in his tone and a quickness as if time were growing much too short. 'They're all coming home again.' He moved quietly and stood right beside me, and put his arm behind my shoulders, resting the palm of his hand against one of the posts of the verandah. He spoke quick and softly. 'Oh, my darling,' he said, 'let me kiss you once.'

I was so surprised that now I let him do it. It reminded me powerfully of the sunshine and the tractor out in the fields. I shut my eyes and tilted my head back and he put his arms around me, and he went on so long, I thought the outboard must have landed already, but then we heard the voices echoing up from the dock, and he stopped. Then he put his hand on my shoulder, and dug his fingers in, and stood beside me while we looked down the path to watch for the people. 'And now there is talking to be done,' he said to me softly, 'and sociability. It seems to me we have never been really alone since we were children, except today: and now it is over. But never mind,' he said, putting his cheek against mine, 'I got what I wanted. Or at least, a little bit of it.' Moved by fondness for him, I turned my face, as I was going to kiss him again; but Mr. Whiting suddenly shouted up the path.

'Hi there,' he called. 'Put on the lights if you're there.'

We switched on the light, and they came up the rest of the way. 'Enjoying the view, eh?' said Mr. Whiting as they all came through the door.

'Enjoying the moonlight,' said Peter.

'It's magnificent, isn't it,' agreed Mr. Whiting. 'There's nothing like the Lake of the Woods! Well, we've had a splendid day.' He began to tell us about it, and so did Ross and Sarah Ann, as they all dumped their things on the verandah. Noise and confusion rolled all around. As Peter said, the day was over.

Chapter Eight

THE next morning, moved apparently by *joie de vivre*, Peter and Ross got up really early and went swimming, or so they told us; and then they took the outboard and careered off across the lake—looping the loop a bit, said Ross — and went to Kenora to see what they could find. They found some mail that had come in on Saturday, and brought it home for us.

They were quite pleased with this effort, though Mr. Whiting pointed out that as Peter had to go back to Kenora very shortly to catch his train, they need not have bothered. We were sitting at breakfast when they came in and they gave us our letters and sat down. There were two or three for me. I leafed through them, and saw that one of them was from Alexander. I put it on top, and went on eating, keeping a careful eye on it the while.

'Who's the letter from that you keep looking at so coyly?' asked Peter across the table.

'It's a prayer letter from Alexander Mackintosh,' I told him virtuously. He looked down at his plate again, and I knew he was annoyed: but I did not mind. Somehow, I just felt like hearing from Alexander this morning.

He was, after all, so very very masculine, I thought, getting on with my toast: and there was something in me today that could really appreciate that. After breakfast I took the letters away with me, carrying Alexander's carefully like a little treasure. When Sarah Ann and I had finished work, I

164

took it onto the verandah to read. I sat in the corner, a nice place full of sunlight and the shadows of the leaves outside. After I had been sitting there for a while, Peter came out too, and sat down near at hand.

He had all his things ready now, he said. In a little while Ross was going to take him back to Kenora. The rest of us were not going with them, however, as it had been arranged that the Williams family would come and swim with us, and stay to lunch.

'I leave you, then, reading your religious post,' Peter said to me now.

I was really enjoying Alexander's letter and could almost see him standing before me, in his kilt, and I did not like Peter to speak like this. I thought I would try to set him right a little before he left. Evading the question of Alexander to start with, I set to work to try to make Peter sympathise better with my missionary outlook.

As he did not interrupt, I chattered on: and, after a while, I took the plunge, and tried, yet once again, to make him see some of Alexander's virtues too.

I approached this part of the task with real enthusiasm. Peter knitted his brows. He did not say anything for a while: but then he suddenly asked:

'Do you really think I want to hear all this, this morning? And just before I have to go away, too?'

'You seem to be listening,' I said, folding my hands contentedly over my sacred letter.

'And this man really occupies your mind?' he said slowly. 'I mean, when you got up this morning you may well have said to yourself, I wonder if I'll hear from Alexander? Nothing interesting seems to be happening just now, you said to yourself: but perhaps all is not lost, I may get a letter from Alexander?'

'Well, yes, I often feel like that,' I agreed.

165

As Peter did not seem to understand it very well, I tried again. I spoke some more about my enchantment and dreams of holiness, and how, of all the models of goodness in the world, I felt Alexander to be the foremost. He sat and looked at me with a rather odd expression.

Suddenly he said, very slowly and emphatically: 'You know, it's amazing, but you make me feel tired.'

'You're never tired,' I said.

'I am,' he replied. 'I feel distinctly tired just now.'

He sat and pondered for a minute or two, and then he went on: 'You know what I feel like? I feel like that man in the Bible who made love to his sister: and in the morning, to his surprise, he didn't seem to like her any more. That's what I feel all of a sudden. Grey, and ill at ease.'

I looked at him a bit wildly because I didn't think there was anything like that in the Bible. 'You made that up,' I said.

'No,' he said slowly, 'I didn't make it up, and I didn't make up the feeling, either.'

Once again he sat and thought for a bit, and then he began to stretch himself. 'Well,' he said, 'I guess I'm looking forward to getting back to work. Not that I'm sorry I came to the lake. It's been quite an experience, really. And if it's really managed to cure me, well, that's not such a bad thing.'

'Cured you of what?' I asked.

'I don't know,' he said, looking at me rather oddly again. 'Just an idea I had, perhaps. It seems to have faded out, now. It's suddenly gone, you know, like at the pictures when the film gives out. It all fades out into a grey pot of porridge.'

'You chat to yourself long enough, and you'll hear something really interesting one day,' I said.

Somehow I was getting irritated; and in myself I wanted

more and more to be left alone with Alexander's letter. I didn't know what Peter meant when he talked about making love and getting up and seeing things grey the next morning, for I was feeling particularly well and particularly interested in men today. The whole arrangement of men in general had never looked better than it did to me this morning: and what more opportune than a letter from Alexander. Peter made me impatient with his criticisms and strange remarks. 'Hurry up, Peter,' I said to him. 'Hurry up and catch that train. I have a lot of praying to do today.'

'You make me feel so tired,' he said again, as he stood up.

He went away now to fetch his things, and came back in a minute with Ross; and the rest of the Whiting family came on to the verandah too, as it was time for him to go.

And then, after Peter had thanked them, and invited Ross to come and visit him, which Ross accepted, we all went down to the dock, and watched the two of them get into the outboard.

Ross climbed into the back and sat down, and then Peter stepped after him. 'Well, so long, Peggy,' he said as he stood in the boat. 'I'll see you again some day. It's been nice seeing you, though. Really, I mean it. Goodbye, then, goodbye. Goodbye!'

He said these goodbyes very firmly while he shook my hand up and down hard: and then he sat down with a distinct air of relief, and, in a minute, broke into a great smile at Ross, who was joking about something. Then Ross jerked at the rope once or twice, the motor broke into a confusion of noise and gas fumes, and in a moment they were off, while we waved them goodbye.

The outboard ran smoothly out into the lake: and there it met the wake of the great *Argyle* as it passed by, its silver paint shining in the sun: and the little boat bobbed up and down in the waves and troughs behind the steamer, and then straightened out, and headed away to Kenora. It disappeared: and as far as I was concerned, that was splendid.

I hoped, actually, for an interval in which I could go on reading, but unfortunately the Williams party arrived almost immediately afterwards and it was necessary to be sociable. At last, however, they departed after lunch, and I was able to retreat to my room and sit down on my bunk and start again.

Alec and his brethren had travelled down to the U.S.A., he said, and were bearing a mighty witness to the Lord among the heathen there. I wondered who was supporting them financially for so long a tour; but this remained one of those inscrutable mysteries. However, this did not matter: I was quite satisfied with the letter, which reflected the holiness of his personality in every sentence. 'And if a man is religious, you know he is *sincere*.' I meditated: 'Alec would never flirt with you.'

Quite certainly, Alec did not flirt! I remembered with a warm glow his inviolable chastity, walking about on those two magnificent legs, and admired in retrospect his persistent refusal to flirt with women at all. But if you could manage to get him to give it up, I suddenly began to think, reseeing his splendid figure as vividly as day. What if you could manage to mislead him?

The idea descended on me with quite unaccountable violence. I found it overwhelmingly attractive. My face burnt as I sat and considered it; and I got up, and went out and strolled into the woods. My thoughts followed me and ran among the trees beside me, little populous ghosts. If you could mislead him? they said. But how far, I wondered, how far did I want to?

Well of course, my mind answered, you would have to marry him. I felt better at this: my cheeks began to burn a little less. That was the answer, yes, I thought, making my way slowly and thoughtfully to the top of my little hill. That was the thing! I reached the summit. To marry him, yes! I said to the view of the lake. Then I could live with a perfect saint for evermore, share his great ambitions, learn from his holiness: and possess those beautiful legs. Whichever way you looked at it, the idea was perfect. And oh, I continued, if Alexander could only visit me at the lake! We would be engaged, of course, and standing on the verandah, watching the moonlight, how passionately I would kiss him. Of course, he had never kissed anyone before — well, I would soon teach him. And then the many golden years in India, the little family, the whitewashed church, the well-appointed mission house! Whichever way you looked at it, it was perfect.

It must be so, I thought, descending the hill again at last, it must be so. I desire it, it must be so. I came down through the woods, my thoughts running after me like little shadows among the trees; and moving a little way off beside me I saw the real inhabitants, the deer, quietly descending the hill in single file, turning their gentle heads from side to side. Go softly, little family, I said to them, I am in love. I am in love, I have been in love all the time, and I never realised it before. I stopped and put my arms around a fir tree and leant my head against its grey-brown bark and thought, It must be so, it must be so, I desire it, the mission house, the whitewashed church, the bells, and Alexander's beauty and holiness to be mine for evermore. I walked off again, kicking up the pine needles that made a dry silky flooring under my feet. And is this what Peter meant? I wondered. But he was talking about sex: and I am in love. He meant something else then: but still, I must marry Alexander, it must be so, it has to be.

I wandered around the woods for as long as I could: and then came home in time for supper, and spent a restless evening with the Whitings. We went swimming, and played cards on the verandah, but my heart was not in it. The evening grew dark early, and as the sun disappeared behind the banks of black cloud a very bright golden light gilded the view, so that although we had had to turn the electric light on in the verandah we could still see the bright gold lying over the lake. When we had finished playing cards, we went to bed early. Now I can think, I said to myself in my bed, closing my arms firmly around my pillow; now I can dream. But I had not half furnished the little mission house before a great wind came up through the trees; and then a most unholy storm broke over the lake. I lay on my back and listened to the rain lashing against the roof over my head, and pretended it was the Monsoon falling in India. The exultation that used to seize me in the mornings, reading the Bible at college, began to possess me entirely now. Of course, I thought, desiring the rain to beat faster and faster against the roof, this was what I was meant for, a dedicated life, as they say, and a perfect, holy, and beautiful man like Alexander. I have that kind of nature: only the most idealistic situation will do for me. I crossed my arms and hugged myself in joy as I heard the fir trees sobbing as the wind tore at them. Some of them would fall tonight and thereafter die and lie whitened among the other trees: perhaps I would hear them crashing in the woods. I could hear the wind howling: there were sure to be trees crashing somewhere tonight.

I was burning with excitement. It is guidance, of course, I thought, my meeting and falling in love with Alexander. All my life I have been waiting to fall in love with Alexander. I resaw myself from earliest years, a small child with no other end before her but to find a man like Alexander. And if only he were here now! I threw myself over on my stomach. We would be married, of course, and so ... I was about to elaborate this idea, when I heard Mr. Whiting and Ross talking together. Ross had apparently just come into the cottage, and he and Mr. Whiting were discussing the storm.

Then Mr. Whiting called out, 'Peggy? Sarah Ann?'

'Hullo!' we called back to him.

'Do you mind the storm?'

'No,' I heard Sarah Ann say as she came out of her room. 'Peggy,' she called, 'do you mind the storm?'

'I love it,' I called.

'Aren't you frightened of storms?'

'Usually, but not tonight,' I replied, appearing in my doorway. Mrs. Whiting emerged at the door of her room, and after a little chat all five of us went out to the verandah, and we watched the scene on the lake. The troubled moon was doing her best to keep clear of the clouds that swirled around her, and in her light we could see the great waves forming out on the lake, and the water fairly lashing and boiling over the dock and beating up against the side of the boathouse.

'We'll be lucky if that dock is there in the morning,' said Mr. Whiting. 'And the waves will be high inside the boathouse, too. I think Ross and I should go and pull the boats out of the water.'

'Just let them be,' replied Mrs. Whiting. 'A tree might fall. Or you might slip at the edge.'

'The boats might be badly damaged by the morning,' he said.

'You're more important to me than any boats,' she replied. 'Just stay right here.'

It was almost an hour before the storm died away into a fine rain. As it began to calm down, Mrs. Whiting went away and heated a pan of Red River cereal, and brought it to us in bowls with cream and brown sugar. Red River cereal was a very gritty sort of porridge — refined gravel Peter used to call it. It was very warming, and after our helpings we felt better able to go to sleep, so we said farewell to each other and went back to bed, and fell asleep to the incessant dripping of the wet trees.

In the morning, although the rain had gone now, the water was still dropping from the trees and the roof; and the little cave under the verandah had suddenly become a muddy pond full of doomed moths and leaves. We went down to the lake: the boats had survived, with some damage to their paint, but a couple of planks had broken away out of the dock and it was now looking more like lace than woodwork. 'Put that right when things are dry, will you, Ross?' said Mr. Whiting, who had to leave that morning.

'O.K.,' his son replied. He and Sarah Ann went to see their father off as he began his journey back to Winnipeg. I went up by myself through the woods. They were wet and dripping on every side, and they were empty too, empty of all illusion. The long reaches of the lake, seen from the hill, had lost their dreams, they were only water and rocks and trees. 'There is no life for me anywhere without Alexander,' I said. I went back to the cottage, and in the afternoon I wrote him a letter, telling him how I was supporting him in prayer and what an inspiration it was to get his news.

Then I got out my diary and counted out all the days until college began again in the fall. But there was a stepping-stone to look forward to in this marshy waste, for just before term began I was going to spend a couple of weeks with Edith: and this meant plenty of opportunity to discuss Alexander. I ringed these dates in my diary and began to await them eagerly.

When my holiday with the Whitings was over I departed on the train, after profuse thanks from me and invitations to stay on the farm, and cordial exclamations all round. I returned to Merrilee and spent some time with Grandma. I went over a good many times to visit Joe and Wilma in their cabin on the pretext of wanting to help Auntie. The prospect of helping Auntie was rather more congenial when it was shared with Wilma, and Wilma was glad to see me, too, and to show me her arrangements in her little house.

After this, I went to stay with Edith in Winnipeg. We went for walks, Edith and I, and shared our thoughts together. We walked along the banks of the Assiniboine, where the willows grew and the thick grass, and the golden-rod now beginning to turn white and feathery. I was thinking to myself that Alec must be back in Winnipeg now, and suggested to Edith that we should go along Portage Avenue, as I was hoping that we might bump into him unexpectedly; but she preferred to enjoy the works of nature, down by the Assiniboine, rather than partake of fresh gas fumes in the heart of the city. Of course I preferred not to tell her outright that I hoped to bump into Alec: so I also contemplated the golden-rod and the autumn leaves of the willows.

But at last term began, and I went back to the college residence. Here I found I had a letter from Wilma. She wanted to tell me that Grandma had had one or two dizzy turns since I had left. 'But she is better now,' she said, 'and no need to worry.' So I wrote to Wilma, and wrote a letter to Grandma which I hoped would cheer her up.

And now it was time to attend the Meeting: and there was the really overpowering thrill of meeting Alexander again, and the joy of seeing him just as beautiful as ever, and the joy of hearing his voice loudly raised in prayer and praise. He shook my hand warmly and thanked me for my letter. I had taken particular pains with my appearance and I noticed that he took in the result. As the other women of the Meeting always took pains not to look pretty, I felt this would be a great advantage to me. I hoped, again, for something to develop between us. But alas for dreams, Alexander's heart had apparently not been made any more susceptible by his long preaching tour.

And this, I found, was very difficult to understand: for I was so convinced by now that the Lord had guided me to fall in love with Alexander, that I could not understand why He delayed and did not make Alexander fall in love with me. It seemed to me monstrous that I should love him and yet he did not love me.

My mind could not accept it, it pushed the dark thought away. It seemed to me to be preposterous; and if it must be accepted, life was become a travesty. Nothing was real any more: feelings had no fixed place or meaning, images no substance, colour and shape melted and ran at the edges, all gathering into a whirlpool underneath into which I would tumble if I looked too long. I took refuge in ritual, and sang hymns and said prayers with the Meeting, seeking salvation from drowning by each separate word, only as an empty sound, an act that might keep me occupied. And in the intervals between the ritual, time in which I was required to live and act, I sank into a long agony, knowing that I could not bear to live in this state any longer: and yet knowing that there was nothing I could do to alter it, since I had already done everything a woman could do.

Or swinging suddenly out of the agony, I entered into a false hope, rushing forward into dreams where the whole world was recreated, living and walking in a fantasy that in the end left me even more exhausted. And it was all sustained on such small things: odd encounters, exchanged sentences, listening to his conversation with others, hearing him preach to a meeting: small insubstantial things, yet each separate and precious, to be taken out and treasured and drawn upon as fuel for my fever, living as I went in a dream wound about his smile and his voice and the sun's spun glory in his hair: treasuring these things that seemed precious to me, but were really only small gilt coins, and counterfeit materials.

But now Wilma wrote to me again. 'Grandma has had one or two more dizzy turns,' she said. 'She feels rather low. Do you think you could pay her a visit? Mrs. Ransom looks in on her once a day, but I think she misses you and Peter. If you went to see her it might cheer her up. It would be a real change.'

It would be a change for me too, I decided, and I needed a change; so I journeyed out to Merrilee on the next Friday. As I walked from the station to Grandma's house, carrying my little grip, I met Mrs. Ransom. She greeted me.

'Well, Peggy,' she said, 'so you've come to see your Grandma. That's a good thing, for she's not been well at all. She's keeping very low-spirited, I think.'

I spoke to her for a few minutes and then passed on. Between the gaps in the houses, one could see the bare expanses of brown field around Merrilee: a very cold wind was blowing, and only a few solitary birds passed through the sky. One or two people waved to me from their cars; and some of the dogs we knew came up and wagged their tails as I went past, greeting me after my absence. Then I came to Grandma's gate, and looked over it.

Someone was feeding the hens in the hen-houses, so I went in and walked through the garden and crossed the patch of grass towards the sheds. It turned out to be Mr. Macdonald, the farmer who had brought me to the house after the fire. He straightened up and looked at me, setting his buckets down on the ground.

'Well, Peggy,' he said, 'your grandma isn't keeping very well, I'm afraid.'

'And you?' I asked.

'I'm doing very well, thank you,' he said. 'Bought a new refrigerator for my wife the other day. And how are you doing at college? Going to be a teacher, eh?'

'Yes,' I said, but not telling him that it was the dusky Indians of Asia that I meant to teach, and the eternal glories of salvation that I proposed to impart to them. 'Who feeds Grandma?' I asked.

'Oh, she does for herself well enough,' he said. 'She gets her little bits and pieces, and Mrs. Ransom comes over very faithful like. I'm just giving her a hand with the hens because it seems a shame for the old lady to come out of doors.'

'Are you coming in to see her now?'

'No, I think not,' he said. 'I've got work to do back at my own place. I've had a word with the old lady today, so I'll just finish feeding the hens, and you go in and cheer your grandma up.'

He went on with his task, and I walked back to the house and went in at the front door. I put my grip down on the lino in the hall and went in to see Grandma. She was sitting by a log fire in the parlour. She rose to greet me, and she did not really seem to me to be so very ill. Paler perhaps, and rather more lined: slightly bloodless-looking, as if she could do with a tonic.

Her voice was quiet too, and she folded her hands very gently and slowly as she sat down again, and then unfolded them, and pulled her shawl around her with particular concentration, rearranging it carefully this way and that and not saying anything to me while she fiddled with it, but keeping all her attention on her task. When at last she had got it all twitched about suitably, she turned to me again. 'Well, Peggy,' she said, 'I'm very pleased to see you. It's good of you to come. But don't just sit there. Bring us some coffee.'

I brought two cups, and we settled down to talk. Looking at her, I decided that what was really wrong with her was that she was very tired. She had probably been up to some sort of mischief, interfering with the affairs of the world, and had caught a chill, or strained her constitution in some way.

I decided to encourage Wilma to come and see her as often as she could, and perhaps bring a cake or a pie when she came. And to begin well, I persuaded Grandma to take her supper in bed, with a fire lit in the fireplace in her bedroom, downstairs, and a hot-water bottle tucked in beside her.

I ate my own supper from a tray as I sat by her, and Grandma was innocently pleased with this arrangement and the company it brought her. When I took the trays away, she sat back well satisfied, and folded her hands again carefully on the top of the white coverlet, with a few delicate quiverings of her fingers here and there until they subsided into stillness.

When I came back she had fallen asleep, sinking down into her pillows. I sat in the firelight until she woke up, an hour later, and then helped her to get ready for the night. Once ready and lying well down in the bed, she closed her eyes immediately; so I went away and left her.

Next morning, after we had had breakfast, I told Grandma to stay in bed; and though she said several times that she would certainly get up, it amounted to nothing, and she simply sat where she was. On a thought, I brushed out her long white hair for her, and coiled it up in plaits again, and smoothed out the bed, and dusted the room.

Then I looked through the house and found all the pieces of sewing that needed to be done, and sat by her fire and mended them. She sat in her bed watching me. Sometimes she spoke to me, and listened thoughtfully to my reply.

Most of the time, though, she simply sat and looked, or closed her eyes and dozed again.

In the afternoon Mrs. Ransom came to see her. 'You must come and visit my house tomorrow evening, Peggy,' she said, 'as my eldest granddaughter is staying with me, and my great-grandchild.'

'Your great-grandchild!' I exclaimed.

'Yes,' she smiled. 'My great-grandchild. Such a sweet little thing. You go and see her tomorrow and I'll come and sit with Mrs. Donovan.'

I thanked her, and left her to sit down with Grandma, and went for a walk around Merrilee. I went along the road and out through the countryside, but the wind was so cold I soon regretted it and returned to our house. Mrs. Ransom was now leaving and she pressed me again to visit her house on Sunday. Then I passed another quiet evening with Grandma; and a quiet Sunday morning and afternoon.

Later in the afternoon, Joe and Wilma arrived in Uncle's car, with kind messages for me from Uncle and Auntie. While Joe sat by Grandma's bed and shared a kind of dumb communion with her, I had a few words with Wilma.

'I'm glad to see Grandma is getting a real rest,' she said.

'Yes,' I agreed, 'I'm afraid she must be very tired, she says so little. She needs building up. I hope she gets enough to eat.'

'Mrs. Ransom is very good to her,' said Wilma; 'and Joe and I drive over as often as we can, and so does your Uncle Arthur. Joe is so very good-natured,' she went on. 'The more I see of him, the more I realise there was never a better-natured person than Joe. I'm sure he is just the best-natured person in the world.'

'He's the best-natured of my cousins, certainly,' I said. 'In fact, he's the best-natured of all us four cousins.'

'Well, you know,' she said, 'I think he's the cleverest

of the boys too. Now old Mrs. Donovan is so sweet, and I just love her, but she's always going on about how clever Peter is: and I really think Joe is the cleverest.'

I looked at her, knitting my brows faintly. 'Peter is clever in an *academic* way,' she said, 'but Joe is so practical. You can always trust Joe to look after everything. There's nothing he can't see to. I always rely on Joe.'

I remembered Peter's fiendish ingenuity, the elaborate preparations he made to entrap Benjamin, his ability to make machinery go if he wanted, and equally well, to break down if he wanted, and remembered, also, the deep thought into which Joe used to be cast at the problem of the best way to take one knot out of a piece of string. But I said nothing to disturb her serenity. Evidently this person of whom she spoke was her Joe, so let it be.

Instead, I told her about Mrs. Ransom's invitation, and she agreed that it would be very nice for the three of us to pop over for a little while, for Grandma certainly would not wish to talk to us all evening. She was looking very pretty, I thought as we discussed it, in a green wool dress and her hair all curled up and shining, and her skin had a sort of milky colour to it. I thought she and Joe were doing very well together.

When Mrs. Ransom had come, and had sat down in Grandma's room with some knitting, the three of us went off in the car. Coming out of the quiet house, we broke into noise and high spirits, and Wilma and I chattered briskly while Joe grinned merrily as he drove the car.

We arrived at Mrs. Ransom's house and found Mr. Ransom there and his granddaughter's husband. His granddaughter was out of the room, getting things ready for the baby's bedtime. They would come in and say goodnight, though. Mr. Ransom and his grandson and Joe fell to talking about farming. In a little while, however, the granddaughter came into the room, and crawling on all fours methodically behind her came their baby. She was about a year old. She was a rosy little thing, with a little soft, reddish hair on her head, and bright innocent blue eyes. She wore a pale blue jersey hand-knitted in baby wool and a pair of blue rompers with a bib and crossover straps. On her feet she had small white socks and small soft white leather shoes.

She crawled well into the room, bringing with her her little pink rattle; and then she paused and looked around at the company. Her blue eyes fell on Joe. She did not need more than her small count of years to enable her to recognise an attractive man. In an instant, she was in love. She was like the figure of my youthful imagination, who saw at a glance the ideal person. She opened wide her little mouth and uttered a song of love.

'A-ba-ba-gug-gug,' she said.

Overcome by the passionate words she had spoken, she bucked up and down where she knelt on all fours, and then she lowered her head and in an ecstasy rubbed her forehead on the carpet.

'Ga-ga-gug,' she said.

She looked up. He was still there. Happy, happy woman! How often the object of our fancy has suddenly disappeared. But no, he was still there, smiling at her. She was noticed, she was preferred. She began fervently to make her way across the carpet. In the middle of the floor she collapsed, tripped by the necessity of never for one moment abandoning the rattle. But love drove her on. She heaved herself up, arms first, knees next, proceeded on her journey, and arrived with a triumphant sparkling little face at Joe's feet. There she gazed up at him, a little round rosy lump of adoration.

'Ba-ba-ba?' she said.

Joe accepted her modest little request. He leant forward

and held out his hands. She seized one finger and with the aid of this she heaved herself up on to her feet. Victorious, she struck him violently on the knee with the rattle.

Joe seized her around the waist with both hands. Getting a good grip on the layers of blue cotton romper, blue jersey, wool knickers, plastic pantie, nappie, vest and plump little baby, he elevated her and stood her up on his knees.

She had arrived! She was there, in his arms. Happy, happy little woman. Never was there such a wedding feast. She banged him on the head with her rattle. She banged him on the face with it. She seized a lump of his dark brown hair and tried to pull it off his head. She did her best to poke his eyes out. Then with her little pink hand she patted softly at his sunburnt face. 'Da-da-da-mum-mum,' she said.

It was evident she thought him beautiful.

Her two parents sat there beaming with startled pride. Joe bounced her up and down on his knees, and then he enfolded her in his arms and patted her on the back, while she peeped bewitchingly over his shoulder. And in the end, so great was the little creature's possessive love for him, Joe had to carry her off with her mother and help at her bath. Wilma did not want to spoil his hour of well-deserved admiration by intruding, so she stayed in the parlour with us; but when we had returned to Grandma's house and Joe was saying a few last words to Grandma, she spoke to me with pride.

'Now wasn't that cute, Peggy!' she said. 'Wasn't she the dearest little baby!' I agreed with her. She blushed prettily. 'Doesn't it show,' she said, full of anxious love and enquiry, 'that Joe is just a *natural* father?'

I had actually felt that the little soul, transported in her love for Joe, had been looking on him as an equal, someone to entice, someone to display her femininity to, not as a father, but the practice of withholding comment — so necessary to live peacefully with Grandma, or to achieve self-preservation at the Meeting — bound me fast, and I smiled at her.

'And isn't it lucky that he loves little children,' she went on, 'and they take to him too. Of course everyone takes to Joe, there was never a more popular man; but I'm so glad he gets on with children, because we're going to have one next year.'

I congratulated her fully. She received my congratulations with joy, and promised to make me a sponsor at the child's christening. Then she and Joe said goodbye to Grandma and drove home happily. I helped Grandma, and then went to bed myself. I had a book with me which I had meant to read, but after turning its pages to and fro I put the light out and lay down and began to think.

The truth was, I was jealous. Here was Wilma ready to provide Grandma with her first great-grandchild, which she would show off as proudly as Mrs. Ransom did hers: and there seemed to me to be something wrong about it. Surely Peter or I should provide the first great-grandchild? And what if Grandma grew very attached to it, and began to think more of it than she did of Peter? What had Joe done to deserve this?

And what a fantasy this was of the innocent Wilma, making Joe out to be such a great saint, when of course you could not be a saint unless you were saved, and even then you had little hope of being as holy as Alexander. And how would Alec look as a father? Supremely well, I thought. Small babies, especially his own, would take to him at sight. He would be a shining example to his children all his life, and perfect holiness would reign throughout the family circle.

With the proviso, of course, that I could manage to learn to be perfectly holy too. I would get started on that as soon as I was back in Winnipeg: it would at least give me something to do while Alec made up his mind. And perhaps this

was why the Lord delayed, and did not make Alec love me:
He was waiting until I realised more deeply my own need
for sanctification. Well, now, under Wilma's influence, I
realised it: so perhaps things would get a move on. I became
impatient to be back at college.

And when I had said goodbye to Grandma, now up and
pottering around the house again, and had had a few words
with her neighbours and encouraged their plans to look in
on her, and had returned to college and made my way to the
daily prayer group held by the Meeting in one of the chap-
lains' rooms, it seemed that a miracle had occurred: for
Alexander's conversation with me took on a new and private
note.

He took particular pains to catch up with me as I left
afterwards, and, walking along beside me with his graceful
step, he asked me where on earth I had been last Friday. 'I
hope you are not going to give up being regular at the
Meeting,' he said, looking at me with a faint sort of anxiety
around his brow; but he did not add that this would dis-
credit the Redeemer, and I could only think that he really
cared whether I attended the functions of the Meeting or
not, and that the miracle had truly come about, Alec was
taking a personal interest in a woman.

I was glad for my interval at Merrilee that had won me the
backing of Heaven at last: and I looked at him sweetly and
said the Lord had called me out to the prairie to look after
my Grandma. He smiled, very sociable and attentive, but
I did not feel it had made the impact that it should, so I
changed about, and said, 'And of course while one wishes
to be absolutely faithful in worshipping the Lord, still as long
as one is in This World these calls will inevitably come, and
I am sure that there have often been times when you yourself have been torn between your work for the Lord and

the needs of your relatives.' Having got this out, I was almost struck dumb with it, it had such a ring of Edith about it. However at this moment dumbness was no disadvantage, for this was just the sort of thing Alec wanted to hear.

His face lit up, and he began to tell me very eagerly about himself and his family, and how they had at first resisted his evangelistic calling, but gradually with judicious praying and hoping on his part they were beginning to come round. I thought this was the time to improve my knowledge of him by finding out what sort of family he had, and how many brothers and sisters: so I asked him how many of his brothers and sisters were saved; and he told me he had two sisters that were saved and one brother.

How many, then, I asked, were still in darkness? One sister and two brothers. That made three of each, I calculated. And how many of their children were saved, I asked. Well, he told me, only his two unsaved brothers were married, but they had three children each, and he and his two Christian sisters were happy to find that they were really able to influence them.

I said it would be wonderful to understand better how to bring young souls up in the nurture of the Lord; to lead them, in short, to the Throne of Grace. He said that that was a most important subject and he felt that he would be as well justified in talking about it as in spending the afternoon according to his original plan — that is, in writing an essay. The Spirit bloweth where it listeth, he said, and when an opportunity like this came up one should seize it. We were now near Portage Avenue, and he suggested that we should go into one of the drugstores and have a cup of coffee, and so, of course, I agreed.

We went in and sat down with our coffee, and he told me most enthusiastically about his efforts to convert his nephews and nieces, and in fact about everything else that occurred to him. I did not listen to him quite as intently as I might have done, because I was so thrilled at the opportunity of looking at him really closely, and especially of studying his face. There was no doubt that he was extraordinarily hand-some. And since because of his years in the army he was a little older than some of the other students, he exuded what I thought of as an enchanting masculinity.

He sat very straight and he was heavily built without being fat at all, of course it was all bone and muscle, and his voice was deep and his glance very forceful and direct. When you remembered the fact that he had quite certainly never so much as held hands with a woman in his life, the combination was irresistible. I could hardly wait until we got around to it. And you could see he would have a natural talent for it; I knew enough about men to judge that. The inclination was there in him all right, it just needed bringing out. And as he had never done anything like that before, he would be very grateful to one for introducing him to this happiness, and would never look at another woman in his life: so one would have this great big bundle of charm to oneself for ever.

'So this is what my choice has finally fallen on,' I thought, looking at him carefully. I had chosen well, I decided. He was very large, very handsome, very black-haired, very intelli-gent, and extremely holy. I could not do better.

Alexander meanwhile gulped his coffee and told me all about his work for God. After he had talked for about an hour, he began to flag a bit. I asked him then how many souls he had saved on his preaching tour and whether he had not been greatly conscious of the support of the Meeting bearing him up in prayer. He said that his whole tour was a great matter for rejoicing and there was nothing he would like better than to share with me his happiness over it. But at present he really should go and finish his essay. We might meet again, though.

He got out his pocket diary and fell silent as he looked through it, and I studied the beautiful line of his hair where it grew around his forehead, and the shape of his hands, which were very finely made for such a big man. At last he said that it really looked as if the best time he had — and here I waited breathlessly — was tomorrow. In fact we might have lunch together tomorrow, and he mentioned a place halfway between our two colleges. Obviously, he said, closing his diary and returning it to the inner pocket of his jacket, giving me a good opportunity to estimate the width of his chest, which I put at about forty-two inches, for he was a very large man, obviously if the only time he really had free was tomorrow, then the Lord (who regarded Alec, one gathered, with especial attention) was leading us to meet again *tomorrow*. This was a piece of reasoning with which I heartily agreed: I felt he could hardly have expressed things better.

After this a happy time began. Probably when Alec first spoke to me on the way out of the prayer meeting he had not meant to embark on anything serious: but once he had experienced the joy of paying attention to a woman, and even of being more or less alone with her, he seemed to be unable to resist it. No doubt he had some inward struggles, but obviously, on the other hand, he always found some excuse of meeting me again. And lest it give rise to gossip, I took the trouble to tell the other members of the Meeting that he was advising me about my future in India. 'And my friend as well,' I added, hastily introducing a chaperon into the scene. At first I was pleased with this little piece of duplicity: but then I began to worry in case someone told Alec about it in such a way that he realised that I had been saying something that was not entirely truthful. If this happened, I felt he would have nothing more to do with me: for a man of such irreproachable purity would not go about with anyone who was a liar.

For a day or two I became quite fretful with worrying about it and could hardly eat my breakfast: but nothing happened, and I began to be able to enjoy his company again. It was not, of course, that we met every day, or for very long at a time, since he still made himself a programme for each day, and could not always justify himself in fitting me in. But he spared me a good deal of time — and what, for him, was a miraculous amount of time. So we met for lunch or for coffee, or for a Coca-Cola or even for supper, and he talked to me. I usually only listened when he was telling me some personal detail about himself. I did not listen to his long religious dissertations, or even to his descriptions of spiritual activities which he had attended, for I was not even yet sufficiently sanctified to enjoy an uninterruptedly otherworldly conversation. When he talked like that, I looked at him, bemused, admiring his beauty and thinking of our home and of how many children we would have. And when I realised that all my dreams were now within my grasp, I would sometimes almost shake with the excitement of it.

One day, Alexander suggested a special expedition to me. In a day or two, he had to go and preach in the evening at a meeting in a little town outside Winnipeg, and he was going to drive there in his father's car. He thought I might like to come too. 'You can support me in prayer throughout the meeting,' he said hopefully. 'It is absolutely essential that on occasions like this one should have some faithful, spiritual person with one, interceding all the time. And who knows? Many many souls may be won during the evening.'

Naturally I agreed, and I was almost beside myself at the idea, for if Alexander was going to drive me alone in a car, it seemed to me nearly to amount to a proposal. I put on my best blue frock, with rather a tight bodice, and a full skirt; and a nice blue coat that I had bought for the winter.

Alexander was rather quiet during the drive there and I enjoyed this, as I could sit snugly wrapped in my new coat and enjoy his presence, and look again and again at all the details of his appearance which I liked to learn over and over by heart. So we drove quietly through the countryside, and I was really rather disappointed when we drew up outside the hall where the meeting was held.

And once inside, Alexander was swallowed up by a crowd of people, and I had to sit with a number of worthy ladies who immediately took charge of me and wedged me down on a chair between themselves, and really it was very difficult to adjust myself to this sudden wave of femininity, and delicate clucking, after sitting in the car and staring all the way at Alexander's profile, which was far from ladylike, and which aroused thoughts which were not at all ladylike either. With coming out of the dark into the electric light, and out of my thoughts into the honest sunshine of a Christian gathering, I sat on the chair blinking both physically and mentally. But Alexander preached most powerfully, and out of the stern concentration of the drive down he seemed to have wrought a wonderful testimony to the Lord.

After his talk we all repaired to a rather smaller room, and were served with coffee and cakes. I hovered about talking to the ladies. Every now and then I glanced at Alexander. I noticed that he frequently glanced at me. Then towards the end of the coffee party he managed to make his way around the room, and to stand quite near me. It was obvious that he was looking at me a good deal. In fact his gaze was so persistent that at last I looked up and looked squarely at him. While the other people all chattered together, he was standing and staring at me. He was looking at me with a bold bright eye. I knew that look in men very well. It simply meant, Bed. Bed was fairly sparkling and dancing in his eyes and in the muscles at the side of his mouth. Well, I looked right back at him. On him, I liked it. I wasn't planning to go to bed: but I knew you could have a grand time just talking it over. I began to make up the sentences with which I would, later on in the evening, express amazed surprise at his forthright suggestions. Then I recollected myself and remembered that he was a pure holy man and the Meeting's foremost evangelist, and that it really seemed extremely unlikely that he himself would actually suggest anything at all forthright, whatever his eyes said and the little muscles at the side of his mouth. So I hastily scratched earth all over my sentences, but they came popping up again immediately, proliferating as they came. Faced with that look, there was nothing you could do but draw yourself together and start planning. A wise girl always looks ahead, as Grandma would say.

At last the end of the meeting came, and everyone began to go home, shaking Alec's hand heartily before they left, and he turned to me and said, Well, perhaps it was time to drive home. We made our farewells and came away.

By now I was all agog. I expected, of course, that he would drive very fast until we were a short way out of the town, and would then park the car and proceed to waste no time. But instead, he drove very slowly, and kept on driving, and he asked me how I had liked the meeting, and whether I thought many souls had been saved, and other questions of that kind. The only difference there was from his normal behaviour was that this time he waited to hear my replies, looking at me as I answered, so that I could see the excitement still shining in his face.

I could not understand what he thought he was doing. It did occur to me, rather wildly, that perhaps he did not

189

even know *how* to kiss anyone and did not realise that there was anything he could do to relieve the state he was in. But I dismissed that thought as nonsense, for how did he get the look he had been wearing if there was no knowledge behind it? No, he had been looking like a man who knew exactly what he wanted. So I was very puzzled as we proceeded homewards in a leisurely way.

However, we arrived at last, and he parked the car under some trees just along the drive that led to the front garden of our residence. And now, I thought, we would surely have a more interesting time. But no, he still behaved with perfect propriety. He turned a little, and put his arm along the top of the seat behind me. After a moment or two he moved so that his arm was actually touching me. Even with so small a contact, I could feel that he was burning; and he was breathing short and deep and heavy so that I wondered he didn't suddenly come out in wreaths of smoke like a volcano. Then he put his other hand around my arm, and offhandedly, as though he were not doing it, moved it down and finally closed his fingers around my wrist. His skin was about red-hot. And all the time he kept on talking about the Lord's work and the saving of souls for the Kingdom. The more excited I could feel him get, the faster he talked about the Lord's work.

After a while I ceased to want to kiss him at all, and simply began to feel uncomfortable, for it seemed to me I was in a situation one could not possibly know how to deal with: something unspecified by Havelock Ellis, or at least those parts of Havelock Ellis of which I had turned the pages. So then I took a despairing plunge, and said that I really must go in now.

He came to with a start, and said Yes, he supposed I must, and got out of the car and opened the door on my side and helped me out, and walked up to the front door of the house with me, and he took a great many long deep laborious breaths of the night air as though they were exactly what he needed. At the door he stood and squared his shoulders and looked down at me and took a few more breaths of fresh air, and I observed regretfully, as the moonlight shone over his black head, how devastatingly handsome he really was, and how, translated into a normal Cola-drinking baseball-playing man, he would certainly be the most desirable catch in the university. I bade him a polite good-night and thanked him for a remarkable evening: and he thanked me for coming and shook hands with me chastely, and in I went.

In my room I pottered around for a while, dropping my clothes here and there in a vague way and finally putting on my pyjamas, and trying to work out what had gone wrong. But in the end a feeling of admiration for him began to steal over me. There was no doubt, disappointing as it was, that he had the most fantastic self-control. Even if you did not like it, you had to admire it. In fact, when it had seemed to me that he was a saint, I had been quite right, he *was* a saint. He could do things other men could not possibly manage to do. By the time I climbed into bed my regard for him was soaring. And my hopes for the future soared in proportion. 'Give him time,' I thought, 'just give him time, and the wedding bells are practically ringing. In fact they are ringing already, for we almost held hands, and members of the Meeting never do that unless they are engaged.' Just before I fell asleep it occurred to me that once I got married to him I would try to persuade him *not* to go to India. Now that the prospect was becoming imminent, I felt that a church in some Canadian city might be better. Surely he could find enough heathens there without, after all, dragging both of us to India? But then I fell asleep.

The morning dawned, therefore, with radiant expectations. Judging Alec's feelings by the code of the Meeting, I was practically engaged to him; and only time was required to make it certain. In a few days he would probably propose.

At the end of the week, there was going to be an evangelistic party at the house of one of the members who lived in River Heights: Alexander had mentioned it during the drive into Winnipeg, and he had suggested that I wait for him outside the front door of our college, and he would fetch me in the car. I felt sure that something would happen on that evening. Last night, no doubt, on the way home to Winnipeg, he had not liked to stop and propose so late at night. On the other hand he knew, being a Christian saint, that he could not kiss me unless he proposed to me: so he did neither. On Saturday, after the party, he would probably do both.

I spent the rest of the week in preparing my appearance for this evening. I meant to look really stunning. I brushed my hair very frequently, and I washed it early in the week so as to give it time to be tidy by Saturday, and then I washed it again later in the week so that it would still be clean by Saturday. And I went down to Portage Avenue and spent a long time in one of the stores where they had a counter with little glass stoppers which you could rub across your wrist, so that you could tell what sort of perfume they had for sale.

I wanted something subtle and elusive, not making it obvious to the whole Meeting that I was wearing perfume, but having a powerful effect on Alexander. There was one called Desire, and another called Nights of Passion, and another called Redhot Fever. I didn't feel any of these struck quite the right note; in fact they seemed, under the circumstances, a little unnecessary. I looked hopefully to see if there wasn't a perfume called Proposal. Or even Wedding Bells. Then I began to wonder what governed the names on the little sample bottles. Did they really bear any relation to the effect of the perfume at all? To find out, I asked, in a round-about way: 'Say, do they have a perfume like Waffles and Maple Syrup? Or Frosted Malted Milk?'

'Well, I guess not,' said the girl, 'though those are good smells right enough.'

'How do they make up the names on the bottles?'

'Mostly for men, I guess,' she said. 'They make up names that men like to give to girls, like Amour, and that sort of thing. Men feel it gives girls the right ideas.'

That seemed to explain the absence of perfumes called Wedding Bells. 'So the names don't have anything to do with the smells,' I said. 'So what's the big difference in the smells?'

'Well,' she said, 'there's the perfumes that make you smell young and innocent; and then there's the perfumes that make you smell old and wise.'

'And which is a man most likely to propose to?' I asked, getting around to the point.

'Why don't you try mixing them?' she asked. 'Try a bit of each. One down one side and one down the other. Then if one doesn't have the right effect, get him round to the other.'

This seemed to me to be very sound advice, and as I got out my purse I couldn't help feeling how much I was enjoying this practical and straightforward conversation, based on down-to-earth common sense, instead of having to talk about absolutely nothing but religion. I sighed for my continuing lack of sanctification and hoped Heaven was not listening in just at the moment: and I bought a bottle of lavender water, which the salesgirl told me was a lovely smell and at the same time as innocent a perfume as you could get, and bound to remind a man of apple pie as his mother made it: and a bottle of a scent one of my friends used to use, called 'Oui.

Oui. Oui.' It smelt, I remembered, like well-tried pemmi-
can laced with sandalwood, and I guessed that altogether
it was as old and wise a smell as the market held. I thanked
the girl and returned home. And so, we see, by Saturday I
was very well prepared for the evangelistic meeting.

This evangelistic party was by way of being a subtle bait.
I had been to such parties before. They began as real parties,
with games, though not dancing, and with food and drink.
Then later on, what the members of the Meeting would call
a more Serious Note would fall, and with an off-hand and
artless air some Christian person would drop a remark
bearing on some religious topic. The other members would
seize on this eagerly and keep it going, and perhaps the
unsaved who had been invited to the party would join in
and produce an argument, and then, before you knew
where you were, you were in the middle of a religious
meeting.

At these occasions the members of the Meeting did a great
deal of talking. They really preferred the unconverted not
to argue too much, but to assume the role of eager enquirers,
thus leaving the Christians an opportunity to Testify. To
Testify generally meant to tell everybody What Jesus Has
Done For Me. This sometimes quite stunned the unsaved:
but for myself I was prepared for an evening of this kind,
and only hoped that the testifying and everything else would
not go on too long, because I wanted to have plenty of time
after the party for my drive home with Alexander.

Fortunately the games and the food did not take up too
much time this evening. Alec was looking unusually handsome; and I felt very proud of him as he moved about, and
was happy when he smiled at the women, because I knew
that it was me that he preferred. And then we all settled
down, and conversation flagged a bit, and it was time for the
Serious Note to fall. It fell, duly, and quite a useful little

discussion got under way. But then one of the unconverted spoilt it. He started talking about sex. This caused the Christians a bit of embarrassment at first, because they hardly ever, except in direct reference to the Bible, talked publicly or even privately about sex. However, they eased themselves into it, and the topic kept going. The unconverted man got very argumentative. He was almost rude. The Bible was a lot of balderdash, he said. The Bible was something a guy just couldn't take any notice of. Now there was that verse, he said, about not looking after a woman to lust after her, because if you did it was adultery. Now don't tell me, he said, that I'm to go through college and never lust after anybody, because, heavens above, I can't manage it, especially the way dames dress nowadays. I muttered to myself, very gently, that that didn't apply, because the Bible was talking about adultery, and Jesus was speaking to people who were all married: or else they would have been too young to be listening to him. And none of us was married, I whispered to myself, and must we waste time arguing about this verse?

But the members of the Meeting insisted on taking the verse, as they always did, as not meaning adultery but fornication, and as being very relevant to college students, and they talked an awful lot about it this way and that, and the unconverted man kept on saying, Gee whiz, never in my life will I get so that I don't want to give a dame the glad eye. And then Alexander sat up straight, and it was obvious that he was going to testify. And a hush fell around him, because like Lucifer his beauty distinguished him before all the throng. He sat up straight, and gave us the full benefit of his magnificent figure, and his striking colouring, and the nobility and earnestness of his expression: and when he was sure everyone was listening to him, he spoke right out and testified with an air of controlled manliness.

'I can honestly say I never desire a girl,' he said. 'Jesus keeps me from it.'

There was the most audible silence I ever heard. The Christians were overcome at Alec's honesty and forthrightness at Testifying so clearly on the subject of Sex and witnessing for Jesus in a worldly gathering. Everyone else was just overcome. But as for me, everything rocked. As people began to speak again, I backed away a little, and found myself beside the window, and I drew the curtain aside an inch or two and looked into the blackness of the windowpanes with the snow falling beyond them. I felt as though I had been hit on some mental funny-bone and was dancing about speechless. Alec had told a thundering great lie. This could never be undone or altered or repaired: he had told a most tremendous lie and he was not therefore perfectly holy. He was, in fact, just like everyone else. And he had told a lie that shut me out. He denied his feelings for me.

And then I began to see it more coldly and clearly; he told the lie to gain himself a good reputation; and for that end he was perfectly willing to deny me, or anything else. At this, I began to feel as if an avalanche were preparing itself inside me, and I got up, and very quietly so that no one observed me drifting past the people standing about at the back of the room, I went into the hall, and got my coat from the room where I had left it on the other side of the hall, and opened the front door softly and went out into the garden, and began to walk aimlessly down the path. And now that I was away from the other people and had no need to hide anything from anybody, the avalanche came tumbling down, and all of a sudden, in a minute, irreparably, everything crumbled and cracked. All of a sudden in almost no time at all, I understood altogether that the perfect saint that I had invented did not exist; and that Alexander was only a very vain man who would do anything in the world to put himself in the limelight, and that all his special doctrines were only a means for him to think of himself all the time. And it only took a minute for me to understand it, because it was the truth and all the rest had been an illusion.

And in the same moment I saw that all the rest of the members of the Meeting were vain and conceited and thrusting too, and that I was growing just like them. And for myself and the other members of the Meeting I did not care at all, but for Alexander I felt a terrible and burning pain, because he was so beautiful and I had thought him so good, and it was not true at all. And it was not now a question of forgiving him or of deciding to overlook it or of saying, 'We all lie too, look at the lies I tell', or even of proving somehow that he had not actually been lying: it was simply that I realised through and through that the image I had loved did not exist, and that he was just a person like anyone else, and that as a person I did not care anything about him; in fact I now had to admit that as a person he really bored me. And I could scarcely keep from crying, because I had been so fond of this image; and I did not know what I was going to do without it.

I decided that I had better go home, and that the best thing to do would be to walk along and cross the Maryland Bridge, and then take a street-car. So I left the party behind, and set off along the street, moving through the shifting curtains of snow that piled themselves up on the pavement, and edged the pitch black trees with soft white lines, leaving recumbent white cushions at every criss-cross of branches. I could have been sick at any minute. But it was a fine soft sighing snow whose whispering kept my mind from turning into itself; and I came along the roads through its moving patterns until I mounted the Maryland Bridge, and stood there for a few minutes to listen to it. Edged in the light of the lamps it came down all around me still whispering to itself; and over the Assiniboine, still unfrozen, it fell on steady and purposeless, reborn as water instantly it met the surface of the river.

And there below me, the water moved away in little flickering silver and black wavelets, an indefinable superficial purposeless fluttering on the surface and a remorseless restless hasting forward beneath: a great sweeping body of water coming, it almost seemed, from nowhere, and continuing nowhere. It existed for me only as the river passing under my feet. There were floating branches caught at the edges and trying to break away; and long thin bent stems of grass making their own useless ripples as they leant over the water, I could see them, fragile and pathetic, illuminated by the light of the lamps. And one night in an instant, a hair's breadth of time out of the winter, it would all freeze over; and the branches would be imprisoned, half seen above the ice: and the grass would be left perpetually bending into the river. I stood and stared into the dark moving water. So I have flung so much time away like the water, I thought. It is not the pain, I said to myself (although that was not true), it is the regret. To lose so much moving time! I do not care about him now, I said (although it was not true), he does not matter any more. Now he is a thing that is cold and quiet like the snow, melting away as soon as it meets the living water. But the endless regret! The time gone by, the wasted years! They were months, truly, but I would not spoil things for a date or two. And the tears met and melted in my eyes, and ran down my face to make infinitesimal puddles in the snow piled on the stone railing of the bridge. And the lights danced on the snow and the water; and snow and water together whispered to me as they made their patterns, perpetually the moving snowflakes, perpetually the meaningless wavelets on the river — until I walked on, and went home to bed.

Chapter Nine

AND then there was a cold clear bright morning opening into a pale blue sky and still banks of piled snow on every side: and life was all to be built anew again at nearly twenty years old. I began to rebuild it in my best green skirt and my green cardigan and one row of beads; they were both quite a dark green, and they showed up the dead paleness of my sombre face very well.

Taking a walk through the fresh white snow on Sunday, I decided that for the time being religion would not play any part in the reconstruction. When I looked into my heart, I did not feel that it would do to discard religion entirely, as it had really been with me since the earliest times, and there was no need to throw it out altogether just because of the members of the Meeting. But the difficulty was to reconcile the difference between religion and religious people; since, while I liked religion, it was now necessary to admit freely that religious people did not appeal to me as they should. But if one took a great interest in religion, one immediately became a religious person — that is to say, the sort of person that often seemed to me quite detestable, especially at the moment.

I did not know what to do about this, so I decided that for the present it would be better not to run after religion any longer, but to wait until it ran after me: and if it caught up with me, I might join the United Church; but if it did not, that could not be helped. And here there was a mystery, as there were feelings, on one side, that seemed to be true, and people, on the other, that looked to me untrue, and I did not know what to do about it. To try to understand the problem was like trying to hold water in your hands — it slipped away to the ground at once. It was real water all right, but I could not hold it. Or you could say, There was some sort of vision there, for certain, like light in the distance, but the clouds kept rolling over it. However, I thought I might see further into the matter some day, if I waited, and, who knows, might even join the United Church. And I might learn something, too, by studying Mrs. Whiting more closely. I began to think she might have something there after all, if I could learn it.

In the meantime, however, there were all my former employments to be dealt with. I decided to go on visiting the babies — I liked them so well. But apart from that, I got under way by ceasing immediately to go to any of the prayer meetings, Bible studies and the rest held by the Meeting. And as well I had a farewell chat with Alec. He rang me up, not on Sunday for that was his busy day, but on Monday, and asked me if I had not been feeling well, since I had not waited for him after the party. I said, no, I had been feeling tired. He said he was sorry about that, but no doubt he would see me at the Bible study this evening.

I replied that I was still feeling tired, and that it looked as though I was going to be tired for a long long time. After this we started an argument about whether or not I ought to go and see the doctor, so when Alec suggested we meet for coffee in the afternoon I agreed: and there I told him firmly that I had decided that I was neglecting my studies and must pay them more attention and not go to the Meeting, and that it was time to remember my dear old Grandma out on the prairie, who was supporting me with her cash and

looked to me to bring her honour and joy during her de-
clining years.

I felt that this, which was quite true, was the best way to
put it, because he was such a big man, and so overawing in
his appearance, that it was too frightening to try to explain
the events of Saturday night to him. However he replied
that nothing, absolutely nothing, should stand between oneself and one's service of the Redeemer, and to let a mere
matter of cash distract one from the worship of the Lord was
to bow before Mammon, to sell one's soul in fact for thirty
pieces of silver and buy with it a worthless potter's field,
'Which was rightly called,' he said, 'the field of blood. . . .
And we remember Ananias and Sapphira,' he continued,
'who withheld their goods from the Lord.' I said Yes, but
these were my Grandma's goods; and I had begun to feel
that this was the right time to direct them to the end she
intended, which was not the support of the Meeting.

He looked at me hard, with something of a nasty glint
appearing in his eye, and said that the faithful servant of
the Lord must always be ready to speak the truth in love,
however painful to himself this might be, for only the truth
could serve the honour and majesty of our great God and
King, and so he really must let me know that it was not
becoming for a young girl to be pert and argumentative.
And probably this was the first time he had ever been contradicted by anyone in any way connected with the Meeting.
But I said to myself, 'Oh, you great big six-foot-two talkative
lump,' and wondered how it had ever been possible to bear
his conversation, which had always been like that: and although he was looking particularly handsome that day, and
his legs as always were remarkable, it now had no effect on
me at all, except to fill me with regret and with a desire never
to see him again.

And on finding himself contradicted, and finding that I

would not give in, he began to get annoyed, and it was obvious that he really had quite a nasty temper, though as long as people would listen to him he could manage to conceal it. So by the end of our meeting I think he had really begun to dislike me, and to ascribe my position to the workings of the Devil: for he could recognise no difference from his own views that was not due to the influence of the Devil. And so we parted without any desire to meet again.

But for myself, I could not help a sort of sadness lingering round me, because it was impossible to dislike him entirely. I could not help feeling that with all that ardour and enthusiasm, and that burningly devoted nature, he could have been a good man, if he had found a way of life that did not encourage him to think about and admire nothing but Alexander. But meanwhile we were oceans apart in heart, since we were no longer agreed about his perfect holiness, and it was no use thinking of him any more. I had evidently made a bad choice again; and it began to seem to me that in every way romance was continually misleading me.

Edith I managed to deal with quite easily. I simply told her that I would not be coming to the Meeting again as I had started taking classes in Roman Catholic doctrine and would probably in the end become a nun: and out of sheer spite and malice I added that the desire to devote my life to the Lord in this way had begun to grow in me when we had both walked together by the Assiniboine studying the handiwork of the King; and for such a Creator, I said, surely only a lifetime's oblation would do. And had she truly, no *truly*, studied the inward significance and meaning of the Mass, so very much in accordance with Scriptural teaching?

To Edith, a Roman Catholic was a human being who could still be saved if they had been born a Roman Catholic, and then they could be snatched as a brand from the burning, if you could actually manage to snatch anyone from the grip of the Catholics. If anyone deliberately became a Roman Catholic, however, that was another matter, something quite as bad as it seemed to the Roman Catholics if one of them turned Protestant: so greatly did all these Christians love one another. I might as well have told her that I was taking up prostitution or going in for homosexuality; after the initial moments of horror she also felt no desire to see any more of me. And for very shame it was unlikely that she would tell the other girls in the residence about it, though she might whisper the news to the members of the Meeting: so I was safe from her now.

While I had been busy with the Meeting life had moved on. Just recently, when I had been seeing so much of Alec, Sarah Ann and Don had become very friendly. Don and I had always remained on speaking terms, but, somehow, now that he and Sarah Ann were always talking to each other, and sat together in the canteen discussing things and drinking Coca-Cola, I did not feel that it would be a good idea to join them, as it might have been if she had taken to sitting with some other man.

Whenever they saw me Sarah Ann would wave and say, 'Hi, come on over and sit with us,' but I would wave back and say that I was sitting with someone else. Of course, there were plenty of other people at the college, but at a time like this, when you had received a shock, you felt like sitting quietly with your oldest friends, people who would understand you thoroughly: and I found Sarah Ann's present preoccupation a difficulty.

And then, there was the drawback that for some time I had let people know that they need not ask me out on dates, as to go on dates was not the habit of the members of the Meeting. And as most of the social life in Winnipeg and in the university depended on dates with men, and it was almost unthinkable to go anywhere important with a woman, an absence of dates was a great impediment. But one could not really boldly tell men that they might now ask one out on dates, after giving so many rebuffs, which I had really enjoyed, turning my spiritual nose in the air and explaining that I was above going to the pictures or to the Gordon Bell School production of Gilbert and Sullivan, or the university Shakespeare play. To gain dates, it would be necessary to be seen out on dates; but it was difficult to know how to get started.

There was time, therefore, for reflection; but the trouble with reflection was that it made me think wistfully of the days when I used to be happy in admiring Alexander, and thinking about the glory and perfection of his character, and this made me sad.

And as sadness grew on me, it occurred to me one morning that I ought to write to Peter. He was one of these people whom I knew exceedingly well, and I thought I would like to get a letter from him. I felt that it might help to fill the gap. And so I sent him a note. It said: 'How are you? I have been a bit depressed lately. I hope you are fine and so is the cement. Perhaps I won't be a missionary,' and one or two more things of this kind; and then I posted it off as soon as it was written.

I looked for an answer at the end of the week, but there was none, which was disappointing; so now I turned my attention to the Christmas exams, which were approaching fast; and it really did seem to be time to pay attention to my college course and continue to give Grandma a good return for her outlay. I got out my notebooks and sat down to work. I was an attentive note-taker, and heartily disagreed with the students who wrote in the *Groan* complaining that we should come to university to read and to think about the courses and not to copy down lectures. I hoped the professors never read these articles. These students should keep their big mouths shut, I thought, settling down ready to learn my notes off by heart and once again come top in the examinations.

After a day or two of study had gone by, I was sitting in my room in the residence in the evening, sorting out pages of notes to learn the next day, when two of my friends, two girls called Linda and Joan, burst into the room.

'There's something waiting for you downstairs,' said Joan.

'What's it like?' I asked.

'Well,' said Linda, 'it's about eight feet tall and six feet wide with black hair and a come-hither look. If you can't use it I can.'

'Not a religious look, I hope,' I asked suspiciously.

'No,' said Joan, who knew Alexander by sight, 'this is about two inches shorter than the religious one.'

'Six feet then?'

'In actuality,' she agreed, 'just under six feet. And he has a sensible, discerning expression, not at all like the other.'

I made myself attractive and went downstairs. Peter was waiting in the hall.

'Peter!' I exclaimed. 'What have you come all the way to Winnipeg for?'

'It's not all the way,' he replied. 'I told you I would be working on a project in Manitoba.'

'And my letter caught up with you?'

'It looks like it, doesn't it?' he replied.

'What's the project?' I asked.

'Well, it's by way of being rather private at present,' he said. 'And anyway, dear, you wouldn't understand if I did explain, would you? So never mind. Have you got a date tonight?'

'For *once*,' I said firmly, 'no.'

'Good. Put your coat on and we'll go out to supper.'

'Have you got any men with you?' I asked. 'If so, bring them too. I'd like you to meet some of the girls.'

'Thank you, Peggy,' he said sweetly. 'I don't want to meet the girls. I'm planning to take you to supper alone with Uncle Peter.'

Having done my best for my friends, I was really better pleased to be alone with him, and I got ready and he drove me off in the car he had brought with him, borrowed from one of his friends at work. 'I'll save up and get my own car soon,' he said, as he pointed out the features of this one to me.

We went to a small restaurant near the centre of the city, nicely lighted with shaded lights and decorated with tanks of tropical fish. Peter put my coat in the cloakroom and looked approvingly at my dress, and then we sat down and he ordered dinner. 'And now,' he said, as the waiter went away, 'what has made you depressed? Have you been eating too much?'

Feeling exceedingly comfortable and cosy, and well pleased with the restaurant and the fishes flickering in and out of the waterweeds in all their rainbow colouring, I hummed and hawed a bit and put the matter to him briefly. With a few pertinent questions, he managed to draw the whole story out of me.

At the full description of Alexander's prowess in the car, he shut his mouth very hard, but a look of veiled merriment and vulgarity mixed gathered around his eyes and he was obviously trying, on the one hand, not to laugh, and on the other, not to make some unprintable remark, such as would have raised a deep chesty guffaw among the engineers. He ate rapidly and intently for a moment or two, and then he looked up at me, the dark blue of his eyes full of pleasure, and said, 'The man was so thoroughly pure-minded, so why did you object? What on earth are you looking for? A male soprano?'

'You misunderstand me, Peter,' I replied. 'I was quite disappointed because I wanted him to kiss me.'

'I don't find that at all flattering,' he said, returning to his dinner. 'What has this man got that I haven't got, that you want him to kiss you? And if you ask me, it sounds to me from his performance that he hasn't even got what I *have* got.'

'Well, at that time,' I explained, 'I thought you should only kiss someone if you were planning to marry them, and so it seemed all right with him. But after the Saturday evening I told you about, when I saw that he wasn't such a saint after all, I didn't want to marry him any more.'

'As for that occasion,' mused Peter, 'I don't know if there wasn't some truth in what he said. It doesn't sound to me like what I would call desire.'

'I told you, he was sweating,' I said.

'Probably with terror,' replied Peter. 'But never mind. You realised that he was a skunk, and that's sufficient. I told you he was a skunk and I'm glad you've seen it.'

'Well,' I said cautiously, 'he's not really so bad. He's no worse than the rest of us. The trouble was I thought he was *better* and then I was disappointed. But you have to admit we all tell lies. Except that when I tell them I just call it imagination.'

'It's not because he tells lies that I say he isn't any good,' replied Peter. 'It's because he and all the rest pretend that they don't tell them. And they tell them, not because it's expedient and makes the social round go smoothly, but because they are frightened. But this is a very boring subject. Let us put it out of our minds for ever.'

After this we passed a pleasant evening, and then Peter went to spend the night with a friend, telling me that he would get up early in the morning and drive back then. The week went by, and I got on with my studies.

But on the next Saturday morning a note came from Peter, telling me to expect him towards the end of the afternoon. Sure enough, he arrived, with a car belonging to another friend of his. 'I can hardly wait to buy my own,' he remarked. He suggested that we might have supper later, but should first of all go for a drive, perhaps round the Assiniboine Park and back along Wellington Crescent, or something like that.

'Well, here we are,' he said as we drove along in a leisurely way. 'As you see, I have been doing some thinking.'

'What about?'

'About whether or not I should come and take you out.'

'Do you want to, then?'

He looked away from the road for a moment, and smiled at me. 'Very much,' he said.

'When did you think of it?' I asked.

'I don't know,' he said. 'It's one of those things you can't put your finger on. It grows and grows and you take no notice of it, and then all of a sudden there it is, all complete, and you don't know why you let it happen. Like at the wedding, you know: it really struck me hard then.' He drove on a bit. 'A chill fell on me at the lake, though,' he went on: 'a distinct chill, in fact. I thought it was permanent, but now it seems to have thawed out.' He looked at me. 'Surely some little idea of it has seeped across to you?'

'I don't know,' I said. 'I don't know at all.'

'Well, never mind,' he replied. We went on, talking a little; and then he continued: 'The way things are where I work, I might not be able to get up every weekend. But I think I could manage every other weekend. But you needn't worry about that: you could still go out with other fellows the other days. I wouldn't mind.'

'Peter!' I said. 'Do you mean you are planning to go steady?'

'Something like that,' he replied.

'It would be incest,' I replied.

'Heavens above!' he said. 'Is that how you spend your dates?' He took his hand off the wheel and patted my arm in a kindly way. 'No wonder you found that Alexander so unique,' he said maliciously.

'You know I don't mean that,' I told him. 'You know what I mean.'

'What do you mean?'

'Well. Well, you know what I mean.'

'People who go steady often get married, that's what you mean, isn't it?'

'Yes,' I said.

'Well, that wouldn't be too bad,' said Peter. 'Cousins often get married. After all, a bull can even be its own grandfather.'

'I don't believe it,' I replied.

'I'll prove it to you some day,' he promised. 'Anyway, it's quite a good plan, isn't it?'

'I don't know,' I answered. 'I don't know. . . .' I thought things over but I still felt confused. 'Now take Alec. . . .' I suggested.

'I don't want to take him anywhere,' Peter replied sharply. 'I told you from the start the man was a skunk.'

'But he was so handsome!' I murmured.

'So am I,' said Peter.

I glanced at him. Certainly, if his face had not been so familiar, you might have thought it passable. That is, if you liked men really sunburnt. 'You can look hard,' said Peter, easing the car round a rather sharp bend. 'A lot of women have looked with considerable interest at what you are looking at now. A lot of women are very regretful that they couldn't hook your Uncle Peter.'

'All the same,' I went on, still trying to get things sorted out, 'you see what I mean, don't you? Whatever he may have said about it, Alec knew I was a *woman*.'

'I wasn't thinking you were a cow,' said Peter.

'But still,' I said, 'I wouldn't really say that you *desire* me.'

Peter began to whistle gently. He cruised the car along, whistling through his teeth: and then he suddenly said: 'Nonsense! Nonsense. How silly can a dame get?'

'Did you really mean it, then?' I asked.

'Certainly I meant it,' he said. 'And the only thing that stopped you knowing I meant it was sheer wilfulness on your part. Sheer downright determination not to believe it.' He thought a bit, and then went on: 'I remember even when I came and stayed with Grandma. My, that was a fine round hole I made in the bedroom wall.'

'You have a dirty mind,' I said.

'I certainly have,' he agreed. 'Certainly! There's no use pretending otherwise, and anyway, I don't want to pretend otherwise. But you just said that was what you wanted.'

'And your father used to be a drinking man,' I added, changing the subject, which was getting too much for me.

'And so was yours,' he returned smartly. 'But mine only burnt the farm down, whereas from what I used to hear tell from my Grandma, yours set the whole nether regions alight with his liquor.' I had to laugh at this, because it was so exactly what Grandma had been in the habit of saying. 'But it doesn't matter, Peggy,' Peter went on. 'Point out all the faults you like. That's the great advantage. You know all my faults already. You'll never get disillusioned.'

'There must be *some* illusions, though,' I said stubbornly. 'There must be some sort of enchantment.'

'How did I get into this conversation!' exclaimed Peter. 'I come and ask a girl to go out with me, and before I know where I am she's discussing our marriage. It makes a man blush. But never mind. I'll be up again to see you on Saturday week. We'll have a good time in a quiet way. But no incest. I'm just an old-fashioned man. Besides, I need my strength for the drive back.'

'You're a brute,' I said.

'It comes of growing up on a farm,' he agreed.

We spent Sunday together as well as Saturday evening, and then Peter returned to work. The examinations started after this, and by the time Peter came again, two weeks later, they had finished: and in fact it was now the Saturday of the Christmas Dance.

I had told him this in a little note, so he came prepared, with his good trousers and his tuxedo in a suitcase, and he took me to the dance. I was very happy about this, partly because I enjoyed dancing with him, for he danced very well, and partly because it now displayed on all sides the fact that I was prepared to go to dances, and not only prepared, but also able to find myself a partner and one who gathered a lot of lingering looks from the females. And from the men too, because Peter seemed to have the advantage over Alexander, that ordinary men admired him too.

Later on in the evening he took Sarah Ann for a dance, and that left me with Don, who seemed quite pleased about it. 'Sarah Ann tells me,' he said, as he steered me round the floor, 'that this well-set-up personality who has tempted you off the path of virtue is your cousin.'

'My cousin Peter,' I said, pleased to be dancing with Don again, but thinking that his slender and elegant figure was not, to me, half so comfortable to hold on to as Peter's.

'That will be another grandchild of that remarkable old lady I met out in the bush?' asked Don.

'That's right,' I said. 'There are four of us. There was my uncle and my mother, you see, and two boys that died when they were young. And she did have another son too, but he never married, and then he was killed in the war, so he didn't have any children. So four of Grandma's children died.'

'I thought you told me once your cousins were a bunch of hicks,' remarked Don.

'Well,' I said, 'this one seems to have grown out of it. Or rather,' I added, remembering how important Joe managed to look to a nice girl like Wilma, 'perhaps I'm beginning to grow out of the idea.'

'Well, when you come to think of it,' said Don, 'there's not much class distinction between meat-packing and meat-growing, is there? And nowadays there's money in farming, too.'

'Not as much as in meat-packing,' I replied: 'but it happens this one's an engineer.'

'Oh, I see,' said Don, 'a college man.' He looked at me with a big smile as the music ended. 'Very suitable,' he said. I wanted to tell him that he should not get any such ideas and that I had already explained to Peter, so I hoped, that it would not be at all suitable to me: but Sarah Ann and Peter had arrived at our side, and I left it.

After the dance Peter drove me back to the residence. We will, as they say, draw a veil over this drive, which was very interesting, really. After that we spent a quiet Sunday; and on Sunday evening after he had gone I packed my things for the Christmas vacation. Peter had told me that he would not be able to be at the farm for Christmas. It seemed that he had to keep an eye on things: but he would arrive just after New Year's Day. I was going to catch the train on Monday morning. Late on Sunday evening, however, Wilma telephoned to me.

'Oh, Peggy,' she said, small and distant, 'are you coming first thing to-morrow morning?'

212

'Sure,' I replied, with visions of miscarriages and other such events floating before my eyes. 'But why?'

'Well, it'll be a good thing if you can,' she answered, 'as Grandma's had a shock.'

'Oh!' I said. 'And what shocked her?'

'Oh well,' she said, 'you know what I mean. What folk call a stroke.'

'You mean she's ill?' I asked.

'Yes. She was out at the farm today, and when we took her back, just at her gate she took a stroke. But if you're coming it'll be all right.'

I wasn't at all sure about that. I had not understood that strokes were to be cured so easily; and I found the journey to Merrilee a worrying one. Joe met me at the station. 'I thought I'd give you a hand,' he said, as he drove us round to Grandma's house, 'and I can take Wilma home now. She spent the night with Grandma.'

'What does the doctor say about Grandma?' I asked.

'He thinks she'll be all right if she's quiet. People often last a long time after a stroke.'

'And sometimes they have another one very soon and just go off unexpected,' I replied.

'Never mind about that,' he said.

'And what are we going to do when I go back to college?'

'Grandma's got money,' said Joe. 'She'll just have to pay for a helper of some kind, I guess. She's likely to be in bed a long time, so we'll have to make some arrangement. 'Tisn't as if it were a case of Wilma sitting with her a week or two and then she'd get up. Wilma's going to have a baby,' he added happily. 'She's looking prettier than ever.'

Wilma was very pleased to see Joe and myself when we arrived. Her skin and her hair were shining even more than before, even though she was looking tired at the moment, and the baby was beginning to be rather obvious. After I had greeted Grandma, she and Joe drove away.

Grandma was propped up on her pillows in her bed. The stroke had only affected her on one side: she was still able to talk, though more slowly than usual, and to use her right hand. The doctor had left a note for me, giving me some instructions, and telling me the times when the nurse would be able to call. I read the note, and then put my things away in my room, and made lunch for myself and Grandma.

After that there began a quiet vacation. On Christmas Day Uncle did drive over from the farm with the family, but they only stayed for a couple of hours. Mrs. Ransom and other friends of Grandma also came for short visits at different times. They used to suggest that I should go out somewhere, perhaps over to the farm, or to visit people in Merrilee, but I was quite contented to stay in the house.

I felt slightly apathetic, like one who has lived too busily for some time; and as my college career would finish with the ending of our fourth year, at Easter, in a vague way I felt that it was about time to decide what I was going to do after college. How life does run on, I thought: it is only yesterday that college seemed like the end of every ambition, and now it is nearly over.

Of course, I was young: most of the people in fourth year were two or even three years older than me, and the ex-service students at college were even older: but still, at nineteen, the age of twenty, which was only a week or two away, seemed quite formidable. It was time now, if it was not too late, to decide what I was after all going to do with my life. This mood of mature reflection fitted in very well with the need to sit with Grandma and to attend to her.

Early in the morning I would light the fire in her bedroom, and then would bring her breakfast, porridge and stewed prunes or stewed apricots or one of the other things she liked, with cream and brown sugar for the porridge and with a pot of tea, for Grandma was ever faithful to tea. I poured out the tea and arranged everything so that she could take it easily. Then it was time for a little wash, and then I tidied the bedroom, and cleaned the rest of the house.

Grandma would enquire anxiously and hoarsely after the house if she thought it was being neglected. 'Have you, have you,' she used to murmur to me, and then take a deep breath and get a better grip on things and speak more loudly: 'Have you set the front parlour to rights?' 'Yes Grandma.' And then, 'I hope you dusted the china.' 'Yes Grandma.' 'I hope you didn't break none of it.' 'Not a piece, Grandma.' And then a long pause while she stared ahead at the wall beside the fireplace, a wall now taking on a cheerful yellow glow from the dancing flames of the logs burning in the fire, and rejecting the stark white light of snowy Christmas-time outside. 'That's good china,' she said. 'Every piece I brought from Ireland with me. Some of it Henry bought me and some was my mother's before me.' And then she would sit and think, and one day she remarked suddenly, 'I lost three boys and a girl; and my grandchildren are three boys and a girl.'

'Yes,' I said. 'That's good, Grandma.'

'There was a boy called Peter,' she said, 'and the girl's name was Sheelagh.'

'That's good names, Grandma,' I said.

'It's a pity when they die,' she said. 'But you and Peter have done very well at college.' I was pleased at that, because a chill had begun to run down my spine, suggesting that she did not know who I was. But now she fell asleep; and then later she suddenly woke up and blinked and looked about her, and asked me, 'Have you seen to the chickens today?'

'I told you, Grandma,' I said. 'Mr. Macdonald fetched

them away the night you were taken ill. He fixed it with Uncle, to save coming here so often to see to them; and Uncle was glad to agree. They bring us a good share of the eggs.'

'But what a strange thing,' she said, 'to take my chickens away without so much as asking me.'

'It saves him the walk, Grandma,' I said. But now it remained a perpetual surprise to her, and she kept mentioning it. She was thinking about it even on the day when, after the New Year, Peter was expected at the farm. In the afternoon I was sitting with her, and most of the time she was sleeping. She seemed to have become very drowsy since the New Year. I was mending some things, and the fire was flickering up the chimney. Grandma awoke and watched me intently, and said, 'I hope you're taking proper care with the mending.'

'I think so,' I said. 'I'm doing it with real trouble.'

'I hope it's not dull for you here,' she said.

'It's not at all dull,' I replied. 'I'm having a really enjoyable visit. How about you?'

She did not answer, because she had started to think, and, plucking faintly at the white coverlet with her good hand, she announced: 'I must see that man about the chickens.'

'He meant really well, Grandma,' I said.

She leant her head back and began to close her eyes. 'What a most extraordinary thing,' she said, 'to come and take away my chickens.' After that she fell asleep. I went into the front parlour after a little while, and piled some wood on the fire which I had lit to keep it warm and aired. Very soon I heard a car draw up, and, looking out of the window, was glad to see Peter in Uncle's motor, with the chains hung on its wheels against the bitter weather that was freezing the roads. Peter got out and waved to me with his fur-gloved hand, and then came indoors and kissed me gently and began to take off his heavy overcoat.

'How's Grandma?' he asked.

'She's asleep,' I said.

'This is not much of a vacation for you,' he remarked, hanging up his coat in the hall.

'It's all right,' I replied. 'After all, this is my home, and I'm enjoying it. Grandma isn't too bad, really, and we get on well. I think Grandma and I understand each other.'

'That's fine,' he said, following me into the parlour. 'Well, I'll go and have a word with her, and then perhaps you'll make me a cup of coffee.' I nodded, and sat down by the fire while he went away. After a while he came back into the parlour and looked at me oddly.

'She's dead,' he said.

I stared at him. 'I don't believe you,' I said.

He nodded. 'I'm afraid so,' he replied.

'She's been all right,' I said, 'except that she was sleepy.'

'They seem all right,' he replied, 'and then another small stroke comes, and they're dead.' I got out my handkerchief as my eyes were full of tears. Peter went and looked out of the window.

'It hits you, doesn't it?' he said. He stared at the barren snow for a long time. 'Oh God, they'll all die some time,' he said. He sat down suddenly in one of the hard chairs by the window, facing me, and tilted his head back with a sigh. He looked very pale in the light reflected through the net curtains off the snow in the garden outside.

'My God, this house is cold,' he said. 'I never felt it so cold before.'

'But you've been in it in the winter before.'

'Of course,' he answered. 'A thousand times. But I never thought it was such a bleak house before.' He heaved another sigh and sat for a long long time staring at the floor. Then he scuffed a little with his foot at the linoleum.

'I guess Grandma was a peasant,' he said slowly.

'What's a peasant?' I asked.

'Someone who really likes outdoor plumbing, and doesn't know about nuclear physics,' he said. 'Oh, I don't know. Someone who's always Irish or Scots or Norwegian or something and never a real Canadian at all.'

'She helped send us to college,' I replied.

'I know that, I know that,' he answered. 'That's a funny thing. She sent us to college to destroy her world. Oh, well.' He put his arm on the window-sill and stared out of the window again at the garden where the light was beginning to fail. Then he looked back at me. 'Grandma wouldn't have liked me to take you on dates,' he said. 'Especially,' he added with a faint smile, 'if she thought we went dancing.'

'I told you it was incest,' I said.

'No, it's not!' he answered, perhaps rather sharply. 'She just had a different set of ideas about things like that. Just a different way of looking at things, that's all.'

'If it's all just a way of looking at things,' I asked, 'what does anything ever matter at all?'

'I never saw any answer to that,' he replied, 'except for a man to get on with his own family, and find himself a useful job. Oh my God, I'm glad I like my job.' He stood up. 'Well, I suppose I'd better go and tell Dad. But I can't leave you here alone with Grandma.'

'We can't leave Grandma alone.'

'We'll ask one of the neighbours to mind her,' said Peter. We put on our coats and scarves and gloves and went out. Now it was the early winter twilight, passing over into darkness, with only a tinge of red on the snow here and there by the side of Grandma's white-painted house to remind us of the sun, and without a bird in the sky or an animal moving anywhere. We went out through the gate, which creaked dismally in the quiet evening, and a cold breeze caught us, coming out of the shadows that lay over the open country past the little track where the horses had run away on the morning of Joe's wedding. Across the road, we knocked on the door, and the goodwife came to it, the light streaming out with her.

'Well, good evening, Peter Donovan!' she said. 'It's a long time since I've had a word with you.' In the room past the lighted passage behind her there was a rattle of cups and the small barking of a dog, woofing to itself but not ready to leave the fire, and a man called out, 'If that's Donovan's eldest boy, bring him here for a cup of coffee.'

'Thank you, Mr. Nielsen,' called Peter. 'Not this evening. I'm on an errand.'

'We have the TV,' said Mrs. Nielsen. 'The two of you should come and see it.'

'Not today, thank you very much,' said Peter. 'My grandmother's dead.'

Mrs. Nielsen was very upset and went to tell Mr. Nielsen, who came to the door with his coffee, and stood talking to us there. In a minute or two we took Mrs. Nielsen back into Grandma's house, and then we drove away to Uncle Arthur's farm. We swept up the track and into the front yard, and before Peter switched the lights off I could see the farm buildings illuminated, and then, climbing out, discerned the bare trees in the little bluff around the house, and the small bushes of the scrub, and the bare desolate expanses of snow lying in the dark.

'I remember when the horses got hit,' I said.

'Yes,' agreed Peter. 'It was a bloody mess.'

He went ahead of me into the house and I hung about in the back kitchen, which was a much smarter affair than the one I used to cook in before the fire. When I thought he had finished telling the story, I went on into the kitchen where the others were sitting.

Then there began a busy time making arrangements, first of all telephoning the doctor, and then making a bed for me in my room upstairs. Auntie got supper ready for all of us, and Wilma promised to lend me a nightdress to save fetching my things.

Peter meanwhile insisted that it would be he who would return to Merrilee and spend the night with Grandma. He had already flatly refused any arrangement that allowed me to return to Grandma's house, and he said he would be perfectly all right by himself. But, said he, since Mrs. Nielsen was waiting, he would not stay for supper, but would return to Merrilee right away. I began anxiously to tell him where to find food, but he patted my cheek, and said, 'Never mind, I am able to find myself an egg. Even if I have to lay it.'

I had followed him into the smaller kitchen, and he stood with his hand on the outer door, and cupped my chin in his other hand, and said, 'Stop fretting,' and began to kiss me in the half-darkness of the little room. 'They'll come out of the kitchen and see you,' I whispered. 'What if they do?' he whispered back. 'Is it a secret?' 'Of course it's a secret,' I said. 'And with Grandma dead and everything.' He laughed, and went away; and I went back into the kitchen for supper, resolving to have another talk with him and show him it must be a secret, since I would never marry him and therefore it would do no good to tell the family. Especially Auntie.

'Now, I am not crying like I did when Benjamin died,' I thought, climbing into my old bed. I decided that it was because I minded so much more, that it was better not to cry about it. And then for the next two or three days, there were more arrangements and plans, and then there was the funeral.

Ernest managed to arrive for this, and of course Mrs. Ransom came to it, looking very sad and puckered, though she cheered up when we asked after her little great-grand-child and told her about Wilma's baby; and the rest of the inhabitants of Merrilee came too, except those folk that we didn't know, because they had such strange ways. On the day after the funeral I went into Merrilee with Peter. He had to call on the minister and pay one or two other calls, and he left me in Grandma's house to pack up my things and to take them back to the farm for the rest of the vaca-tion. And I thought that at the same time I would take the pieces of embroidery Grandma had put aside for me, and wrap up the shamrock table-cloth and give it to Peter, to make sure that he got it and Grandma was not disappointed.

It did not take long to do my packing, and to parcel up the embroidery and the things belonging to me which used to be left behind in the house during term time, and to put Peter's cloth in tissue paper and in coloured paper left over from Christmas. After this I took a walk around the house because it was quite likely that I would not come into it again. After I had looked around, I went into Grandma's bedroom, and stood there alone at the back of the empty house, and looked about. The snow lay piled on the window-sill, and the inevitable transparent row of icicles hung at the top of the window frame, with their little fellows solemnly standing in a row below, reaching upwards, and snow lay along the bars and crossbars too and in one corner had drifted half across the window-pane, thick at the edge but dying away to a mere smear of frost in the centre, frost spangled with tiny crystals, each of them radiant.

The curious dead light of daylight reflected off snow shone bleakly on everything inside the room. The linoleum was reddish brown with red lines running this way and black lines running that way. The bedstead was brass, with sharper lights from the window and colours from the room caught on its golden surface, the bedspread white, the rag rug by the washstand black and white, a bold pattern invented and worked out by Grandma. The washstand had an unusual top, pink veined marble which when it was wet used to shine with deeper shafts of colour as perhaps pink jade might shine, and it carried a set of washing things, basin, jug and soap-dish, in bright shining green.

Then there was the wardrobe and the chest of drawers containing all Grandma's clothes which were so familiar to us. On the chest of drawers stood her mirror, and a number of snapshots of her family.

Here, for instance, were Uncle Arthur and Auntie standing in front of our barn when it had just been built, soon after their marriage. Here was Uncle Arthur's brother in Winnipeg who was killed in the war. Here was myself in my graduation dress for Grade XI. Here was Peter as a little boy, hanging over a gate. There was time to look at everything carefully. I looked at it all most scrupulously, but the life was out of it. I began to see it and to feel the house devoid of all the memory that gave it meaning, the busyness we had built around every inch of it.

There had been nothing lifeless in it before; even its smallness and its frustrations had been an excitement, helping to drive me to Winnipeg and to college so that my life was now something new and different partly because of this small house and its narrow view of the fields and gardens and the neighbouring houses. But I lost the sense of all this now and of all the memories and saw it like the scenes created in plays or films, of other people's frustrating lives, showing how barren and bare and narrow are their lives and their environment — barren and bare, that is, to the authors, who had completely failed to see what life was to them. And now I saw the house like one of these artificial scenes, no longer the warm snailshell in which I and Grandma lived, where even the hideous linoleum was something peculiarly part of ourselves, a pleasure to Grandma and a perpetual warm familiar enchanting and precious source of annoyance to me: no longer full of memories but a cardboard construction on the TV demonstrating what life is like — to the author — out in the bush.

Here is the life of people living in a small way out in the bush and here is the linoleum they brought out here before the flood, before or after or during or between one of those wars which, though a fixed part of history, we do not now clearly remember, and we cannot tell near to which war it was they laid down this strange linoleum: for since we have lived through our own war the memory of all other wars is ineffectual now. It is time then to go into our own kitchen and get a snack out of the refrigerator. It is time to pour out a couple of drinks.

Now here is also the strange jug and basin out of which these people wash for they do not have running water. We see here a cardboard ewer and basin and a cardboard pump outside the window and soon a cardboard woman will go and pump at this pump.

We do not see the real pump with the sunlight lying along the side of the handle and the iron of the handle burning hot under your hand, with the yellowish grass and the yellow-flowered silverleaf growing around the base and the tiny procession of red ants making its way solemnly past, and the drops of spilt water marking the dust in dark brown circles, like a handful of children's toy coins scattered at our feet. We do not know anything about this pump: we see a cardboard pump and we know we simply do not wish to pump at such a pump. How wonderfully the author has recreated the very atmosphere of life out in the bush, what a genius he is, how fervently we now know that we do not wish to live out in the bush, where all the appurtenances and necessities of life are created of cardboard. It is time to pour another drink. And just so I stood and saw it all empty and barren and bare: and could not recapture anything that gave it meaning.

Then Peter came in at the front door and called out to me. I came into the hall to greet him. It crossed my mind for a flash of time that there was nothing I would like to do better than to spend the night with Peter. It would be so warm, so comfortable, I thought, so real and alive: we could find so much to say.

The idea was there for a moment, perfectly in focus, and then it was not there any more, and I could not understand why I had felt it so violently, for now it was just Peter and I standing in a hall and talking as usual, something that had happened over and over again since the very beginning of time. He was clapping his hands together because he had been walking around the garden with his gloves stuffed into his pockets, and his fingers were frosty.

'Cheer up, small pale ghost,' he said. He put his arm around me. 'Where are your things?' he asked.

'All neatly put in the parlour,' I answered, 'and a parcel for you, a table-cloth. I did it up nicely, so don't open it. Keep it till you get back.'

'All right,' he said. He put everything in the car and we both got in, and he began to drive back to the farm. 'You know I have to go tomorrow,' he said.

'I know,' I replied. 'The vacation's nearly over, anyway.'

'I'll come and see you,' he said. 'That'll be nice. We'll keep each other company.'

He drove on, humming to himself: and I resolved again to

make it quite clear that this was not to be a real romance between us.

'Though I don't suppose he's serious when he talks of marrying,' I thought. 'He can't be. As I said, it wouldn't do at all, cousins like us marrying. Who know each other so well too.'

But it was not the time to talk about it, a better time would come, so I remained silent, and Peter went on humming gently, and we drove back to the farm to end our Christmas holiday.

Chapter Ten

AFTER this there came the winter of discontent. It closed around me at the farm, when I began to think that once Uncle Arthur had sorted out Grandma's things and sold her house, the farmhouse would count as my home, and I did not want it to do so.

And though Wilma was very pleasant and nice, and Joe in a very cheerful frame of mind, and even Ernest managed to be amusing, before he went away, with his description of his correspondence with Wilma's cousin, which was still continuing and looked like lasting for a long long time, I felt that the person I had really been fond of was Grandma, and that they could not take her place. 'And you can be fond of someone,' I thought, 'even if you get annoyed with them. Fondness is one thing, and annoyed or not annoyed is quite another. But I get annoyed with Auntie, without really being fond of her at all.'

Auntie was a funny woman: she was always so busy, and always so sharp, and always so absolutely *right* about everything. But she thought she was right, even when she was wrong, because she did not understand what the other person was saying: whereas Grandma too often understood it and did not care at all, so that you could give way to her with a sense of respect, as one defeated by a superior force, instead of having to endure the frustration of having an antagonist that could easily have been defeated, but would never consent to bring her mind into the field of battle.

'I do not respect Auntie, that is the trouble,' I thought. 'In short,' I concluded sadly, 'though Uncle and the boys are fond of her, she is not my own flesh and blood. We are not the same sort of woman.'

The question of money did not bring any difficulty. Grandma had left an orderly will, dividing her money judiciously between the four of us. And she had had a good deal of money, for Grandad had brought capital with him from Ireland, used it well, if not always with the strictest honesty, and eventually invested the gathering surplus in a way that survived the depression and increased in value afterwards.

Before she made her will, Grandma had gone to great pains to work out what the farm would represent to Joe when he eventually took it over while Uncle Arthur retired on his own savings and his own inheritance from Grandad, and as well, what college had meant to Peter and myself; and she had made a will that levelled it all out as well as she could.

I had thought that she might be going to leave all her money to Peter and me, in which case I would have given something to Joe and Ernest; but Grandma's will rebuked me for supposing that she might fail to do what was neat, orderly and respectable. And in fact as things stood Ernest came out the winner: and out of sheer contrariness Auntie, who had been so cross when Grandma decided to send me to college, now shook her head over a young lad like Ernest having so much money to play about with; and complained that he would probably spend it all on drink, women, flashy cars, and new neckties.

After she had said this a good many times, especially when clumping meals on to the table, or getting in my way when I was bringing in the food, Uncle Arthur, sitting by hungrily, took his pipe out of his mouth and asked whether he was ever to get another meal in peace or was it to be forever nothing but women complaining; and anyway the money was in trust until Ernest was twenty-one, and he and Peter were the trustees. 'In which case,' said Joe (for he and Wilma often took their meals in the farmhouse), 'Peter will buy *himself* a car, for he's fairly longing to have one. And I expect he wouldn't mind a woman too.'

At this unexpected venture into wit and irony he was delighted with himself, and sat grinning with his splendid white teeth illuminating his sunburnt face. I tried to suppress my own smiles, because I could see that the remark, though I thought it was funny, was equally annoying both to Uncle, as a businessman, and to Auntie in her role of solicitous mother. And there seemed to be some distressful flutterings on Wilma's face too, as she wanted to think as well as possible of everybody and didn't know how to do it if Peter was going to buy himself a woman with Ernest's money: while the hired man, sitting at the end of the table, gave one or two very knowing looks. Ernest was obviously fast assuming the position of a poor little outcast nigger baby, oppressed by everybody including Grandma who had inconsiderately left him money. But Uncle, who wanted to pay all his attention now to his beef and pickles, put the matter right.

'Peter has his own money,' he said firmly, between mouthfuls, 'and as long as he makes a good job of engineering and doesn't take too much drink, he may get himself anything he likes by way of cars or neckties or women. Even if he goes out and picks up a Red Indian squaw out of one of the reservations.' 'They smell,' said Joe. 'You're damn right they do,' said the hired man feelingly. 'You two be quiet,' continued Uncle: 'and what was that heifer bellowing all morning for in the barn? Couldn't neither of you feed her in good time? And as for trustees, if Peter's a trustee that's so as he can do the paperwork. I suggested it to

Mother myself. Don't give me any paperwork, I said to her. What have we trained Peter in mathematics for? I've paperwork enough to do myself with this blasted Government interfering with me all the time. So what it comes down to is, Ernest will not spend a penny until you and I are agreed on it, Mary. So that is the end of that subject for good and all. I don't want to hear any more about it. Pass me the pickles.' This was enough for Auntie, who never mentioned it to Uncle again, but began instead to say to me: 'Well, as long as I have full control of Ernest's money, that's all right, but Mother should have made that clearer in her will': and out of sheer desperation I let her say it.

So money was no problem and there was enough to pay any college bills that were left and to give me a start in anything that I decided to do afterwards. But it seemed to me now to be a burden even to have to finish my college course, for without Grandma I did not feel that I cared whether I passed examinations or not.

And back at college, my disfavour with everything piled itself up, with the farm and with the city and with religious people and with irreligious people like anarchists and the like, and with the professors, always talking so slow and deep and portentous, and the girls in the residence, always yattering high and fast and trivial, and with drab thoughts because they were drab and romantic thoughts because they were misleading. 'And what it all boils down to,' I said to myself, 'is that my coming to Winnipeg has not in any way achieved anything I really wanted.' Except a lot of excitement, I added grudgingly, but that is beginning to wear off now.

The thing that struck me most, as I sat and thought about it soberly, was that I had always supposed that in coming to Winnipeg it would be possible, somewhere in the bounds of the great city, to find something, a way of life even, that

I could regard as life itself, the centre of things, after which one need look no further. But the centre kept moving away from me, as if it were the horizon, constantly disappearing as you made your way towards it: and while I walked on looking for the centre, the horizon which in this case I was trying to get away from, kept catching up behind me, and the feeling of being on the outside edge of the world persisted.

'And the truth is,' I said, facing it, 'that even Winnipeg is on the edge of the world, in a way: it seems to be hanging there, ready to drop off.' Blow the wind too hard, and Winnipeg would blow over the edge in a moment, leaving behind the rocks and trees and the bare Laurentian plain. 'And nobody would miss us,' I said. 'They would ship their grain from somewhere else, and never miss us, because we haven't become any sort of a legend yet.'

Now the North was a legend, and Old Quebec; and the Yukon and New York and Boston; and the Hebrides, Ultima Thule, which the Canadians still behold in dreams — and the cities of Europe like Rome and Paris and London, England. And if these places accidentally fell into the sea, people would go on thinking about them just the same, so tenacious of life were their names. So surely in places like that one would find oneself in the middle of life at once? And one's life would become important, because one had lived in such a place?

And at about this point in my reasoning it began to dawn on me that probably in some place like Europe, if I visited it, I would come upon a sense of satisfaction that so far I could not altogether say I had discovered in Winnipeg: and having found it, could perhaps bring it back with me, and keep it for ever. But before there was time to think it out, Don and Sarah Ann added power to my discontent by starting to drift around the college arm in arm, beaming smiles at everyone, and announcing that they had got engaged.

This made me feel supremely left out. And I knew what would happen now: there would follow Showers, at which we would give Sarah Ann presents, and then long evenings admiring the presents with her, if she had any evenings to spare from Don; and long walks round the stores with her choosing her trousseau; and then their wedding when college finished, and wedding photographs, and the new furniture to admire in their home; and then of course there would be the expected baby, and then the arrival of the dear child into a welcoming world; and then when sobriety had scarcely re-entered the scene, the next baby would begin to make itself felt.

As a practical, useful friend, ready to discuss the world with me, Sarah Ann was lost to me more or less for ever.

But I congratulated them suitably, and fourth year held a little dance for them, and Mrs. Whiting had a number of teas, and Don's parents held a party in astonishing magnificence in their home on Wellington Crescent. Peter came to this party with me, looking very elegant in his formal clothes. He brought his own car which he had just bought, and spent most of the evening telling me about it: so there was little time to unburden my complaints to him.

But after the party, I started some serious discussions with Linda and Joan, who were going to set off for Europe as soon as the college year ended. Another particular friend of theirs, a girl called Mamie, was to travel with them; and of course they would probably meet other student friends on the way along. The tour of Britain and Europe was becoming all the fashion. We were always hearing from people who had made it in the summer vacation. Or if you wanted to spread yourself, you could go for a whole year and get a job over there.

As far as one could judge, the Canadian men made the tour to see Britain and Europe, and the Canadian women made it to keep an eye on the Canadian men. So a student would thankfully say goodbye to his family and his acquaintance and set off to see Europe with two or three of the boys. And when he had panted his way, maybe, up the Eiffel Tower, at the top as smart as paint in her lipstick and new cotton frock he would find some gay, laughing girl he thought he had left behind in Saskatchewan or Alberta. And then they would meet again in the Pyrenees or bump together, by accident, on the Matterhorn. It was worse than Interpol. And towards the end of the summer, as the fall approached, everybody would drift into Paris or London; and you could hold parties then that were just great, just the same people almost as a party at home, except that one or two of the natives might have slipped in by mistake, lessening the tone a little.

And surely, I thought, in London, England, in the fall, with the leaves falling through the rain off the plane trees in Sloane Square, and the artists making their way in bare feet along the Chelsea pavements, and the Beefeaters out and about, and the Chelsea pensioners, and the Lifeguards riding by with their white plumes rising and falling, dimly seen in the mist as they disappeared through Hyde Park on their supercilious, polished, caparisoned and supremely elegant horses, surely there between mist and falling leaves there must be some kind of poetry to be distilled out of the air, some wild dream the very essence of romance, that would seize the wakeful inhabitant of London, England, and teach him to find the very meaning of life itself? Then such an inhabitant must I be, perhaps not barefooted — I drew the line at that — and not, on the other hand, clad in the useful woollen stockings that were the sole legwear of the remainder of British womanhood, no, nylons I would take with me and a year's supply of face powder, but, anyway, with my hands outstretched to feel the rain and my heart eagerly seeking, I proposed to find my soul in London, England. It looked, though, as though it would not be possible to find a passage until the fall itself, so popular had the journey now become. By then Linda and Joan and Mamie felt they would have seen Europe. They would join me in London, we would all find work; and we would be happy together.

I told Peter about it one Saturday evening when he had come to see me. He smiled at me. 'You always have some dream,' he said. 'I suppose it keeps you happy. But how does one earn one's living out of a dream?'

'I can get a job there,' I replied. 'But for the time being I don't have to earn my own living unless I want to, anyway.'

'No,' he said. 'Money is a very useful thing. Doesn't this car go sweetly? I was lucky to get her, a bargain, and just one or two things that needed setting right which I managed fine.'

'Lots of guys go running after new cars,' I said.

'That's all right if you don't know anything about cars,' he replied. 'And when the year's guarantee is up you trade it in for another, I know. It's fine if you can keep paying the difference, and then you always have a new car and the repairs paid. But that's for people who don't understand machines. I'd rather have an old car off a scrapheap and make her work and think it was my own doing.'

'Can't get much speed out of a really old car,' I said.

'I don't care about speed half as much as setting right a difficult piece of machinery. Speed is too easy a challenge for me.'

'And what about my going to London in the fall?'

'You won't go to London in the fall,' he said. 'You'll

233

have had a dozen other plans by then. Besides, you'd get seasick.'

'I want to go to London,' I said.

'Wait until I've made enough money to satisfy me and I'll take you. Then I can hold your hand when you get seasick.'

'Will you have enough money by the fall?'

'Gee whiz, I'm not going to leave my job right now.'

'So what will you do if I go to London in the fall?'

'I'll knock your little block off,' he said. 'Now look at that monstrous car over there. What on earth is the use of anyone designing a car like that? Now if we just sidle through the traffic here we can catch up with her and then I can look her over. Dammit, it's turned off down Broadway. Well, here we go.' He slid ahead and turned left down Broadway. 'I thought you said you were taking me to eat in a place along Main Street?' I said. 'So I am,' he replied, 'but I want to see what that car is like.'

'Peter,' I said, 'do you know the price of gas?'

'Peggy,' he replied, 'have you heard a word called matriarchy?'

'I heard it dimly somewhere,' I said.

'It means a place where women are always the boss. Like the U.S.A. And they do as they like all the time and the men come running after and say Yes, honey, and No, honey. That's a matriarchy and I don't like it.'

'I'll see the day you run after a woman and say Yes, honey, and No, honey,' I said.

'Exactly,' he replied. 'But let's have a minute's peace while we look at this car.'

I fell silent while he stared at the car, no doubt memorizing every feature of it. 'The sensation seems familiar,' I thought. 'It feels just like being driven round by Peter in an old wooden cart, ten years back.' Then when he was satisfied, he turned our car aside, and started to cut back through the side streets to Main Street. 'Peter,' I said, 'why should women give way to men anyway?'

'It makes them feel good,' he replied. 'And then when they feel good they turn round and make women feel good, and everybody is happy.'

'But that's only putting it a little further back,' I said. 'What is it about men that you have to give way to them to make them feel good?'

'It's something to do with sex,' he said. 'If you order a man around all the time, you make it so that he can't enjoy it and he goes off and finds another woman, and, well, if she's bossy too he finds another, and then you have driven him promiscuous. Or on the other hand you drive him to get tired of sex altogether.'

'This is getting too complicated for me,' I said.

'Good,' he replied, 'I wouldn't like you to grow up rude-minded. Now look at that thing ahead of us, that's not a car but a crate on wheels. Do you see her, just turned down Garry to Portage Avenue?'

'Peter, honey,' I said, 'how extremely clever it was of you to have thought of taking us to Main Street to that marvellous restaurant that everybody is talking about nowadays and wishing they had been there. It takes you to find a good restaurant. And I just love Main Street, too.'

He started to laugh and he put an arm round my shoulders. 'I prefer you in front of all other women,' he said, as we passed by Garry and Fort Street, and reached Main Street again.

'But still,' I said, 'at the moment your great love is your car.'

'At the moment my great passion is my car,' he answered. He looked at me swiftly. 'My great love is you,' he said. But at that for some reason or other I started to blush; so

I did not say anything more until we had arrived by the restaurant.

'All the same,' I thought in the evening when I was back in my room, 'his mind is all on his car now like at the lake it was on his new job. His mind is always preoccupied. And what my great love is I don't know, but my passion now is to go to London and I don't think Peter understands that very well.'

So after that I did not say too much about it to him, but just mentioned it now and again: and he would say, 'But of course you won't go,' and then we'd change the subject.

And then there came such a spring, with a wind blowing tumultuously about us; and with the thaw all the old copies of the *Tribune* and the *Free Press* that had been dropped on the snow during the winter, and all the cigarette packets and ice-cream containers and everything else that had remained dormant, took on new life; and as the water thawed and trickled off them into the gutters they began to move about the pavements, and then they took wings in the wind and rose high above our heads, taking the news of Europe for a ride in the sky over the roofs of Winnipeg. As always the scene seemed to me exceedingly sordid. I did not think I could bear to find a job in Winnipeg during the summer. I did not even want to stay in Manitoba at all. The blowing papers repelled me, making me long to go somewhere more beautiful even for that little time. Perhaps to the Rockies. 'Peter,' I said, 'I think I'll go and be a waitress in Banff for the summer.'

'No you won't,' he said. 'You'll find something to do near me.'

'The Rockies would be so peaceful and cool,' I said. 'And I should like to see that really mountainous country.'

'Don't be silly,' he answered. 'Our whole lives will depend on what we do now. You stay here with **me.**'

He will grow out of the notion about marrying me, I said to myself for the hundredth time. Indeed, I'm surprised that his car hasn't cured him already. And I should like to see the Rockies. I *will* see the Rockies. 'I shall go to the Rockies,' I said to him again.

'You keep your mind on your examinations,' he replied. 'And by the way, you remember I told you I was going with some of the boys on a fishing trip?'

'Yes,' I said. 'When do you leave?'

'Just before the end of your term. It'll be a couple of weeks. I'm taking a proper holiday.'

'All right,' I said. 'I'll expect to miss you.' I fell once again to planning my summer at the Rockies. But then I began to work out that if I did go to see them it would leave me very little time before I sailed for Europe in the fall; and when it came to the point of actually having to make up one's mind, I decided that it would be nicer after all to stay somewhere near Peter. So, instead, I began to think over various plans for a summer in Manitoba.

But then, all of a sudden, Mamie's mother fell ill. After great discussion, it was decided that Mamie could not go to Europe. 'There you are, Peggy!' cried Joan and Linda. 'You can get her passage.'

'But gee!' I said. 'I haven't my papers ready or anything. I don't suppose I could get them through in time. For one thing, the exams are just coming on, and I have to think about them.'

'I'll see to that for you,' said Don, who, with Sarah Ann, was sitting in the canteen with us. 'One of my father's secretaries will do it for you. He'll be back from Chicago tonight. I'll tell him about it.'

I thanked him and accepted his offer. That left me with the problem of telling Peter: but I did not dare to do it.

I saw him again, and he said goodbye to me, for he was to

leave, at the next weekend, for his holiday, and still I could not manage to tell him. I told myself that until everything was definitely arranged it was just as well not to tell him. But in a day or two more it became clear that there would be nothing to hinder me from taking the passage. So I wrote and told them about it at the farm; and then took a deep breath, and wrote Peter a letter that would reach him before he left for his holiday.

I supposed that when he got the letter he would decide not to go fishing at all, or else would cut his holiday short, and would come to see me. I was not surprised when he did not reply to it immediately, as he was not at all fond of writing letters: he would, I expected, simply send a note that would arrive just before he did.

Meanwhile my excitement and expectation of our voyage was mounting every day, and I whirled about preparing everything, shopping and packing and looking at maps and visiting friends before we went. I rushed out to the farm, too, taking with me the luggage that had to be left there. When I got back, though, it suddenly dawned on me that there were only three or four days left. I *must* hear from Peter tomorrow, I thought: but out of sheer impatience I wrote him another letter and posted it. Then I realised that it would have to be forwarded and might not reach him for a day or two, if he was still on holiday — but surely he was not still on holiday, but had come back now, and was preparing to come and see me for these last few days? But the next morning there was still no letter from him.

I was now at the residence, which was not closed for the summer vacation yet, so that it was possible for me to stay there for my last days. This morning, as I went through the things I had left there to pack and take with me on the train, I came upon a moment of astonishment. I found my first letter to Peter. I had not posted it. At that, I felt quite sick.

But I did the only thing possible. I sent him a very long telegram explaining everything as well as I could. I waited with extreme impatience and late at night I had a telephone call.

'This is me,' said Peter. 'Your telegram has been phoned up here. What the devil do you mean by it?'

'I mean what it says,' I said. 'Are you coming to see me for the last two days? Surely you are coming to spend the last two days with me?'

'How the bloody hell do you think I can?' he asked. 'There isn't a plane to be got here. There's not even a post office where we are, you know: this phone is miles away from us and they had to come and find me with the telegram. It was lucky that they would bother to. And it will take me ages to get back to Winnipeg. But it doesn't matter. You're not going.'

'Of course I'm going,' I said. 'I've paid for my passage and everything.'

'Well, God damn you altogether,' he said. 'What train are you taking from Winnipeg?'

I told him. He was silent a moment as he was thinking. 'Do you realise,' he said angrily, 'that the only connection I can get will only just have got into Winnipeg by then?'

I was distressed at that. 'But it's two or three days,' I said.

'Peggy,' he said, cold and patient, 'none of us has got a car here, and as for trains, there just aren't the connections to get me there any quicker. But never mind, I'll get to the platform in time. I shall have a few things to say to you.'

He rang off. I was not at all happy, but time was going by so fast, there was no time left to stop and consider. Every minute was full of things that had to be done or people that had to be seen. The days went by in a whirl; and then all at once it seemed, I set off to the station to catch the train.

Linda and Joan, who lived in Ontario, were joining the

train at Toronto, so I went in the taxi by myself; but on the platform there were a number of people I knew, come to say goodbye to me and to other friends of ours who would be leaving as well. After they had greeted me, I left them all talking to each other, and went and hung about looking for Peter. And then he arrived, with a drawn face and a hard expression.

'Well, that was a damnable long journey to take when you wanted to hurry,' he said. 'I felt I would like to get out and push the train along. Come on, we'll go on the platform, but if any of your friends come up you can tell them to go away.'

'They're down the other end,' I said. 'They won't come. Not if they think it's a private goodbye.'

'It's a goodbye all right,' said Peter, 'you needn't think that if you go travelling around Europe for the next year I'll be waiting for you. Waiting and saying Yes honey, no honey, do just as you please honey!'

'Oh, Peter,' I said, 'I do so want to go! Don't be so proud about it.'

'It's not that I'm proud about it,' he said. 'It's that I can't bear it. A whole year! How can you? How *can* you? It reveals something to me all right. I see that you don't care for me at all. Or how would you face a whole year? And I suppose I was just a fool to hope that you might be getting to care for me.'

'But it's *only* a year,' I said. 'And we'll both be so busy, it'll easily go by.' But now that I was on the platform, and the moment of parting had come, which in all my plans and excitement I had never stopped to imagine before, it was quite true, I did not at all like the idea of a whole year without Peter. 'But I can make it shorter,' I said, 'when we've had a good look round, to make it worth going there. Just when we've seen Italy, and Germany, and France, and then London . . .'

'And the whole of the rest of the damn caboodle,' said Peter. 'Don't stint yourself.'

'Oh, Peter,' I answered, 'you can't ask me just to throw Grandma's money away. Just to go there and back for the ride and nothing else. She wouldn't like it one bit.'

'Well, I don't like it one bit, and you don't care, do you?' he said. 'I've told you all along that I don't like it. This is a time that matters to us: you can't just take it and throw it away, throw it into the sea and say, all right, in six months' time, say, we'll be back, and start all over again. If you *had* to, maybe, if it was a war or something: but you don't have to, and that's what makes me sick.'

'I wanted to go on this trip,' I said. 'I thought it would be exciting.'

'You don't need excitement,' he said savagely. 'You're far too excitable already. My God! When I think of you wandering around Europe, getting more and more excited . . .' Speech failed him for a minute. Then he went on: 'And God knows what unspeakable Italian or Britisher or what else you'll think you have fallen in love with. Some bloody ape who only wants to seduce you. And it'll be another crazy romantic dream for you, though there isn't a bit of real substance in it. All the things you go chasing after. Fantastic things! Why the devil can't you be contented with me?'

I didn't say anything.

'You just don't think I'm adequate, do you?' he said. 'You want a thousand things and I don't match up to any of them! But I have one advantage. At least I'm solid flesh and blood. At least I'm *real*.'

He turned away with a little snort and began to walk up and down the platform, striking his hands together. I trotted after him.

'Peter, I believe you're going to cry,' I said.

'Maybe I am,' he replied.

'Brighten up,' I said. 'I'll write you. Maybe I'll telephone you from the Old Country. And I'll be back as soon as can be.'

'I won't be available when you get back,' replied Peter. 'I'll have found myself a girl.' He looked at me blackly. 'A really *nice* girl. There are nice girls by the handful in Manitoba, you know.'

'Find yourself a hundred girls,' I retorted. 'What does it matter to me? You're only my cousin.'

His eyes widened and went black. 'I could kill you,' he said. 'I could beat you into a thousand little pieces.'

He looked so angry that I did not feel like saying anything more. I sniffed. In a moment tears would be trickling down and I didn't know what I should do with them. But fortunately there was no more time left for goodbyes, and I had to climb onto the train. As I stood in the doorway he put up his hand and stroked my face.

'I'm sorry, darling,' he said. 'Write me a letter, anyway.'

The train moved off and I sat disconsolately in my seat. He might at least have kissed me goodbye! I had really been looking forward to it. And now there were all these months to go and never a chance for all that long time. Well, never mind, I thought, thrusting my hands deep into my pockets, I'll find someone in Europe and kiss them. There's people that are better at kissing than Peter! However, I knew perfectly well that there weren't, and if it had not been for the travellers sitting opposite me I might have burst into sobs of misery.

But I held them back, and then my nerve began to stiffen. Peter was a brute, I said to myself. I got out my handkerchief and wiped away what still remained of the tears. Peter could not possibly understand a person like me. And the fact that he had not kissed me was of no importance at all. It was quite unreasonable to regret a thing like that. And there was nothing poetical or romantic about him when you came to analyse it; in fact if you thought about it, the way he got up a grip that nearly cracked your backbone once he got going, it was downright indecent, really. Especially in a cousin. I was better away from him. I straightened my skirt, patted my hair, sat up straight and began to take an interest in life again.

This burst of resolution lasted for a little while; and then my spirits began to sag again. It was, as Peter said, a very long time. I had never stopped to imagine it before, as for most of the time I had been thinking about a journey in the fall. And now that the summer passage had come upon me so suddenly, this moment, when it was now too late, was the first real occasion I had had to take in the fact that I actually would not see him for a good many months.

And now that I had time, and sat still and thought about it, I did not like it at all. And this surprised me, for in the past such months would not have mattered to me. But now they did. And so, evidently, things were not at all what they used to be.

And while I was thinking this over in surprise, something else began to creep over me, and that was the realisation that it was not actually to be a question of months at all, but of for ever. Peter had meant what he said. Peter was not only angry, he was also exceedingly hurt. It was very likely indeed that he would go and console himself with somebody else.

At that I felt as though I should like to turn the train round and go and stop him. But then I said to myself, What right have you to go and stop him, when you do not intend to marry him anyway? And looking at the matter face to face, I realised that since I had always meant, some day, to part with Peter, and to make it finally clear once and for all that the idea of our marrying was a very silly one, now that I had parted with him it would be ridiculous to wish to undo it. I had just been putting off the day of a final goodbye: now that the goodbye had crept up on me unawares, I must just accept it.

At that I began to feel exceedingly sad. But I said to myself over and over again, As it has to come some time, you must accept it now that it has come. After this, I took on another burst of resolution.

But this fell away before the terrible image that began to threaten me, of the other woman whom Peter would marry instead. For even if he did not find someone while I was away, he would certainly find someone else in the end — especially now that I had said goodbye to him, and would not be going out with him any more — and would marry her.

I tried to imagine it happening, but could not bring myself to picture it clearly. It is unimaginable, I said, and so it must not be. But it was certain to be: especially now that I was going away in this fashion. And so the unimaginable would have to be believed in. But it will destroy me, I thought.

And I thought, as well as I could, about this other woman, and about how Peter would propose to her; and then they would get married. And then he would make love to her. And then, I thought, she will think she knows all about Peter. And even though she knows nothing about the things that mean something to us — Grandma, Benjamin, the good days, the big days; the bad things, like the horses' blood that spread over the dry yellow grass and drowned the small ants, the small, small things even down to the crickets' thin whispering all night long, everything that makes up a whole lifetime's vision, the very substance of living itself — still she will believe she understands Peter entirely. And she will think that I do not. But I am not such a fool, I do not imagine that I understand him entirely: but I am ready to kill the woman who thinks that she does.

And then when I saw that I was thinking like this, I began for the very first time to wonder seriously whether I would really like to marry him or not. And the answer was forced out of me, that I would love to.

But no, I said, I must not torment myself like this, for I cannot marry my cousin, with whom I am so familiar; and as well, and this is the great instrument of battle, the argument with which I have always stifled myself, we are not the same kind of person at all, and so it cannot be.

And even if it could have happened, I added, I have put an end to it now by going away like this. And then I said to myself again, Do not even say 'even if', we are not the same kind of person at all, it could not possibly happen.

And while I continued this argument with myself day and night, we were passing through some magnificent scenery: and we steamed alongside Lake Superior, with its water like a whole country and its timber booms the size of islands, and the shadows and colours of the sky above reflected on a surface that stretched far away beyond the horizon, making the steamers and the other boats and their drifting smoke seem pointlessly small and unemphatic as they sailed across it. And we proceeded on our way by the hills and trees, and at last reached the station at Toronto, where I was to meet Linda and Joan. I seized upon their company and their conversation. Gee, they were looking forward to the trip, they said. Well, gee, I was looking forward to it too, I agreed. And I had to, or else I would begin to think — isn't it going to be wonderful, I said loudly — of the things that would never come now, not with him, the house, the garden, the family, the ivy and geraniums on the window-sill, the days and evenings, the nights, especially that — of course to be educated you *must* go to Europe, I said — and who knows, even in the end a small cabin with a basket chair and an old black stove, retirement, peace, the hens at the door and the long gold light of evening falling across the empty plain: here then, silent but not desolate, a world to ourselves. There is, I repeated, *something* about Europe. So civilised. So full. Linda and Joan agreed with me: Europe had something special. From Toronto to Montreal we told each other what it was about Europe. And then we finally arrived at Montreal; and our luggage was shepherded away to the dock; and there was time for us to go and buy postcards, and to have a quick look at the city, and to drink a bottle of Coca-Cola.

After this, we made our way towards the ship. We came down towards the riverside, talking gaily, and myself talking the most gaily of all. And in a minute we must pass the barriers and be swallowed up in the whirl that would at last disgorge us, respectable and accredited passengers, into the ship. I stood still.

'I'm not coming,' I said. 'I don't want to go on the water. It doesn't look substantial to me.'

'The water's the worst of it,' said Joan. 'You'll feel better when you get to the Old Country.'

'What does it cost to telephone home from the Old Country?' I asked.

'Several dollars a minute.'

'That's too much,' I said. 'It won't be at all convenient. I'm not coming. I'm sorry, but I just can't come with you.'

Now that they began to see that I meant it they were full of exclamations. 'You're never going to cancel your trip!' cried Linda. 'You won't get any money back now.'

'It's my own money,' I said. 'Every cent of it. I can do what I like with it.'

'And when'll you be able to afford to see Europe again?'

said Joan. 'Think of it, Peggy! All the places we're going to! All the wonderful old culture — the poetry of it! You know you just love poetry.'

'I'll make up my own poetry,' I said. 'I can manage that very nicely. I know how.'

'Never mind about the poetry,' said Linda. 'The fact remains that you'll probably never get a chance to look at Europe again if you throw away all your money now.'

'I'll look at Canada, then,' I replied. 'I guess it'll still be visible.'

They were still amazed. But I put it to them as well as I could, that I had begun to realise that if I left for Europe I should be unbearably homesick. And then Joan began to take my side, for she probably saw a little way into the matter, and she said that if one's heart were not in a thing like this it was much better not to do it. 'And if Peggy is miserable,' she said to Linda, 'we'll be miserable too.' Linda wanted to argue, and to tell me that I would soon get over it, but I told her there were no arguments that would avail, I was absolutely determined. 'Well, of course,' said Linda, giving in, 'you come from the land, and they say people off the land get terribly homesick.' 'That's right,' I said, encouraging her; 'when they took soldiers from the Hebrides Islands in the war, some of them just sat down and pined away and died. Going home was all they were longing for.' 'Well, for mercy's sake,' replied Linda, 'don't pine away and die on us. But I'm sorry about your money.'

I told her that the money was nothing in comparison with my necessity to stay behind. And so we went and got my luggage, and arranged to have it returned to the station and checked in there. And then for decency's sake I waited and saw them onto the ship, though it took a long time and the day was wearing on and I was burning to be gone. And then, when it was all done, I left the dockside, and turned round for one final look at the big ship, and waved goodbye to it without a pang.

Then very slowly and luxuriously I strolled up towards the city. I had everything planned. First of all I would book a place back to Winnipeg on the train. Next, as the day was so far gone and the night had to be arranged for, I would find a room in a nice hotel. I would wash and I would take a cup of coffee. Perhaps I would go for a little walk round and about, deciding exactly what to say. And then I would telephone very conveniently to Peter.

THE END

PRINTED BY PURNELL AND SONS, LTD.
PAULTON (SOMERSET) AND LONDON